The Girl From Stretchneck Holler

Inside Appalachia

A novel by

Betty Dotson-Lewis

and

Kathleen Colley Slusher

Published by
Brighton Publishing LLC
501 W. Ray Road
Suite 4
Chandler, AZ 85225

The Girl From Stretchneck Holler

Inside Appalachia

A novel by

Betty Dotson-Lewis

and

Kathleen Colley Slusher

Published by
Brighton Publishing LLC
501 W. Ray Road
Suite 4
Chandler, AZ 85225
www.BrightonPublishing.com

Copyright 2012

ISBN: 13: 978-1-62183-013-9
ISBN: 10:1-621-83013-6

Printed in the United States of America

First Edition

Cover Design By: Patricia McNaught Foster

❧ *Dedication* ❧

The Girl From Stretchneck Holler
Inside Appalachia
is dedicated to the children of Appalachia.

❧ *Prologue* ❧

Appalachia: A Culture in Conflict

What is so fascinating about Appalachia? Everything. Appalachia is a state of mind. A place both physical and spiritual. A place people go away from and long to come back to. A place that shapes the thoughts and actions of those living there or who have ever lived there. A place in the heart. A place of violence, abject poverty, and natural rugged beauty. A place of horrible strife, survival, and resilience.

Buried deep in the hollers of those majestic Appalachian Mountains, along the narrow creek banks and on the sides of the steep hillsides lives the coal miner, the symbol of the working class. The discovery of coal's riches has hung like an albatross around the miners' necks for more than two hundred years. These struggling workers have been pitted against big business, absentee landowners, and ruthless coal barons. The growth of the coal culture—a culture colored by violence and killings, by threats, by abuse, and by the rape of mountains—has forced this reclusive, independent, tenacious people into subservience. They serve the coal that provides their livelihood, but the consequences are great.

Rising out of this state of colonialism is male dominance, which is one accepted norm. Sons learn from their fathers. Daughters learn from their mothers. The pattern of domestic abuse is prevalent up and down the hollers as the cultural flaw repeats itself generation after generation. Behind the walls of the little four-room houses stuck on the side of the hill are many hidden secrets. Children raised in Appalachia become a product of their environment. Gracie Justice and Kinu Raines Ransome are products of the Appalachian coal culture.

❧ *Chapter One* ❧

Return to Stretchneck Holler
Gracie

Gracie blew a kiss and whispered "Goodbye" into the wind for dispersal to all the wonderful people of Luray. They had taken good care of her during her ten-year stay. She'd said her goodbyes to co-workers at her art shop, shed tears with close friends, and accepted well-wishes from clients for the past three months since it had become public knowledge she was moving back to the mountains of her childhood. Cliff and Helen, the nice couple who had leased her apartment, were impatiently waiting for her to vacate. Finally, the day arrived and Gracie was ready to roll.

She packed her four-wheel drive vehicle from top to bottom with personal belongings, including her precious art supplies, carefully packed in the old army locker she'd taken to college. The locker also contained a shoebox of unopened letters. After making one final round inside the apartment and finding no forgotten items, she pulled out her old quilt—her favorite—pressed a faded square to her cheek to intercept a tear, and then tossed it over her good clothes. The one-way U-Haul trailer she was towing was securely connected to the Jeep's trailer hitch. The local weatherman gave her a safe winter advisory report. She climbed in. Gracie tilted her head back for a good view of her smile in the rearview mirror. She applied more Cherry Red lipstick, smoothed her eyebrows, and brushed her hair to one side. It didn't matter where she was going, top of a mountain or a nice restaurant—she always wanted to look good. She thought about how people let age, little numbers, control how they look and feel. She wasn't going to participate.

"Yeah, yeah, yeah," she hummed. "I don't ever plan on getting old or officially retiring, but this new feeling of complete freedom from the nine-to-five job stint must be on the positive side of aging," she said to herself, referring to her transitioning status.

Hairs bristled on her arms and back of her neck as she pulled the gray seatbelt strap across her shoulder and lap. She gave herself a quick

1

thumbs-up for her gutsy decision to go back to the holler where she came from in a last ditch effort to rescue herself from herself. She reflected for a moment on her status; Gracie—single, mother of two grown children—pulling up stakes and leaving behind a job she loved and could stay with until she died, people and an apartment she loved.

She had tried this same plan of action when her marriage broke up ten years ago. She let her house and job go and moved four hundred miles away thinking: a new place, a new start, a new Gracie. Nothing happened. She was desperate now, and knew time was running out. If she were to ever experience the feeling of being a whole person in her lifetime, she needed to get busy. She had big items on her agenda. Could she have forgiveness from her deceased sister, whom she had failed? Could she have guilt removed based on a childhood dream? Could she gain the respect, acceptance, and love from the mountain people she'd tried so hard to leave behind? She was chasing answers, forgiveness, redemption, seeking love and peace of mind. She was glad people could not look inside her and see half a person. God knew of her fragile mental and emotional state, but apparently he was not on her timeline. Finally she was ready to ask and accept any help she could get regardless of pride, religious convictions, and plain common sense.

For the first time in years she felt a sense of deliverance. Unexpected excitement and a deep longing for "someplace" came over her as she pulled her Jeep into the southbound lane of busy I-81. She headed home to the one-stoplight coal mining town of Stretchneck Holler. She chose nighttime to make the seven-hour trip. As her traveling companions she loaded the passenger seat with Patsy Cline, Merle Haggard, and Tammy Wynette CDs, and she would tune in to her favorite radio station and listen to more country music stars as the night went on. After years of denying her heritage, fooling only herself, she had finally succumbed.

As a child of Appalachia, born and raised in the coalfields and saddled with a backward culture at birth, she carefully groomed and clothed her tall, slender figure to fool the outside world—outside Appalachia. Blond hair, blue eyes, and fair skin easily defined a Nordic connection, but it was her dialect, the "Y'all" and "Kin I hep you?" that defined her Appalachian mountain connection.

During her frequent trips back to Stretchneck Holler to reconnect and find housing, Gracie discovered relatives on her dad's side lived about halfway the distance. She'd stopped by a few times and was warmly welcomed with hugs, a place to sleep, delicious fried apple pies like her mother used to make, and stories of when they were young in the mountains. They were her people and her kind of people. When she told them the date she would officially be moving to Stretchneck Holler, and that she would be traveling at night, they begged her to stop over. They didn't think it was safe for a woman to drive all night alone. Gracie promised she would stop if she felt tired or scared, but instead of yawns, feeling brain fog, or being apprehensive, which happened often on long road trips, she felt alert and charged with energy as the hours fled by and the distance shortened to her new place. The apple pies would have to wait. When the gas gage registered one-quarter tank and she was within sight of the travel plaza, she blinked her signal and pulled in for her one stop of the night. Gracie pulled on her jacket, then gently ran her fingertips underneath her seat and retrieved her "Ladies Special" 38 caliber pistol. She slipped the cold steel into her jacket pocket before unlocking the door. Gracie never traveled alone—her pistol and her past were constant companions. She strained to see beyond the bright lights as she pumped regular fuel into the tank. She even thought she could make out a little house or two on her side of the road, but mostly a familiar feeling in the air signaled she was almost there.

The darkness began to fade as she steered her Jeep around the hairpin curves and climbed to the top of the chain of mountains serving as the landmark to the entrance to coal country. Clumps of grayish-white clouds, fluffy as baking-powder biscuits, hovered over the low-hanging layer of fog that covered Stretchneck Holler in the early morning light. Gracie could imagine—more than see—the blurred outlines of the courthouse, stores, diner, and hotel across the river. They were a short distance from the fork in the road leading to her house, a one-lane gravel road, which followed a small tributary of Stinking Creek. She slipped her Jeep into four-wheel drive as she approached the steep incline leading to her house. It was the dead of winter. She pulled the trailer up close to the back door, and before she got out issued a prayer of hope and thanks. A heart-shaped hand-painted "Welcome Home" sign hung on her wobbly front door, and a ragged, hungry Calico cat stood guard, wearing a bell on a red ribbon. Gracie felt humble to be accepted. She unlocked the

3

front door and flicked on the front porch light, standing for a moment in the half-day, half-night light, eyes embracing a dirty looking snow-covered hillside with love. Stretchneck Holler looked like a tired old coal miner with gray whiskers and a hump back, cloaked in the December chill. The town sat down in a round bottom in the shape of a tin cup with a long handle attached, like her grandma used for drinking well water. Hills surrounded the residential and business district, starting low and rising to steep, commanding, sharp peaks. But the peaks were alarmingly fewer due to mountaintop removal mining.

When Gracie was a child her family, like the other coal mining families, was surrounded on all sides, entombed within their natural environment—mountains. Hardwood trees, naked and shapeless since losing autumn's glory, lined the riverbank where coal barges pulled in, docked, and waited to be loaded with the rich, black coal. Narrow one-lane roads jutted out from the town's streets and followed the outline of ridges leading to the hollers and steep hills named Slope and Paradise. There, four-room houses were built butted up against the bank because of the lack of flat land. The coal company houses, all constructed the same, were wedged with a river or railroad track, or both, on one side of the one-lane dirt road and a steep bank on the other side. The coal tipple was usually within walking distance.

Gracie could see the ground around her house was soggy due to the continuous low-hanging mist in the air, and a thin layer of gray snow covered the top. She would be careful not to pull the trailer off the gravel and get stuck when she was ready to unload. Electricity was the only utility turned on. She pulled the rough, hand-stitched denim quilt used to cover her clothes, a pillow, and a sheet out of the back of her vehicle. An old couch, clean but faded, sat in front of one of the long front windows. She piled the bedclothes on top of the couch, spreading the sheet over the cushions, pillow at the top, quilt on top of sheet. Every bit of her five-foot eight-inch frame slumped down. All at once Gracie felt the sting of an all-night drive and an unknown future. She buried her tired eyes into the pillow as she pulled the quilt over her for warmth. The L&N six a.m. train whistle sounded in the distance. She had come home to roost on top of a mountain in Stretchneck Holler.

Gracie fell into a deep sleep, fully clothed, including shoes and socks, on the old couch as the train wound around the holler walls. The forgotten sound of the click, click, clicking of the steel wheels on the rails was like a cradle rocking her to sleep. Once again she dreamed of life as a girl in Stretchneck Holler. From the time Gracie could remember as a young child, she had dreams—vivid, active dreams. Her dreams came from her lifestyle in the mountains even when she no longer lived there. She remembered many of those dreams—pleasant dreams were just that, pleasant dreams—Mommy or Daddy holding her on their knee, or the excitement of actually getting that big new doll she saw in the Christmas catalog. The pleasant dreams made her smile inside, but the majority of Gracie's dreams were not pleasant.

One recurring dream from childhood Gracie referred to as "The Tillman May" dream produced images she lacked the courage to talk about, paint, draw on canvas, or convert to words on paper. The Tillman May dream was like a curse on a little girl in bib overalls with pigtails. She and her family lived in Stretchneck Holler at that time.

Through the years Gracie had tried different DIY (do-it-yourself) techniques to remove the dream from her memory bank, but to no avail. She came to the conclusion that dreams have a life of their own. The Tillman May dream did not age, nor did it change. The dream clung to her like a second skin. During her pre-teen and teenage years Gracie seldom spent the night with friends or had friends over for the night, for fear something would burst out of her about the dream. Everything in the nighttime vision was the opposite of how she wanted to be perceived. She was a genuine, loving, caring person, with a gentle persona. Did another person also live inside her? She read that dreams are the specific expression of your unconscious thoughts—thoughts beyond your control.

Childhood trauma was the most logical explanation for The Tillman May dream, but try talking to a dream, pleading for it to go away. When Gracie was five or six, her mother took her to a neighbor's wake. The dream came for the first time that night when she returned home and went to bed. In Gracie's dream she saw her own young, pretty mother lying in the casket instead of their neighbor, Tillman May. Her mother was in excellent health. Can anyone imagine the burden of a dream like that placed on a little child's shoulders with no one to make it go away? Instead of magical fairies or sugarplums dancing in Gracie's young head, fear came each night at bedtime in that cold, lonely room.

5

She dreamed of seeing her own mother lying dead in a tin coffin. That was what she had to look forward to after the sun went down.

Back on Stretchneck Holler, Gracie lay there on the old couch, fully clothed, covered from head to toe with her worn denim quilt and the six o'clock L&N clicking steel against steel. As she drifted into slumber land, The Tillman May dream unfolded.

❧ Chapter Two ❧

The Tillman May Dream
Gracie

I was five years old, walking with my mother across the back porch towards the kitchen door of Verdie and Tillman May's weatherboard house. An apple tree close to the steps held an empty tire swing. I tried to control my trembling hands and wobbling knees. I pressed against my mother's thigh, wanting to crawl back into the womb for protection from this stranger, Death, I knew nothing about, who'd made an unexpected and unwanted call in our coal mining holler. My mother didn't notice me clutching her dress. She was sobbing into a white, wrinkled handkerchief wadded up in her hand. She and I (her scared little girl) walked as one the length of the back porch, turning our bodies sideways to gain entrance into the small kitchen. Yellow flowered wallpaper covered the walls opposite the tall kitchen cabinets filled with Blue Willow dishes. Women from Verdie and Tillman's Pentecostal Holy Roller church crouched together in a circle, crying and praying aloud in the center of the room. The kitchen table had been moved to one side. They opened their entwined arms and made a path for me and my mother to pass through into the dimly lit dining room. The brown metal coffin stood backed up against the wall away from the long knotty-pine eating table. I kept my head downturned and lifted only my eyes toward the coffin. Fancy, puffy white satin fabric filled the inside lid. An embroidered United Mine Workers of America emblem was sewn to the top edge. Big white buttons held the satin in place. The coffin lining looked like the bodice of the beautiful wedding dress with pleats, tucks, and big buttons I'd picked out in the spring and summer Sears & Roebuck catalog.

Quickly, I lowered my eyes and pushed my chin further down on my chest, pressing against my collarbone till it hurt, so I couldn't see Tillman. I did see Nellie, Tillman's eight-year-old beagle hound, his most trusted and loyal companion with the exception of his wife, Verdie. Nellie's long, tan head lay underneath the coffin directly below her master's head. Her slanted brown eyes were filled with liquid. Several of the drops spilled over and settled in the white patch underneath each eye. Nellie was Tillman's favorite rabbit hound and the only hound allowed in the house. Nellie and Tillman meshed the moment they met. Both enjoyed the early morning rabbit chase and both showed signs of good breeding: happy, good-natured, and playful. An untouched biscuit from the kitchen table lay near Nellie's front paw. She too was in mourning.

Tillman whittled me a wooden soldier doll for Christmas. My mother hadn't told me why Tillman died or where he would go when he left the dimly lit dining room. My stomach turned over at the strong stench of funeral carnations, baby's breath, honey-baked hams, and embalming formaldehyde.

Opposite Tillman's dead body, a row of men lined the wall. Familiar faces to me. They drew slow drags on their Camel cigarettes. With mouths rounded into large Os, the men tilted their heads back, letting rings of smoke drift out of their mouths and noses and filter up towards the pink-flowered, papered ceiling. Some smoke rings drifted and hovered over Tillman's head in the casket. The men spoke in low voices as they sipped cups of strong black coffee in preparation for the night's watch with Brother Death.

One man's breath reeked of whiskey when he opened his mouth to speak to my pretty mother. He attempted to give her a hug, but she pulled away. He was a regular visitor to our house, because he was one of Dad's hunting buddies. The Dingess Family Gospel Quartet harmonized on the chorus of *When the Roll is Called Up Yonder* in the adjoining living room. Lillie Dingess sat in a chair to ease some of the weight of the guitar off her humped shoulder. Verdie May, Tillman's widow, sat in a rocker in the middle of the living room. A prayer shawl covered the upper half of her short, stout body. Her gray hair, pulled back in a bun, had fallen free from hairpins with the convulsing of her head in shock and grief. The unruly hair fell on her shoulders in the same young woman's style I had seen in Verdie's wedding picture on the bedroom dresser. The new widow's deep mourning sounds could be heard throughout the house. Two of her daughters-in-law took turns dabbing tears from her swollen eyes and holding smelling salts under her nose.

I didn't want to look in the box and see Tillman dead, but my mother took a firm grip on my hand, lifting me on my tiptoes even though I resisted. I squeezed my eyes shut tight. Fear washed over me as I bent toward the coffin. Slowly I opened my eyes. There lay Tillman May—hair slicked back and blackened with shoe polish, pale skin yellowed from too much formaldehyde, rugged hands with traces of coal dust around his fingernails, clutching the Bible he always carried. I had never seen a dead person before.

IN MY DREAM—the long brown metal coffin held my own mother. I saw her face, pale and thin with pretty red lipstick on a bow-shaped mouth. Her hair, auburn with a few streaks of gray, was molded into a large row around her head beginning at the edge of her right eyebrow and ending at the left eyebrow, parted on the left side. A brown comb with rhinestones buried in the right side held a few wayward hairs in place. The moment I opened my eyes and looked in the coffin, my mother sprang upright, as if hinges were attached to her hips. She opened her green eyes wide in surprise, staring back at me. She wore her dark blue checked housedress with little black buttons up the front. The same dress she wore when she took my hand and led me up the narrow holler road to meet a stranger called Death at Tillman May's wake.

Sometime during the night after we came home from Tillman May's wake and my mother put me to bed, I got out of my bed and walked in my sleep to the kitchen and crawled underneath the long gray and white metal kitchen table during my dream. My mother heard me crying and found me. She shook me awake, telling me I was having a bad dream. She told me to stop crying. My dad was trying to sleep in the next room. Helping me as I stumbled when I tried to get up, my mother took both my cold hands in hers and led me, shaking, back to bed, without hugging me or saying a word of comfort. I lay there frightened and shaking as she covered me with one of the handmade quilts made from the boys' rough, worn-out jeans. The big, drafty house was cold even in the summer. I cried softly into the quilt. Images of spirits floated in and out of the window at the far end of the dark, bare bedroom. I was afraid of the night, afraid to go back to sleep. Afraid I would see my pretty mother in the coffin again where Tillman May belonged. This dream remained a secret hidden deep inside. A curse on me. My mother never knew. The long line of burdens began at an early age for Gracie Justice.

9

Proverbs 23:7

Following a day of much-needed rest after the move and all-night drive from Luray, Gracie was ready to unload and begin transforming her modest house, in need of many repairs, into a home. She planned on doing as many of the projects as possible before hiring a contractor. Just as she had done with her apartment. Her toolbox was well equipped. She loved the old kitchen cabinet with the flour sifter the previous homeowner left behind. The wooden wall cabinets she would coat with a soft cream color. She wanted new floors when she could afford them, but there was no timeline. She could live with just the basics.

During the weeks that followed, Gracie tackled one repair job after another, calling a neighbor when she got stuck, since she soon realized contractors were far and few between in Stretchneck Holler. She painted, sanded, peeled, varnished, and assembled odds-and-ends pieces of furniture from Goodwill. The pale blues, deep greens, and vibrant shades of red turned the throwaways into eclectic pieces of art instead of the standard pieces of furniture used to furnish most homes. Regardless of how hard she worked physically, she couldn't get the Tillman May dream off her mind, but instead of focusing on the details of the dream as she normally did, for the first time she began piecing together the before and after events. Tillman May died years earlier so she wasn't sure everything she remembered was exactly correct, but she was sure Tillman May's wake was on a Saturday night, because she hurried to church early the next morning hoping Preacher Paul could somehow help without her actually telling him about the dream. She thought preachers could do that—read people's minds.

Their preacher, Paul, was a union coal miner and the preacher at the Baptist Church. Religion and coal mining were the backbone of their community. Gracie constantly heard that Jesus spoke to the people of Stretchneck Holler through Preacher Paul, especially during his Sunday morning sermons. When he preached, he screamed, sang, or beat out the messages of Hell and damnation on the pulpit with his Bible clenched tight in his fist. "Yes, Jesus Loved Her," and was all knowing and powerful, but to the people of Stretchneck Holler and to Gracie, even more knowing and powerful than Jesus was Preacher Paul. He preached at the coal miners' wakes and funerals. He dipped them backward into muddy Poor Fork or Stinking Creek for baptizing. He prayed at the altar with his arm around their neck when they backslid. He led the worst sinners in the county to the Cross, often referencing his own days of being a slave to sinful living: running wild, drinking, swarping up and down the hollers, lusting after loose women, cussing scab miners, and flattening their tires. He was a great man.

Gracie was raised in the church, as were the other children of Stretchneck Holler. She was a young, impressionable mountain girl when sweet Miss Minnie, her Sunday school teacher and Preacher Paul's second wife, led Gracie and the other children in class to Jesus by having them recite the Sinner's Prayer. Each child individually asked to be saved and promised to obey the Word. Jesus became Gracie's Master, Lord, and Savior even though she'd never seen him.

So it was the very next day after the dream where she saw her mother in a coffin that Preacher Paul stood in the pulpit in front of the pew where Gracie sat. She had high hopes she would be delivered. She had no idea what she needed: resolution, atonement? Nor did she know the psychological damage that would stem from this bad dream in years to come from the slant the preacher unknowingly conveyed to her. She stared at Preacher Paul in anticipation. She looked with admiration at his huge, gray, watery eyes, sweaty forehead, and round, red face. Sweet Miss Minnie proudly announced each Sunday that her husband, Preacher Paul, was a Disciple of the Lord. On that Sunday, she felt he knew about the dream with no words spoken between them. Just as she had hoped, he read her mind. That was clearly indicated to her when he stationed himself in front of her pew at the beginning of the sermon, but instead of reconciliation, he made her feel, even as a young child, she'd committed a grave sin when he read the scripture. His special words from the Bible on that day were not sweet parables of love and forgiveness a child could understand, but a passage of harsh reality, adult-themed but meant for her alone and etched on her heart forever. He looked directly into her round blue eyes and held a stare even though forty more people occupied pews. Preacher Paul lifted his Godly Instrument and read from the book of Proverbs 23:7, "For as he thinketh in his heart, so is he." Her young mind's interpretation of this bad dream according to the scripture had one of two meanings: she wished for her mother's death, or she could make her mother die. She looked sheepishly around at little friends sitting next to her—did they know? She made a pact with herself at that moment on that day to never talk about the dream. She was barely six years old.

Gracie purchased a soft blue paint for her bedroom walls when she first arrived in the holler. She had a pretty piece of fabric for curtains that would match perfectly. Family photos were framed and ready for hanging.

The Pleasure of Serving

Gracie wanted to connect with people in the community, so she went to the Baptist church she attended as a child. Instead of Preacher Paul standing at the pulpit, now there was Preacher Paul's son, Preacher Paul, Jr. She added her name to the list to help with the clothing bank run by the church.

She visited the Black Lung Clinic soon after her return to offer volunteer services. The clinic was sparsely staffed. They signed her up on the spot to help out with transportation. The four-wheel-drive Jeep would make it possible for her to get to homes in the hollers two-wheel-drive passenger cars couldn't get to in the snow.

Gracie had seen the effects of black lung first hand. She had family members and neighbors suffering from the deadly coal miners' disease. She drove the disabled miners, their wives, and even their kids back and forth out of hollers into town and to the doctor. Gracie got a lot of satisfaction helping the miners. They were an extension of her family. If one piece of her heart remained intact, these poor miners, suffering from black lung, owned that. They coughed and wheezed with each breath as if it would be their last. Their labored breathing and clumsy oxygen tanks told these miners, without numbers from the D.C. experts, they would surely die of black lung. Miners accepted their fate from the first shift they pulled mining coal. They got little respect and less compensation from coal operators and paid-off politicians for keeping the lights on in America. The public outside the region were blind to this coal country culture.

Gracie's days were soon full. She became part of the community. Announcements of bluegrass festivals, community barbeques, and church dinners arrived in her mailbox. She wanted to go to all events. She'd never allowed herself to enjoy her Appalachian culture before. So many things were simple and beautiful. To her total surprise, a college alumni bulletin came to her new address, and she read it from cover to cover looking for photos or announcements of her long-lost and almost forgotten classmates. Gracie seldom mentioned she attended college.

One snowy winter afternoon Gracie visited the place where they lived when she was little. People living in the bottom remembered her family with all the boys and (gingerly stated) barking hunting dogs. One of the ladies had gone to school with her deceased sister. She didn't know about Gracie's sister's death so she had lots of questions—Gracie had few answers. Now, confronted with outward reminders combined with the nagging inward feelings of regret and failure, the perfect venue was created for a continued nighttime cycle of intrusions. The Tillman May dream seemed to be on a hiatus, but the repertoire grew: she dreamed God was angry with her; she dreamed she crossed to the other side in search of her sister but the angels would not tell her where she lived in Heaven; she dreamed she visited a medium against Preacher Paul, Jr.'s advice.

Gentle hugs with sweet conversation from friendly faces seen at the grocery store, church, and community events made life more bearable, but townspeople wondered why Gracie had come back to this struggling coal-mining place. Her mommy and daddy were gone. Her well-known grandparents had been dead for years. Word soon spread that her sister, whom they remembered best, was dead. Was Gracie having some kind of mental problem? Was she looking for a new man? She didn't look poor, but she didn't look rich either.

Gracie noticed so many needed and wanted help in the holler. There was purpose for her. She was meant to be here. She could do some good, but before she could give it her all she had to unravel the threads of her own self-destruction. "Each day on the mountain is a new beginning," she scribbled at the top of the page as she turned each month on the calendar. Gracie prayed for guidance and courage. Her house was almost finished. She and Cali had survived winter in Stretchneck Holler.

Pictures from the Past

The spring weather lifted her burdens temporarily. Little violets and early lilies poked their heads out from behind bedrocks and rails used for fencing. She looked forward to gardening and mowing. But nights were difficult. Sleep came in spurts. Although the nighttime L&N lulled her to sleep, a hundred coal cars could not haul her worries away. She tossed and turned in the darkness reaching for something or someone, and each time she dozed, haunting tales came.

Gracie woke to the sound of birds singing outside her window. Perhaps it was the break in the nine-to-five office routine that made her lose track of time, plus the fact she was involved in activities not classified as work. She got out of bed and removed the two dim white sheets used to cover the windows each night. She was waiting until she got the room painted and then she would sew curtains. For no good reason she could think of, she kept putting off painting her bedroom. The two gallons of deluxe satin-smooth soft sky-blue paint had sat in the corner of her room for almost six months now. She closed the bedroom door when guests came. Today was the perfect day to paint. She could open the windows and let the fresh early summer breeze come in. She was tired of dim-looking white sheets over her windows. All she needed was coffee and a toasted peanut butter sandwich for breakfast. She would use a kitchen chair to stand on. She had brushes and rollers on hand.

The soft blue paint glided on, transforming the walls and ceiling into a beautiful room of tranquility. Painting was finished by midafternoon. She set up her Singer sewing machine and cut out four panels from the fabric. Quickly she measured and folded the fabric to make a sleeve for the two curtain rods. She then put in a four-inch hem at the bottom, enclosing weights she'd saved from previous drape panels. She cut and sewed two sets of ties from the extra fabric. The room was ready for finishing touches. The cardboard box containing her family pictures was stored underneath her bed.

She used the broom handle to push the box out. Her children's pictures she put in every nook in the house. Her grandparents on her mother's side were on top of the stack. He wore a hat and she had round, fat, pink cheeks. The picture was taken when they were a young couple, before the violence began. Her parents' photo was next. This was a

14

combined photo because the only pictures Gracie had of her dad was with a hunting dog, so the hunting dog was cut out and a picture of her beautiful mother taped in its place. Gracie's sister's picture was on the bottom. She wore a blue sweater set, her hair was dark and naturally wavy, her teeth white and straight—but her most striking feature was her piercing, liquid blue eyes staring straight at you. She had a somber look, as if she were sad. Gracie hung her picture in the middle of the wall collage directly opposite of the head of the bed. She would be the last thing Gracie saw at night before going to sleep and the first thing in the morning when she woke. The room looked polished and inviting.

Gracie sank down on her bed to rest a few minutes before she formally turned in for the night. She dozed off to sleep staring into her sister's eyes, with her sister staring back at her.

❧ *Chapter Three* ☙

Spirit of the Night
Gracie

The lonely sound of the six a.m. whistle from the L&N woke her in the midst of a dream. Gracie sat upright. She caught a glimpse of the shadowy trace evaporating into thin air in the dim morning light. Lavender scent lingered. Was it the spirit of her sister? Who was going to believe the spirit of a dead person was in her room? Fumbling in the darkness, she found the light switch to the lamp on the nightstand. She switched it on and quickly scanned the room. Nothing visible except Cali, her Calico cat, curled up at the foot of the bed sound asleep. Strike six. The clock on the fireplace mantle in the living room resumed ticking. She turned over on her side and moaned, "No sense in trying to get back to sleep now; the coal trucks will start soon." Her thinking was foggy, as if she were drugged.

Again the mantle clock was striking—seven strikes this time. She had been lying there an hour piecing together the strange dream. She had to remember every detail. Was this a message? She rolled out of bed and pulled out a tablet and pencil from the nightstand drawer. Quickly, before one grain of information left her, she jotted down everything that came to mind: a blue room; a former college classmate, Kinu Raines, wearing a pale blue kimono; herself; someone suffering; a spirit. She believed God worked in mysterious ways.

Gracie rolled the rumpled bedclothes into a pile in the middle and promised Cali, who liked neatness; she'd make the bed before noon. The first order of each day since she was a young girl was to give thanks. Gracie lifted her eyes, straining to look beyond the stretch of blue sky and white clouds. "Thank you, Lord, for sending me back to my beautiful, rugged Stretchneck Holler."

She could not hold back the stream of tears that fell as she pulled on her favorite pair of faded jeans and a red t-shirt. The same questions spun through her head over and over like a broken record: could she take any more, was there anyone nearby she could turn to, was she getting close to a breakthrough? She sloshed the frothy, mint-flavored Colgate toothpaste back and forth in her mouth. The road back was one of the easiest decisions of her adult life, but now after six months and still no resolutions her question was, "Was it the right one?" She picked up the soft bristle brush off the sink and gently stroked her naturally wavy blond hair one hundred times before pulling it back into an easy ponytail. Gracie walked out of the kitchen and onto the screened porch—her comfort zone. She sat there in the rocking chair, rocking back and forth and examining each charm on the little charm bracelet she always wore. She gazed out through the screen—two panels needed replacing—the trees, green grass, and jagged hillside with green stems everywhere reminded her of the newness of the season. Gracie walked back into her bedroom and stared out the window, thinking; trying hard not to slip into dejection again, weighing every possibility in an effort to make sense of the dream. What was the meaning?

She pulled herself together. In one morning her emotions had run the gamut. Her long, bare feet moved quickly to her little country kitchen. Coffee brewing, a wonderful smell—she needed her coffee first thing in the morning to get going.

Annie Lynn and Little Jimmie

Glancing out the kitchen window, she saw a late-model red pickup truck coming up her driveway. *Who could that be this early?* she thought. Then, it came to her: Little Jimmie and Annie Lynn, coming after the load of kindling wood she gave them two weeks ago. Gracie smiled; this was a good day for company. She walked out to greet her visitors.

"I'm glad to see you've come to get your kindling wood—take it all. Make two trips if you have to. It's yours. I have enough for next winter."

"We sure thank you, Gracie. Annie Lynn brought you a jar of honey. Hope you like it."

Gracie held the Mason jar up to the light and looked at the light-colored honey with honeycomb left in. "Hey, you've got to come to breakfast some morning soon for biscuits and honey."

Annie Lynn got out of the truck, smoothed her floral dress and adjusted her glasses. Her dark brown hair was streaked with gray. She was pretty, with a round face and round body to match. She and Gracie started toward the house.

Annie Lynn and Gracie had bonded immediately. They were in the same Sunday school class at church.

"How's the Nicorette working for Little Jimmie? I can tell he's put on a little weight. He looks good."

Little Jimmie wore a red flannel shirt with a square blue denim patch hand-stitched on each elbow. The turned-up cuff of his blue jeans exposed hard-toed mining boots. A faded high school baseball cap rested on the back of his crew cut. He pulled his truck around to the pile of kindling, got out and limped to the back, unlatched the tailgate, and started tossing little pieces of wood into his truck. Jimmie's buddies at the mine told him he was lucky to have ended up with only a limp after the roof fall at Big Conover. Three miners were crushed to death. But the perils lurking deep in the dark, rich mountains did not stop Little Jimmie, nor his daddy and his daddy's daddy. It was in their blood. It was the only life they knew—they were coal miners. In Gracie's family men talked of the rush they felt (adrenaline) each time they boarded the mantrip and spun into darkness, traveling for miles to reach the face of the mine, not knowing whether they'd return to their wives and children or meet their maker before they saw daylight. Little Jimmie's daddy died of black lung, and his grandpa was crushed to death by timbers that gave way at the face of a hand-dug mine on Panther Mountain. Annie Lynn put miners on the prayer request list each Sunday at church.

Annie Lynn heaved a heavy sigh and shook her head before answering Gracie. "The last time we went to see the doc he told Little Jimmie he's got to quit smoking. The doc showed the X-rays to Little Jimmie. His lungs are in bad shape from the coal dust and cigarettes. I worry about him so." She sighed again and changed the subject. "What pretty flowers you have here on your back porch, honey. Do you have trouble keeping them alive? I haven't any luck getting Petunias to grow. How often do you water?"

The screen door slammed shut behind them.

18

Gracie stopped by the coffee pot on the kitchen counter. She raised the pot to pour Annie Lynn a cup but was waved off; she refilled her cup before sitting down opposite Annie Lynn at the kitchen table.

"How's Melinda Sue and Donna Jean doing in school?"

Annie Lynn beamed. "We're so proud of our little girls. The Board of Directors at the Baptist Foundation Center awarded Melinda Sue a five-hundred-dollar scholarship towards college. Donna Jean made head cheerleader. She's in the tenth grade this year. Both serve the Lord. How about your little children, are they doing all right? I thought I saw their vehicles here a few weeks ago."

Gracie's children were helpful and would try to meet any of her needs, but there was a part of her life she lived alone. She wanted it that way.

"Yes, they're doing great. Both have good jobs. That's hard with this economy. I don't see them as often as I'd like. I miss my children when I'm away from them for any length of time, but they have busy lives. I'm so proud of their achievements. Even with their hectic schedules, we still make it a point to spend time together, especially during holidays." Gracie drained the last bit of Eight O'clock Coffee into her cup.

"Are you doing all right, Gracie honey? Someone reminded us at our Wednesday night church service that the anniversary of your sister's death is coming up in a few days. Oh, my, we know how hard that is on you, little darling."

"I think about her all the time, but when that date rolls around each year I feel like I'd like to die too. I have to think this place is my healing ground. I want and need to find myself...rebuild my life. This is where I started. Maybe this is where I'll end. Each day I'm finding out more about the healing process. It's a complicated and lonely journey. An old skeleton will jump out of the closet when least expected. A hurt or transgression buried for years will suddenly appear and linger on in the middle of the night. I believe we're all in recovery mode of some kind. The worst thing I have to deal with is dreams.

"Annie Lynn, I hope you can't tell I carry around a secret dream world inside me. When the sun goes down and everyone is resting

19

peacefully, my troubles begin. I'm haunted with dreams, some are recurring. One is from childhood about my mother. I had a dream the other night about my dead sister after I'd painted my bedroom and hung her picture on my bedroom wall. She was staring straight into my eyes when I fell asleep. I'm scared to death to go to sleep at night. I don't know which way to turn. Who can help me?"

Annie Lynn gently touched Gracie's hand, "Gracie, I'd like to try to help you. We're such close friends. Tell me your dream."

"The one bothering me most now is about my dead sister. Are you sure you want to hear, Annie Lynn? It's confusing and borders on the supernatural, but maybe someone like you, someone close to God and spiritual, can help me."

Annie Lynn nodded and smiled, appreciative of being called "close to God and spiritual." She prayed silently that God would use her to help Gracie.

Gracie's voice softened and dropped to a whisper as she recounted details of the dream she'd had a few nights back. Annie Lynn had sensed earlier there was trouble revolving around the death of her sister, although she didn't know any details. It came out in Gracie's face and voice that she was suffering from more than ordinary grief. Gracie was always asking the preacher and congregation at church for an unspoken prayer request. Gracie's lips trembled. She felt she was treading on hallowed ground by sharing this nighttime episode with an outsider. Annie Lynn leaned in, nearly touching Gracie for fear of missing a word. Gracie's round blue eyes stared past Annie Lynn out the window between the white Priscilla curtains, between the peaks of two jagged, steep hills, and into the clouds, as if someone there was looking back.

Gracie spoke: "The illumination of the room is from an unknown source. I'm confined to a straight-back chair, sitting in this soft blue dream room waiting for the spiritual return of my sister so I may beg for redemption. Someone is in the room with me. Someone I barely know. Almost a stranger, but I feel connected to this person." Gracie's voice drifts off into a low monotone. "A girl named Kinu Raines. When I woke up, I felt a spirit or ghost in my room. I could smell lavender. That's how my sister always smelled...like lavender."

Her eyes stared into Annie Lynn's face, searching for answers. Moisture surrounded the blue iris in each eye and formed large drops, which fell over into the lower invisible blond lashes. She brushed away the tears with the back of her hand. Gracie's eyes found the clouds again as she tried hard to remember where she had known the young half-Japanese, half-American girl in her dream.

Again, more to herself than Annie Lynn, Gracie said, "I have this strong urge to reconnect with this girl as if she is part of my healing. I can still see her in my dream reaching out to me, to embrace, comfort me."

Annie Lynn held her elbows against her sides as the shivers ran up and down her spine. Gracie had called her "spiritual," but Annie Lynn was outside of this spiritual gathering. The air thickened with the vapor of another. Annie Lynn, without being obvious, looked around the small kitchen. Seeing nothing visible, her eyes settled back on Gracie. She stared at what she thought was a tiny image of a woman in the blue of Gracie's eyes; she had long auburn hair and wore a kimono.

Suddenly it came to Gracie that she knew Kinu Raines from college. She had read her husband's obituary in the college bulletin. She hugged Annie Lynn tightly. "A breakthrough. Do you think so, Annie Lynn?"

Little Jimmie beeped the horn. Annie Lynn lifted the hem of her flowered dress and dabbed the spilled-over tears from underneath her glasses. She held Gracie's ice-cold hands in her own for moment, then gently placed a kiss on Gracie's forehead and walked out the back door. Halfway down her driveway, Little Jimmie began backing up his truck. Gracie ran out to see what was wrong.

"Did you hear that Judy Bonds passed away? She was a fighter and I guess that's one way she beat cancer—just went away from it."

Gracie, Little Jimmie, and many members in her community were following Judy's story. She was an environmentalist who fought against mountaintop removal, starting in her community. According to newspaper reports, Judy's life had been threatened, but she didn't give up or give in. Then she was stricken with cancer, and that's what took her.

"No, Little Jimmie, thanks for telling me. You know, if that mountaintop removal permit is approved on top of Stretchneck, I don't know what I'll do. I love my little creek down here. It's so clean you can sit and watch the minnows swimming around for hours. I don't want any miner to lose his job—I've got a lot of friends and relatives who depend on the coal industry to feed their families and provide health insurance—but we have to protect our environment. That's Biblical. I know there's a resolution. It's in the hands of our elected officials."

Little Jimmie headed back down the driveway and Gracie started back to her house slowly, thinking of the loss of the well-known environmentalist.

Fried Apple Pies

Two days later Annie Lynn stood at Gracie's back door holding six homemade fried apple pies in a round aluminum pan, still warm, with powdered sugar on top. "I've come to talk about that dream. You wanted my opinion, right?"

Gracie hugged Annie Lynn as she pulled her through the half-opened screen door.

Annie Lynn hurriedly began to explain while still standing, holding the pies. "Gracie, it's like this, everybody here in this holler that's anybody has always known you had a lot on your shoulders with your family and all. That's the way it worked in your family. I don't mean any disrespect to your parents, but you kids raised each other and yourself. I can tell life hasn't been easy for you, not by the way you look or act when people are watching, but it's the sadness in your eyes and that faraway look you get when you don't know anyone is watching. Now you're back home, in the place where a lot of things happened that made your family turn out the way they did. Old memories are bound to flare up...things you've been holding back are unraveling, honey. Things that happened you don't remember...maybe something happened to your mother or dad. Gracie, I'm no head doctor but I watch some of those TV shows that has doctors who talk about things like that and things like that can affect their children. On top of all of that, you have to consider what happened to you since you left this place.

22

"They're all mixed in together, Gracie, you can't control that, but I just know somehow, I think maybe God laid it on my shoulders, someone, somewhere, is reaching out to you. When you started on that dream about your dead sister and you said there was a presence in your bedroom when you woke up, there was a spirit or ghost in your kitchen while you were telling the dream. I felt it Gracie, I just felt it. Then when, out of the blue, it came to you where you knew the Kinu girl...from college...I felt like we were in one of those séances. I was telling Little Jimmie, I felt as cold as ice and hot as fire at the same time. I felt it all up and down my body. Now, just thinking about the way you looked gives me chills."

Annie Lynn held up the arm not holding the pies for Gracie to examine.

"All of this makes me know, don't ask me how, there's a spiritual connection between you and this Kinu. She may be the one reaching out to you. She could very well be your kindred spirit. I don't claim to be an authority on dreams and I'm not book-read like some, but I do keep my eyes and ears open. You know most of us folk here are in tune with God's ways. This dream you're having, especially with Kinu showing up out of nowhere reaching her arms out to you, may be His way of talking to you. Dreams have to be interpreted to get the real meaning. That's what I'm told by my cousin, who dabbles in such things. She said mediums do that, but I don't know what Preacher Paul, Jr. will think of something so strange.

"I watched one named Delores, her last name leaves me, on a television show the other night after I'd been over here. This medium interpreted a dream for a woman in the audience. The dream was similar to the one you told me about your sister. She was sure her dad was sending her a message, because when he died they were on bad terms and she knew her dad would not want her to carry that burden around for the rest of her life. Another person in the audience asked about a kindred spirit. This Delores told that woman a kindred spirit is someone who feels and thinks like you do, even though they may live miles apart. She said they often can help you if you're having problems, because of this spiritual connection. Like that girl, Kinu, who came out of your past to your special dream; she may be able to help you in some way...maybe that way.

23

"After watching that show, I said to Little Jimmie right then and there, 'Some kind of a medium and that girl Kinu may be able to help our little Gracie.' You talked about that strong urge to get in touch with her; call the college and see if they can give you an address. Write her a letter. See what she's like now. See if she remembers you like you remember her. Gracie, honey, if you want to get better inside, you've got to let people on the outside help you. I'm praying for you every day."

Annie Lynn handed Gracie the pan of fried apple pies.

"Gracie, we've got to run; going down to the school for a special ceremony."

Gracie walked Annie Lynn to the truck where Little Jimmie waited. She whispered, "Thank you, love you," in Annie Lynn's ear before helping her up on the seat beside Little Jimmie.

Little Jimmie shifted into drive and leaned his head out the window towards Gracie.

"We'd do anything in the world to help you. We're so glad you come home. We don't care about the reason."

They are such good Christian people—like so many here, Gracie thought as she walked back to the house. She stood there soaking up the warm morning sun before opening the back screen door. Maybe Annie Lynn was right—Kinu Raines, kindred spirit, the girl out of her past, who without any apparent reason stood there in her dream with arms outstretched to Gracie. Annie Lynn could be right.

Gracie picked up her phone and placed a call to her college alumni office asking for a mailing address for a long-lost, almost forgotten Kinu Raines. The address was not that far from Stretchneck Holler.

❧ Chapter Four ❧

An Evening in Draper Bottom
Gracie

Repairing and upgrading the little house she bought, along with her community volunteer services, had kept her busy for the six months she'd been back in the holler. Visitors complimented her on the work she'd done inside the house. She sanded and repainted the kitchen cabinets and refinished the floors in the living room and dining room herself. She hung quilts on the walls and spread quilts on her beds. The freshly-painted white kitchen cabinets glistened against the warm cream on the kitchen walls. The old kitchen cabinet she left as it was. Hand-woven rugs and lots of plants created a warm and cozy home for Gracie and Cali, her Calico cat.

But now money had run out for home improvements. There were no more excuses. The time had come for Gracie to focus on herself—her troubles—get them out in the open. She needed internal repair work on herself—her heart and soul needed mended. That didn't take money but it did take courage. The outside of her body was fine, with no evidence of deep scars and countless hurts. Gracie was ready to dig deep—look at herself—evaluate her life. She knew with the help of the Lord, friends like Annie Lynn, and perhaps even Kinu Raines, she could be strong enough to deal with the pain and feelings of regret, and find a way to fill the emptiness and longing inside her. Mainly she needed strength to find relief from agonizing and beating herself up over her sister's death. This dream, like the childhood dream about her mother, was quickly crippling her.

With a little free time on her hands, Gracie began a ritual—not intentionally, it just happened. Late in the evenings after supper—she suspected as an attempt to suspend the approaching night, which was filled with haunting dreams—Gracie drove around the back roads as if she were tracing someone's footsteps. Her ancestors'? She didn't know. On the narrow road she slowed down to a crawl as she passed the giant coal tipple. The fading evening sun cast long, boxy shadows on the little houses stuck on the side of the hill. Kids dressed in bib overalls and girls in pigtails played in the steep yards, and old people rocked in rocking chairs on the front porches. This scene, familiar from childhood, gave her a sense of where she came from and who her people were. Most evenings, before going back up her holler for the night, she drove down the road into the old cemetery in Draper Bottom. This narrow bottom provided a little patch of hard-to-find flat land to rest loved ones in. A wire fence about four feet high surrounded the graveyard. Old fashioned red and pink roses climbed the wires, weaving their vines in and out. If enough daylight allowed, she'd park, get out, and mull around the graves looking at dates and names, even though by now she had most memorized.

Gracie noticed no one had placed flowers, a teddy bear, or any kind of decoration on a tiny unmarked grave since she had been visiting Draper Bottom. She hoped they didn't object if she bought something for the baby. Gracie found the perfect decoration—a tiny wreath made of plastic with white baby's breath and a big pink bow. She carried the wreath to the location of the two round stones facing each other about three or four feet apart. Baby Darcie Lee lay in the unmarked grave. The baby's mother was a young unwed girl who had no money for a headstone. She had long ago left Stretchneck Holler. Gracie heard the father was married. He had other kids. Exact details of the baby's death were sketchy. Gracie judged by the setting sun which end was the head, because Christians buried their dead facing the East in anticipation of the return of Jesus. She remembered that from Sunday school class. As she carefully removed the tissue paper from the wreath, Gracie wondered, more than questioned, why this innocent life was cut short. She thought about her sister and whispered aloud, "Why was she taken?" Details surrounding her sister's sudden death were still out there. Gracie never knew for sure.

Caught up in this moment in Draper Bottom Cemetery, Gracie tried to think about death but was lost in the meaning of the word. It was too hurtful. She couldn't face it or understand it. Instead of thinking of the reasons and the hereafter, Gracie thought about the rituals of burial and how horrible that seemed. What was it like to be buried, like her sister and baby Darcie Lee, six feet under in total darkness with dirt piled high on top? Why were people dressed in their Sunday best, placed in a coffin, then buried in that deep, dark hole like the baby in the unmarked grave and her sister buried hundreds of miles away? What kind of a ritual was that, anyway? How did it help that poor dead person? Gracie dared to question God for the first time in her life. Why did her sister have to die? She, too, was innocent like the baby. Gracie gently bent over to place the wreath at the head of baby Darcie Lee. Flooded with anger and emotion, she fell to her knees on the hard dirt. Bitter tears fell on the little grave for both innocent souls, the baby and her sister. She covered the little mound with her own body, giving the cold grave warmth and life. She lay there motionless except for a stream of hot, wet tears falling on the Dollar Store wreath she had placed at Darcie Lee's head. Gracie wept for every innocent, helpless person who had died. Gracie wept for any person who had died alone. Gracie wept for her sister. Gracie wept for herself and her tortured soul.

She refused to look up at the sky where her God lived. If this was the way he handled things, she just didn't know if she wanted him in her life or not. He'd not given her peace up to now; her life was a wreck and he'd done nothing about it. Why should she look up with thanks and smiles in this dark hour?

And then it came to her: was she blaming God for her shortcomings? Was she as much to blame as God? Could her sister have lived longer if she'd had a better life, better care? Why did God allow people to be subjected to more than they could stand? Gracie questioned God, but mostly she questioned herself. The part she played in this. Her sister spent the last part of her life in a state-supported halfway house for people who could not be fixed mentally any other way. Was that the best her family could do? Was that the best she could do for someone who had done everything for her? Deep in her heart she felt responsible for her sister's ruined life. She wanted to fix that somehow, even beyond the grave.

Atonement. Redemption. Could she, could anyone, go beyond the grave? Would God allow that?

Afraid of the Night

Following the meltdown at Draper Bottom, Gracie, exhausted, fell on her bed and sank into a fitful slumber. She tossed from side to side in her bed as dreams swirled around in her head, hour after hour, during the darkness of night. Out of nowhere, a bright light shot through her window in a single stream so bright it could scorch your eyes. It woke her. She sat up and listened for the familiar sound of a coon hound treeing on her property or a hunter calling out for Maybell or Dottie, who'd wandered off the path during the chase. But there were no sounds, not even a car or truck going up or down the holler. This time the presence was there with her—within her touch—a long shadowy figure of a woman, the same presence who had visited her before. Gracie was too afraid to reach out to the presence. She felt alone and afraid, not of physical harm, but afraid she would be rejected and remain unforgiven. It was a few minutes past midnight. She cried softly, as if she were a young child again, vulnerable and alone. She wept into the denim hand-stitched quilt she'd thrown over her bed. Afraid of the night. Afraid of sleep, she propped herself up to a sitting position with pillows supporting her neck and back and waited for daylight.

Morning light gently filtered into Gracie's pretty bedroom. An iron bedstead sat catty-corner to reap the benefits of both small windows in the room. The Ott-Lite on a table beside her bed illuminated space at night for reading or crocheting. Three hand-woven rugs, none matching, were scattered on the bare bedroom floor—a housewarming present. The used wicker loveseat and matching rocker were spray-painted white, to contrast gently with the blue walls.

She glanced at the marked calendar on her dresser; on this date five years ago, her sister died. Aside from the photo on the wall, Gracie's favorite photo of her sister, taken during early high school years, was centered at the top of the mirror with a heart on each side. She half-smiled at Gracie from that picture. Gracie had folded and cut the paper with a jagged edge exposed down the middle symbolizing a broken heart. She felt something warm and round on her cold feet. That startled Gracie. She was nervous. It was Cali. The cat raised one paw and covered her eyes, hiding from the new day. Gracie pulled her feet out slowly so as not to disturb the late-morning sleeper. She was glad the cat at least got a good night's rest.

She got out of bed and walked to the kitchen. Not taking time for coffee, she walked across the room to the kitchen table. A few days earlier she had gotten Kinu's address. A small, silver-plated ballpoint pen lay mysteriously on the tabletop. "Who put that there?" she whispered under her breath. Pulling a sheet of paper from the top drawer of the file cabinet, she picked up the silver-plated pen and began writing a letter to Kinu Raines.

Reaching Out

Dear Kinu,

I hope you remember me. We were classmates in college. We only talked a few times but we crossed paths on campus almost daily, so I remember you well. You were a standout beauty with your exotic looks. My most vivid memories are the religion and philosophy classes we had together our freshman year. Do you remember the required classes, outside the core curriculum, since we were going to a Christian college? I was so green I didn't know our professor purposely instigated heated debates in his class with discussions on controversial topics such as "God is Dead" and the Vietnam War. I suppose he was trying to prepare us for conflict in our future. If I remember correctly, we were on the same side in many of those heated discussions. That professor became popular with students by stirring up controversy. I recall seeing his face on the front page of the school's newspaper more than once with his non-traditional views on war and religion at our conservative college. How could we forget him and that class?

I haven't had the time or desire to recall my college days until lately. Yeah, we were college students during the height of "The Decade of Peace, Love, War, and Unrest"—the mid-to-late sixties. I was scared of getting involved in the protest against the war, afraid my scholarship would be revoked, but I was so against the war. I signed the petition after I got word a young boy from my hometown was shot down. So many of our classmates were out there protesting, taking a chance, saying they were against the war. Yeah, little did President LBJ know in 1966 when he authorized the deployment of five hundred thousand troops to Vietnam that he would create a lasting divide in this country.

Oh, Kinu, I'm sorry, I didn't mean to get on my Vietnam War soapbox, but we were at that age, young and impressionable, our minds were forming values that would hang with us the rest of our lives. Oh, my, I could really get started but I'm not writing to discuss our late sixties history, at least not in this letter.

I have to admit one reason I've avoided discussing my college days and connecting with college friends could be my final status at the college, which was "college dropout." I'm not proud of that. I had personal reasons for not staying connected, things that happened at the college I've tried for years to forget. But just the act of writing to a former classmate is bringing back many memories, some pleasant, that I thought I'd lost. Remember our dorm mother our freshman year who guarded us like prison inmates? Wonder what happened to the guy a year or two ahead of us who wanted to give every girl on campus a backrub? That's barely touching the surface. I've gone back to campus only one time. What about you?

Kinu, one thing I remember so well about you—your beautiful clothes. Did your family own a clothing store? I loved that tan trench coat you wore with a blue and green plaid scarf. You always dressed like a model. I envied that.

Someone told me your family came from Mercy Mountain. My roots are only a few miles away in Stretchneck Holler. I'm back now— back in Stretchneck Holler. I've come back to settle up, make peace, and rebuild myself.

It would be nice to reconnect with you for social reasons, but I have another reason for wanting to reconnect which may come across as strange or weird. I agree completely. I'll explain the best I can.

Five years ago my sister died alone in a hospital many miles away. Our family was never able to find out the exact cause of death. I'd acted as her caretaker for several years after her mental and physical breakdown. She became stronger physically over a period of time through good nutrition and care, but she never fully regained her mental capacity. We went from one doctor to the next for referrals and medication. All the fixes were temporary.

Since coming back to Stretchneck Holler I'm having a dream about her appearing to me in spiritual form. (It could be because I want so desperately to communicate with her and tell her how sorry I am for my failures.) Kinu, you are in this dream. You are young, as I remember you in college, and dressed in the traditional Japanese kimono. Would you possibly have some insight into this?

I have to be honest and tell you my life has not turned out as I had hoped or planned. I hope life has treated you well and all your dreams have come true. I read your husband's obituary in a college bulletin. I remember your husband. Were you happy? How did it turn out for you? Do you have children? I can't wait to hear from you, telling me about your life.

A friend from your past,

Gracie Justice

Contestant

Gracie folded the letter in half, placed it in an envelope addressed to Kinu Raines, and hurried down the steep embankment to her mailbox. Her heart fluttered with excitement at the thought of reconnecting—one more piece of the puzzle, possibly. When she opened the mailbox to place her letter inside, she pulled out a flyer without a postage stamp. Gracie tucked the piece of local mail in the back pocket of her jeans.

As she turned back, her heart fluttered again. Mid-June's humid sky hung low and heavy, nearly touching the jagged green mountains. There on the side of the hill between sycamore trees and lavender lilac bushes sat her two-bedroom, twelve-hundred square foot mansion gleaming in the mid-morning sun. She swooped Cali up in her arms and pointed the cat's face up the steep hill to share the view. The scene could easily have been taken from one of her paintings left behind in the art shop in Virginia.

"Look Cali." And this time she painted the scene with words instead of strokes of her paintbrush.

"See the cornfields, the tall green stalks are waving to us in the sun; over there's the beaver dam, in the creek near the edge of the woods.

31

The beavers' tails paddled their sticks to the site and carried mud to hold the dam together; there, to the left, is Buddy Estep's house. His parents built it in the fifties with the half basement, which was a luxury at that time; and across the creek is Caudill's pasture. The horses and cows graze right up to the door of the Pentecostal Church—a beautiful scene."

She stared with pride at her Tara in the coalfields of Appalachia.

Her pleasant thoughts were cut short when four or five birds twittering and hopping from bush to bush towards the white pines startled Cali. Animal instinct took over as she wiggled out of Gracie's arms and made a soft landing on the ground. Crouching low on all fours and slinking through the thick weeds and briars, Cali ran for the trees. Gracie shooed the birds and then called out, "Here kitty, here kitty." Gracie shaded her eyes with her hand against the sunlight to look into the dark grove of trees for her cat, but instead of Cali, she caught a glimpse of a tall, slender figure moving against the shadowy background. She could make out the dark brown, wavy hair and fluid movement of the body. That was her dead sister. She'd seen the image a thousand times before at the most unexpected moments, but lately the presence was always in Gracie's shadow.

When Gracie got home from the mailbox, she pulled the flyer out of her jeans pocket and unfolded it.

ANNOUNCEMENT

Contest Sponsored by KYC Radio Station
Winner Will Travel to New York City
Guest Appearance on the Andrew De Soto Show
featuring the famous medium
500 Word Essay on why you should win
See details on back of flyer for entry deadline or call our station
One entry per family
Must be at least 18 years old to enter

Gracie looked the flyer over again and decided to enter. If she won, she'd request that the medium interpret the latest version of the dream about her sister. She'd ask if he had a message from her sister and she'd ask what part Kinu Raines will play in her life. A medium was what she needed. She remembered Annie Lynn saying there was a medium in a nearby community.

❧ *Chapter Five* ❧

Friends in Need
Kinu

A large white farmhouse sat on a two-pastured hill overlooking the country road which serviced the community of Mercy Mountain. A small herd of horses grazed in one of the pastures, and a chrysanthemum field bordered by three greenhouses occupied another. The graveled approach winding steeply up the hill was bordered by sugar maples and Rose of Sharon bushes. At the top of the hill the gravel road branched; a large, black-painted barn and several outbuildings were to the left of the road. To the right was the six-bedroom spacious farmhouse belonging to Maggie Harris, daughter of Kinu Raines. Seated on the porch swing enjoying the mid-morning sun, Kinu spotted the mailman coming up the country road.

Kinu watched as her son-in-law, Joe, went down to pick up the morning mail. In the peaceful hollow where they lived bordered by two other neighboring farms, the delivery of the daily mail was a comforting social event. Kinu knew tidbits of mountain gossip were often delivered along with the mail; her mailman, a gossipy middle-aged man handicapped slightly by a mild speech impediment, generally threw up his hand in farewell as he drove by the farm. Kinu knew it was his way of signaling to her that she had mail. When she saw his hand go up today, she waited patiently for Joe to come back up the hill.

"A couple of bills and a letter for you today!" Joe said as he delivered them with his usual friendly grin.

Kinu looked at the letter first. "Who in the world?" Kinu said softly when she saw the return address. Then she remembered and put a long-forgotten face to the name she saw written. "Why, it's been years since we knew each other back in college!" She started reading the letter; when she finished, she went inside.

Reflecting on her nearly forgotten memories of her college classmate, Kinu took a few minutes before she put pen to paper.

Gradually, she formulated a clearer picture of a college-age Gracie in her mind: a girl with a wide smile and the tall, slender body of a model, Gracie's blond good looks and soft twang served to make most people initially underestimate the astuteness of her mind. Kinu had been impressed by Gracie's clearly-stated and strong observances on various topics during the classroom debates in their freshman year philosophy class.

Their junior year, they lived in the same dorm, but on different floors. They ran with different crowds, but they always spoke in passing. Kinu thought Gracie was good friends, and maybe more than friends, with a tall, brilliant, political science major who was active in campus government. Another class she shared with Gracie that year was a second semester advanced art class. Kinu's interest was jewelry design; Gracie's was pen-and-ink depictions of coal country scenes of miners, mines, and mountain landscapes.

Kinu began writing her letter, thinking to herself how nice it would be to catch up with an old classmate. They hadn't been best friends or even close friends, but maybe there was still a little connection from those days.

Still writing fifteen minutes later, she raised her eyes from her letter; something on the table caught her eye. She hadn't noticed it earlier. It was her late husband's favorite coffee cup. Following John's funeral service three years ago, she had returned to a home without him and placed his cup high in a cupboard. Who had moved it? Even as she formulated a rational answer, in the back of her mind was an irrational question: John?

An hour or so later, Maggie came in from the mum fields looking for her mother. She was surprised to find her staring out the bedroom window into the lushly forested hills behind the house. When Kinu turned away from the window to face her, Maggie saw the tears on her cheeks.

"Mom, this has got to quit. Dad's been gone for a long time, over three years, and you're still grieving…it's not good for you to continue this."

In a trembling rush of words, Kinu said, "I got this letter today from someone I knew in college; it brought back such old feelings and memories. You think I'm grieving, and I am, but there's something else to this. I haven't told you, but I've been noticing little things. I feel his presence. This morning, his favorite John Deere coffee cup was sitting out on the table. I know it was put up in the top cupboard; I think he's putting things out for me to see, to communicate with me. I know, it's foolish—the dead, long gone and buried, trying to be heard. It's foolishness, isn't it?" Gazing thoughtfully at the letter to Gracie, which was lying half-written on her desk, Kinu wondered aloud, "Dreams, memories, letters from the past...are they God's way of letting his angels talk to the ones they've left behind?"

"I do think the dead can send us messages. I have a friend who knows someone who can communicate with the dead. She told me about this woman, a medium named Delores Lee."

Hearing a beseeching note in Maggie's voice, Kinu looked directly into her beautiful daughter's blue-green eyes. Maggie was the spitting image of her father. She nodded for Maggie to continue.

Maggie rubbed her arms as if she was suddenly cold and said, "Anyway, I went to see her; I wanted to ask if Daddy was still suffering or...she told me to come back and to bring someone who loved him with me. I know you're skeptical, but maybe it would help. Nobody needs to know. Nobody will judge you."

Kinu nodded in mute agreement.

The next morning, as she was getting dressed for the day, Kinu momentarily studied her reflection in the mirror above her dresser. The face looking back at her was somewhat exotic. Slanted, slate-dark eyes under a high brow and tousled red-brown shoulder length hair were accented by high cheekbones prominent in a heart-shaped face. She looked at her image, and for a fleeting moment saw a young Kinu. She shook her head wearily and turned away from her reflection.

The many nights of lost sleep and restless dreams had taken their toll on more than just her looks; she was tired, weary to the bone with recriminations and a sense of deep loss. When John came home from the doctor's office, telling her without preamble that he'd been diagnosed with advanced prostate cancer, she'd collapsed inside. Her way of coping with the enormous monster waiting just outside the door was to throw herself into a whirlwind of domestic activity. Terrified, she worked on and on, hoping her physical exhaustion would finally dull the pain of watching him suffer. Nighttime was the worst; neither of them could find the solace of sleep. Nighttime was still the worst.

Last night had been another long one. Finally she'd given up on sleep and got up to finish her letter to Gracie Justice. Once finished with the letter, she continued to write—writing late at night seemed to calm her nerves. Her notebooks were filled with her poetry and stories, some of which were written as far back as college.

"Now look at me this morning," she said to no one in particular. "I'm tired out and dragging my feet before the day has even begun." She picked up her notebook from the bedside table, sat back down on the bed, and began reading what she'd written in the night. When she finished reading, she wiped her eyes before getting up to make her morning tea.

This feeling of being off-kilter and uneasy for no real reason stemmed from more than just a lack of sleep. The feeling was getting stronger, more dominating, ever more depressive.

Deliberately forcing herself to be optimistic, Kinu gave her usual quick, thankful prayer that she was no longer bound to the wheelchair now sitting unused in the corner of her bedroom. For ten years, through bouts with diabetic foot ulcers, gangrene, and foot-deforming Charcot Joint Syndrome, she'd been restricted in her mobility. The foot surgery she finally agreed to have proved to be a smart decision; for the first time in a decade, she was walking unassisted.

Looking back at her years spent in the wheelchair, Kinu saw a woman trapped by the betrayal of her body. The gradual yet pervasive deformity of her feet and ankles had been a killing blow to her sense of who she was; it nearly succeeded in stripping away her identity along with her physical grace—nearly succeeded in wearing down the fighter in her. John was her strength during those years. Rather than step away, he took a step closer. His loyalty and his love for the grace of her spirit gave her strength and deepened her love for him in the way that only going through fire and hardship together can do. She wanted to tell John this, to tell him how much he meant to her, but she had waited too long, thinking she had time. Time escalated, and then he was gone.

Now, as she stood thinking in her small, sunny kitchen, Kinu knew she needed to talk to John again. She made a leap of faith and smiled resolutely; how happy John would be to hear that she was walking. Yes, she would go to see Delores Lee. She had much to say to him still.

While finishing her tea, Kinu reread her letter to Gracie. Then she prepared the envelope, noting once again the proximity of the Stretchneck Holler address, and waited for the mailman.

King Coal
Gracie

Gracie rinsed her mop out in bleach water before standing it upside down on the back porch in the sun. She shook her head, remembering one unpleasant experience when she worked in public education. That was before she decided to go full-time as an artist and moved to northern Virginia. On occasion at work, when one custodian was not present, she went in the closets where the mops and mop buckets were kept, and there was always a mop standing in a bucket of thick, milky-looking water which smelled to high heaven. She chuckled and pinched her nose, recalling the stench. Why didn't they take a few minutes to rinse out those mops in bleach water or stand them outside in the sun? Every time she mopped her floors, she remembered that scene.

Quickly, she swapped her red t-shirt for a bright pink one, smeared men's Old Spice deodorant under her arms, and applied pale pink lipstick, stroking the stick across several times in a thick coat. Gracie loved lots of lipstick. She smoothed down her out-of-control wavy hair, located her purse behind the chair in the living room, and headed out the back door to her Jeep.

She made a quick stop by the black lung clinic on her way to the grocery store. It was hard to stay away on days she did not volunteer. She felt needed. The receptionist yelled for her the minute she walked through the door. "Gracie, you have a call."

The wife of one of the miners she transported to the clinic on a regular basis was on the phone. She asked Gracie to stop by and visit her husband if she had time. She told Gracie he was feeling exceptionally low that day and she had to go to work.

Gracie parked in a wide spot on the side of the road and walked across the wooden bridge to the little white-frame house. She knocked on the door. A faint voice summoned her in. He was alone. After the black lung diagnosis three years earlier, he was no longer able to work. His wife had taken a job as a clerk at a small grocery story to supplement their meager income.

Gracie felt helpless as she watched him struggle to get up from a lying-down position on the couch after she entered the small, dimly-lit living room. His breathing was labored. He wheezed and coughed. He used a walker in one hand and a handmade cane in the other, to shift his weight to find a way to sit up on the couch. Finally he positioned himself so the bulk of his thin body rested between the cracks in the cushions. That made the pain less. Oxygen tanks were on both ends of the couch and a wheelchair was stationed near the door. He showed her a handful of pills prescribed by the doctors. One was a breathing pill. Gracie stayed until his wife came home. She gave the miner and his wife a hug before she left, hiding her tears. She'd forgotten about her own problems.

On the way back from the grocery store, Gracie stopped by her mailbox and pulled out a letter from Kinu. She raced up the hill, staring at the letter on the passenger's seat instead of the road. In record time, the groceries were unloaded and perishables refrigerated.

Gracie's hands trembled as she opened the envelope. She walked to the kitchen table where she had written her first letter to Kinu. Her voice quivered as she read the letter aloud.

❧ *Chapter Six* ❧

No Bed of Roses
Kinu

Hi Gracie,

It's great to hear from a fellow classmate; it's been so many years. I didn't realize you were from near Mercy Mountain. Yes, I was married. My husband, John Ransome, do you remember him? He was a year behind us in school. He passed away nearly three years ago from prostate cancer. John suffered terribly the last months of his life, and I stayed by his bed. Could this somehow be a connection to the loss that you've experienced? We were married for thirty-eight years. We had three children, but one died at birth. I'm living with my daughter, and my son is working up north. My health is better now than it's been in ten years; I'm recovering from some foot surgery that helped get me out of my wheelchair and walking again. I am disabled from diabetes and have several problems related to that. I was forced to retire early from my teaching job. Now I design and make jewelry. It's sort of a hobby and it keeps me busy.

I don't really know why you would feel an urge to write me in particular, unless you could somehow sense that I am in need of a friend at this stage of my life, too. You said your life had not been a bed of roses. Ditto here. Ever since my husband passed, I've been restless— searching for answers, I guess. Our marriage was full of ups and downs, and I feel like I've fallen short somehow. I don't know what I mean exactly, but if you need someone to listen to you, as I do, please feel free to write anytime. I do remember you, beautiful hair and skin, and you were the girlfriend of a friend of mine, right?

Gosh, you remember my clothes? None of my clothes came from a store; my mother made everything I wore, except for underwear and that coat. We didn't have money to spend on store-bought clothing. The trench coat you mentioned was my prized possession. Mom and Dad scrimped to get me a nice coat for college and I was so proud to have something from a real clothing store.

Tell me what you need from me. Maybe we can help each other.

Your former classmate,

Kinu Raines Ransome

The Campus God
Gracie

Gracie carefully folded the letter and stuck it in the back pocket of her jeans, laced up her walking shoes, and headed for the meadow and the woods. She had picked up her dad's habit of walking to sort things out and to level out her emotions. Kinu's letter opened the door for more communication, and possibly an explanation of their connection.

Gracie could see a vehicle coming up her driveway. When she got closer she could see it was a 1970 Cadillac Hearse pulling in next to her Jeep. Preacher Paul, Jr. had come to call. He drove the old hearse as the church's business vehicle. The local funeral home director had donated the car, and the service station owner installed seats where the coffin ordinarily fit. Church representatives used it for travel, as well as the preacher. Gracie ran up to the preacher and they hugged. It was nothing unusual for the preacher to pay a visit to his parishioners, but Gracie wondered if he had something specific on his mind.

"Gracie, can we talk for minute?"

She hurriedly walked ahead to put on a pot of coffee, and mentally she was taking stock of what was in her refrigerator or cabinets to eat with coffee. This was a surprise visit to Gracie. She wondered if someone had "reported" her to the preacher. She remembered she'd frozen three of the apple pies Annie Lynn brought her. She quickly pulled them from the freezer and stuck them in the microwave to thaw while she fluffed up a pillow on a kitchen chair, pointing to Preacher Paul, Jr. to sit down.

"Now Gracie, don't go out of your way. I just stopped by to talk to you a few minutes...see how you're doing or if you're having any problems."

Gracie didn't know how to respond, but as Preacher Paul, Jr. lifted his cup of coffee to his lips, he lowered it before he took a drink and held it in midair. He looked directly into her blue eyes.

"Gracie, some people at the church said they saw you walking around Draper Bottom Cemetery a few evenings around dark. Some of your family there? I know if Big Daddy was still here he would know how to help you, since he knew about your family. Is there anything I can do for you as your preacher, or just as a friend? You know the Lord is always talking to me."

Gracie handed Preacher Paul, Jr. a warm apple pie. He ate it without either one of them saying a word. She looked at his gray, watery eyes, his round face, and the drops of sweat collecting on his brow. He held his worn Bible in his left hand. Getting up to go, Preacher Paul, Jr. reached for the fried apple pie left on the plate. Pausing with his hand above the pie, he looked at Gracie for permission. Gracie smiled and nodded. Preacher Paul, Jr. took the fried pie and walked to his hearse.

Gracie felt the need to talk or write to someone she felt connected to about her worries.

Dear Kinu,

I told a church friend about you and how I felt this need to reconnect and find out about your life. I wonder why you went to the same college I attended; was it for financial reasons, like me? What were some of your most memorable experiences from there? Did you make lifelong friendships, as I did?

I want to tell you something about my college experience. I want to tell someone who understands the setting, the people, us as poor mountain students, and the fragility of our emotions during that time. Opening up about something so personal could be what I need to begin the healing process. This is hard because I still feel ashamed and blame myself. To this day I've only confided in one or two people about this relationship.

I don't talk about my college life to people. When asked, I only hit on a few high spots. I felt it best to keep this memory as my deep, dark secret.

If you were in the same financial situation as I, then you appreciated the scholarship awarded, making the impossible possible. But I'm still confused over the strange relationship that developed between me and a prominent administrator. I hope you'll try to understand and not be judgmental. I'm sure someone with such confidence and beauty as you, Kinu, would never fall into such a scandalous trap at such a young age and in a Christian environment. This is my story:

When I stepped off the Greyhound Bus after an eight-hour trip onto this college campus, I transitioned into another world. I quietly claimed my Army footlocker when the driver opened the compartment underneath the bus. My brother's name was crossed out on the tag and my name written above it. The dented green metal box contained everything I owned in the world. I'd been on my own since age fifteen when my parents moved out of state and thought it was all right that I stay behind with a family friend to finish high school. I earned my room and board by cleaning for the family I lived with, and earned spending money by cleaning houses for other families in the community. My parents were unable to attend my high school graduation because they had moved again, and college was not in their plans for me. I stayed with my parents for a couple of months during the summer between high school graduation and going off to college, where I had been awarded an academic scholarship. On the day I left for college, my dad took off to the woods hunting without saying goodbye, without giving me money for the one-way trip or uttering a word of encouragement.

I loved the southern look and feel of the small liberal arts college. The big red-brick buildings in white trim with long windows were stately and beautiful. My secret dream or fantasy of attending a large university had faded. I was in college and that was a miracle all its own. More than anything I wanted the American Dream—a nice home, a husband with a good education and good job who could support me. Someone I loved and who loved me and wanted a family. Also, I planned on a career of my own. A college education was a step in that direction. I held on to that. I envied the girl whose mother bought hundreds of dollars' worth of dresses, matching underwear, coats, boots, and shoes for her daughter to take to a big university. That was never going to happen to me. It became less important when I realized I could, and

43

would, go to college without that. I was on the campus of a college; I reinforced that fact to myself over and over. The rooms were small but nice. How could I be homesick for a home I didn't have? My roommate and I were total opposites. That worked to our advantage.

Surely no one guessed my culture shock on this campus. It took hard work and full concentration to cover up my shortcomings. I felt so white mixing in with African-Americans for the first time. Not racially white, but white inside, experiencing my first exposure to racial diversity. Are we living together in the same room, I asked myself upon arrival? Do white girls date African-Americans? I didn't know. I didn't care. But this was new to me. I grew up in the mountains where we all looked, talked, and acted alike. Surrounded by eggheads, foreign students, and gays, I put work into looking well-adjusted, forcing my eyes to turn away from bodies strolling the hallways in togas and turbans speaking in foreign languages with high-pitched accents. Much different from the nasal mountain twang I grew up with, and spoke myself. I felt as if I were in a foreign land, more foreign than Appalachia.

Every student worked. That was part of the scholarship agreement. Dishing out scrambled eggs and half-baked biscuits to students in the mornings for breakfast and wiping tables with a wet rag dipped in bleach got me going for the day. The school cafeteria was entry-level in the work program where I landed. College administrators and professors sometimes took breakfast with the students or joined them for a cup of coffee as a way of getting acquainted. After a few weeks of classes and working in the cafeteria, a hand scribbled note appeared in my school mailbox: "Come to Student Services for additional labor assignment." For extra dollars, I could work additional hours serving at formal dinners to wealthy clients and potential donors to the school, and top-ranking school officials. I gladly accepted the additional work assignment.

Training sessions taught mountain girls like me to serve from the right and not to lean too far over guests. We were expected to be well-groomed, good looking, polite, and reserved. Water glasses were never empty for long. Apparently this position put me in touch with my future benefactor, one of the top administrators at the college, who helped organize these gatherings as well as attend.

Classes were hard-driven, with long lectures and long assignments. Students at the college were there because of their academic achievements. My roommate kept up and excelled in her studies; she hit the books every night. I didn't get involved head-over-heels in my studies, but my grades were fine. I enjoyed dressing up and going to the student union to socialize.

My circle of friends grew and we became known on campus as a clique. A prospective class leader caught my eye early on. He was a serious student, a debater and activist. We began a casual dating relationship. I fell for him. A farm boy with sweaty hands got a crush on me. I didn't want to date farmers, because I wanted to move upward on the economic scale. Upper-class boys liked me, but I had no dating experience, so I was more comfortable in group social settings with experienced guys.

It wasn't long before I didn't have time for boyfriends my age or upperclassmen either, because my benefactor, an older, established, powerful, prosperous-looking Campus God tied up most of my free time. It started out so innocently. Perhaps I laughed at one of his pitiful jokes when he stopped by the breakfast table I was wiping down, or I smiled a wide smile at him when we crossed paths on campus, which made him take notice of me. If so, I did it without purpose, but it took hold with him. He latched on to me early on in my freshman year. It was comforting and complimentary to have someone so important to lean on. From the very beginning he'd say, "You are the most beautiful girl I have ever seen."

I could see him coming from a distance on campus heading in my direction, and when he saw me, his pace quickened. The years have faded some of the memories, but I remember him most in the winter. He dressed in a dark business suit with a white shirt and expensive brightly-colored ties. He wore a long black overcoat with a dark gray scarf around his neck. His head was shielded from the cold with a dramatic, charcoal gray Russian Cossack hat. His dress reflected his comfortable salary. His long Edwardian face with its thin, chiseled nose was dotted with brown pigmentation and his friendly brown eyes were often rimmed with a jaundiced yellow tint, caused by an active case of malaria, I later learned. His smile exposed brown stained teeth, straight across the top, but the small bottom teeth overlapped each other. I could feel the bones in his long, lean fingers when he grasped my hand as we walked together. He walked about campus with an air of money, confidence, and power that superseded any physical flaws.

I bathed in the glory at first. Coddled and teased, I felt lucky to be the chosen one. I'd never received such special treatment. He escorted me from building to building, holding doors open, tipping his hat, and smiling. He couldn't do enough, and he did so with joy and pleasure. Did my friends see me? This man was one of the most important and influential college administrators, not only on our campus, but also in the state and regional educational community, and he was walking with me, helping with books and spirals. He was an engaging conversationalist, telling me of the foreign countries he'd visited. Places I wanted to go to. I wanted to travel. He represented the new world to me. A world I dreamed about and read about in books seemed a possibility for me. My version of the American Dream evolved from the conventional husband, home, and family, to career, travel, fine clothes, and prominent social status. As the days and evenings came and went, my hours increased with him. For the first time, I was privy to a world beyond poverty. A world of attention was lavished on me. What was so fascinating about me? My height and slender build—inherited from my father's family—my Swedish coloring, blond hair and blue eyes—inherited from my mother's family—or my vulnerability, a poor mountain girl? A poor mountain girl who longed for attention, affection, and money.

His office represented his importance on campus. His desk covered half his office. The long sleek boards, sanded and stained to perfection, were assembled in a friendly semi-circle design which both welcomed visitors and presented a figure of enormous power behind it. He immediately walked from his desk when I entered his office, reaching his aging hand to me or gently pulling me into a friendly hug. I responded with all my attention on every word he spoke, with expressions of thanks and smiles.

Weeks became months, and months turned into my entire college experience. My relationship with the Campus God grew stronger. Publicly we were together almost daily. He stopped at my dorm in the mornings to escort me to class or my job on the way to his office. In the evenings, he came into the student union to say something of no importance to me, to see who I was socializing with and which boys might be hanging out at my table.

I remember one of the cold winters I was there, when the winds whipped through the trees and around the college buildings, a fifty-dollar check surprised me in my mailbox with a short typewritten note: "A new winter jacket for you." I was grateful. More gifts arrived. A copy of a book he recommended I read: Pride and Prejudice, with the inscription, "You are sweet and oh, so pretty..." A Christmas card with money for clothing. Money in my checking account with no record of the origination.

As the days and months wore on, in spite of his generosity and my boost in self-importance, I wanted to spend more time with my friends. I wanted to date real boys, especially the one who'd caught my eye, but my attempts were stymied. The Campus God politely warned me over and over to stay away from him. As he put it: "He'll be sorry. You're too good for such a boy. You are better than that. If this goes too far, I have the power to kick him out of this school. Have you heard of someone leaving this place because of failing grades? I have that power."

With words like that I realized the relationship had gotten out of hand. I didn't have an escape plan. I was torn. On one hand, I wanted and needed the money he so generously gave to me, and the social status was nice as well. But on the other hand, I had no life of my own. Even if I got into trouble on campus, my penalties were lifted or lightened. Eventually I told my roommate, although she already knew plenty about us. Word soon got around campus that I was this administrator's girlfriend and so did the jokes, especially from potential dates. Some of the guys would say things like, "I'd like to go out with you, but I need to get my education."

My roommate, who held backroom counseling sessions, started in on me to do something about the situation. My response: "What situation?"

She encouraged me to talk with someone.

I said, "I'm a Christian. Nothing happened and nothing is going to happen. Why would I talk to someone, and about what? Tell them someone important on campus befriended me? When did that become a cardinal sin or a college crime? What more is there to tell? Who would I tell this to? Who'd believe me anyway? What constitutes crossing the line?"

I reasoned with her, "It's nothing more than a casual friendship and I'm cutting back on that."

In the meantime, I was able to send my mom some much needed money for holidays and on her birthday.

I was a poor mountain girl, swept up by money, power, and attention. But I didn't know how to deal with the internal conflict. I felt alone. The object of campus gossip, I was a helpless lamb in a wolves' den. Over time this relationship began eating me alive. I became so conflicted, there were times I wished I were dead. I chanced dating a few times, and on more than one occasion a security guard followed us.

On one of my few trips back to my hometown, I talked with a close relative. I said, "I've something I need to talk to someone about, will you listen?"

She took my hand in hers and said to me, "Honey, no matter what it is, it's not your fault."

She could not resolve the situation, but offered me sympathy and understanding. She told me it was more than a casual friendship on his part.

In one trip to his beautiful home, floored with dark, wide planks and furnished with soft, overstuffed couches and chairs, I admired a painting hanging in his living room. He removed the painting from the nail and placed it in my hands, telling me he would enjoy it more if I accepted it as a gift. I took it back to my dorm room. I later gave it to a friend. He never talked about his personal life. I never met or saw his wife.

I wrote to my mom, but not on a regular basis, and it was always a short, happy, positive letter, regardless of my real status. Never in my wildest dream would I tell my mom or my dad I had a relationship problem. My parents did not engage in lecturing or counseling. You made your decisions and lived with those decisions. They didn't send or offer monetary support. They did not have extra funds, especially for a college education.

A shoebox of unopened letters I received after leaving college remains stored in my old Army foot locker.

Thank you for listening to me Kinu. Hope to hear from you soon.

Take care,

Gracie

❧ *Chapter Seven* ❧

Falling Hard
Kinu

When her son-in-law handed her the thick letter that had come in the day's mail, Kinu knew that she and Gracie were about to embark on a journey together. She'd been waiting expectantly, wondering if her old classmate would rise and accept her offer to listen; gauging simply from the heft of the letter in her hand, Kinu knew her offer hadn't been dismissed.

After she read Gracie's letter, Kinu went to the old rosewood bookcase in the living room and pulled out a thin college yearbook from its place on the top shelf. She located Gracie's junior class picture and stood for a long moment studying her face. The big smile and wide-open eyes of youth were there, but was there also a shadow of sadness in her eyes, a tenseness in the corners of her smile?

Gracie's story of her college experiences had been powerful and candid. Kinu felt a gut connection with the young Gracie. A sister.

After thumbing through the yearbook, she studied one more picture, a group shot of the college's English professors, then put the book back in its place and went to her desk to write her own detailed confession…opening doors.

Dear Gracie,

Thank you for having the courage and taking the time to share your story with me. I've a college experience as well. My story, too, is painful and haunting. I've kept this story to myself until now.

I became a new person when I went to college. As soon as I stepped out of my father's old Buick and put my feet on campus ground, I felt liberated. And exhilarated!

The trip from Mercy Mountain took five hours. Dad used the majority of that time to lecture me sternly about the "nature of boys" and to warn me not to even date. I'd heard all this before; he hadn't allowed me to date at all in high school and although I'm sure he realized it was a useless proposition at this stage, he was determined to make his declarations loud and clear yet one more time. I was uncomfortable with Dad. He was so out of touch with me that he and I couldn't carry on a true, unguarded conversation about anything, much less boys—my overwhelming desire was to get away from all his lectures and suspicious questionings, his dire warnings, his monitoring of my every thought and deed.

When Dad stopped drinking nearly two years before, I thought our relationship would improve and not be so confrontational. I did love my daddy, but I couldn't seem to show him spontaneous affection. We both remembered certain incidents that had happened when he was drinking; those memories put the squeeze on spontaneity. Now, perhaps as a result of my actions towards him during that period, I secretly thought he sometimes considered me capable of wild, unpredictable behavior. There were times when we discussed my school work or daily activities in a normal fashion, but there were also those moments when we were circling each other warily, no longer in an actual fight, but on the ready. I hated to leave my mother, sisters, and little brother, but I was ready to leave Dad. Out of tenuous shreds of filial loyalty, I tried to hide those feelings on the trip over, but they were ready to explode. I wanted to tell him he was wrong about me if he thought I was looking to go wild. He didn't need to try to supervise my every thought and action; he could trust me.

What was he saying now? I was distracted by the beautiful campus grounds surrounding me and all the activity. Fellow dorm-mates were arriving and there were noisy farewells and tears everywhere. He unloaded my new red suitcase, which was my treasured graduation gift from my Aunt Leslie, and stacked the several extra cardboard boxes of items next to them.

Were those tears in his eyes? Suddenly, I felt my own eyes well up with tears. We hugged awkwardly and I whispered, "I'm sorry, Daddy. I'm sorry to leave you and everyone."

51

This seemed to please him and he said, "Just be a good girl and study hard. Do your best. I'm proud of you."

What? Was I wrong about what he thought of me? I hugged him again and we said goodbye.

Those few unexpected words gave me such pleasure. I was determined to make him proud of me, for sure. I had begun not only a new time in my life, but a new beginning with my father.

The next few weeks flew by. Orientation, scheduling, chapel meetings, dorm meetings and, of course, the twenty-one semester hours of classes I'd signed up for. My new optimistic outlook was pervasive. College was great. I wrote home to my mother, "This is my cup of cha." I wasn't the only biracial face standing out in the crowd, for one thing. My Japanese grandmother had lovingly called me her little "hoppa haole"—half white. Well, there were many races and hoppas here on this wonderful campus. I could converse easily with the girls I met in the dorm, and I quickly began to make friends.

Predictably, many of my friends were foreign students; by looking at me, everyone assumed I was one too. They were always surprised to hear me speak fluently in unaccented English, and my Asian friends were equally surprised to hear my extremely feeble attempts at Japanese.

Mother had never taught us much Japanese. For one thing, living in Mercy Mountain, in the heart of the Appalachian coal fields, didn't exactly afford her much opportunity to use the language herself; on the flip side, she never picked up the southern mountain dialect. She spoke textbook English. She couldn't force herself to say words like "hain't" or "holler" for hollow. Mom worked at her speech. After traveling with Dad while he was being stationed around the U.S., she now had only the slightest trace of an accent. The few times she spoke in Japanese were never in public, just around the house. So I knew only a few common phrases: how to count, the words to her favorite Japanese song, the names of the parts of the body, and a few choice cuss words.

At some point during those first few weeks at college, I came to the conclusion I was ignorant in a major way about dating and boys. Within a few days of arriving on campus, I was getting rushed by some upperclassmen. I didn't know how to respond to all the attention. Having never been on a date, I had no idea how to act or what, exactly, was expected of me. I only knew two things—my father's warnings, and that it was time for me to figure out for myself what this was all about.

My first dates would probably qualify as disasters. Awkward conversation, bad campus movies, holding sweaty hands, combined with jumpy nerves, all led to a quick goodnight kiss and the rush to get away safely inside the dorm. Those poor guys probably wondered if they had body odor, or something worse, that warranted my cold treatment of them. I just couldn't warm up and relax; my communication skills disappeared. I don't know what I was expecting, but something was definitely not happening. I continued to get asked out, though, and found that double-dating was more my idea of a good time. No pressure there to be a scintillating conversationalist or to live up to my—so I was told—exotic looks.

I did fall hard for someone; it was the beginning of the second semester of my freshman year. He wasn't a student. As soon as he came into my English classroom, I felt my breath stop; mine and every other girl's in the room. In his thirties, darkly handsome—all female eyes were drawn to him.

When he called the roll and he got to my name, my voice came out husky; he glanced up from his paper and looked my way. His eyes were a dark forest green and they narrowed a little in concentration. He said nothing, though, and continued calling off names. His lecture was as fascinating as he was; I left his class determined to do my best work for him. I left his class wanting him to notice me again. I left his class hooked.

In the following weeks and months I attended every one of his classes. I gleaned scraps of information about him from other students. He was thirty-five and married—his wife was tall, beautiful, blonde, and pregnant. He had the reputation of being a good teacher, hard but fair. His office was located next to his classroom on the top floor of the old wooden building that temporarily housed the English department during some campus renovations. He sometimes had conferences with students in his office after class.

There's always been something stubborn about me. I don't like being forced or pushed to do anything, and now I felt like something beyond my control was pushing me toward him. When class was over, I refused to join the girls thronged around the lecture podium even though I longed to be near him. When anyone mentioned him, I forced myself to say little or nothing, when instead I wanted to gush about how great he was. And other than answering to my name in class that first day, I didn't speak unless he singled me out. The truth also was that I couldn't trust my flustered reaction to him to allow me to open my mouth and contribute something coherent to class discussions.

I was inspired, instead, to write my heart out for his assignments; I wanted to impress him, to let him know who I was in hopes that he'd ask me to "come to my office after class," but although others were invited, I never was—until the day of the final exam. The exam was an exercise in creative writing, our choice of topic, and I wrote about the night I confronted my father over his alcohol-fueled abuse.

I was alone in the classroom with him when I looked up from my finished paper. He walked over to my desk, and I handed my work over slowly, suddenly wishing I hadn't written about that horrible night. He asked me to stay while he read my paper, then as I watched, he wrote across the top of the paper, "beautiful work." I was flushed and pleased and embarrassed; I wanted to avoid his scrutiny as I felt his eyes on me, but then, over the surely audible pounding of my heart, I heard him ask, "Kinu, would you come to my office please?" I hesitated for a fateful fraction of a second, but when he turned and left the room, I followed.

His office was dark and small, crowded with books lining three walls. There were two tall, narrow windows on the wall behind his desk, and in the corner was a worn leather armchair. Motioning to the chair, he invited me to be seated. I perched on the edge of my seat, aware of my stiff spine and the smoky aroma of the room.

With little preamble, he asked me if I would like to work for him as his student assistant next semester. I nodded dumbly. He smiled a little and asked if I would tell him about myself. I talked for nearly thirty minutes, his quiet, skillful questions and comments drawing me gently out of my rigid, somewhat shell-shocked state.

He explained that he'd been looking for a student who showed promise as an English major to help grade papers and to do secretarial duty. His current student assistant was graduating. He assured me he could get me released from my job working in the stacks section of the library. I could barely concentrate on what he was saying; I was drugged by his proximity to me and hypnotized by the sound of his warm voice.

Belatedly realizing I had to leave for another class, I gathered my senses and blurted, "Why me?" I felt his eyes on me once again. He shook his head. "I don't know; I have a feeling you'll work out." As I stood, he reached out to shake my hand. When our hands touched, I felt the connection run through me; and, for an instant, I thought his hand tightened on mine. As I hurried out the door, he called after me, "You'll start next week."

Later that night, when the dorm was quiet and my roommate was sleeping peacefully in her bed across the room, I replayed every word, every nuance of every word, every unspoken word. But what filled me with trembling excitement was the remembrance of his touch on my hand, and the glorious moment that was mine when he said I was his choice.

Would my friends notice my sudden difference in demeanor? Because I couldn't seem to recognize myself in the mirror. What was that silly smile all about? I spent the weekend, not in the library working and studying as usual, but lining up my outfits and doing my nails. On Sunday evening, I came down hard from my high.

I regularly wrote my mother on Sunday nights, and this time when I tried to write, I felt like I needed to cover up something. I'd always confided in my mother, my best friend, but I couldn't tell Mom that I thought I was in love with a married man, nor could I even indicate that I had certain feelings for my teacher, who had asked me to work for him. I wrote a guarded letter, casually mentioning that I was transferring from the library job assignment to one of teacher's secretary. I would be working for Dr. Allen Akers in the English department. This was the first time I hadn't been completely honest with her. I reasoned that I wasn't actually lying; I was deceitful by omission.

I was determined not to let my infatuation show on my face or in my actions when around him. The turmoil of raw emotion that threatened to boil over whenever I thought about him was something I would work to control, just as I'd learned to control other aspects of my life. This potentially dangerous, forbidden love would be my deeply guarded secret. I would not share it with my mother or friends; as a Christian, could I even confess this secret to God? And if it was a deceit and a sin to love a married man, God forgive me.

By the time I went back to his office Monday afternoon, I had myself under control. He showed me my desk, and we talked at length about my secretarial duties. He had a class to go to, but before he left, he carefully selected several books from his crowded bookcase and asked me to read them. "We'll talk about them as you read them," he said. "Is this for a class or something?" I asked. "Part of my hope is that you'll allow me to mentor you, Kinu. And teaching is such a part of who I am, I don't want to miss this opportunity to encourage you in your reading and to prepare you for the teaching career you said you wanted." My heart leaped in a traitorous way, once again out of control. And of course I agreed, rejoicing in the realization that I was graduating from the cut and dried secretarial position to something a little more personal. He was interested in me as a person, in a good way—maybe not exactly in the way I had imagined, but now I was diverted from my schoolgirl daydreams and enticed by the idea that he had actually offered to be my mentor.

That semester I read everything he gave me—Steinbeck, Hemingway, Shakespeare. Each day after my work for him was done we discussed books, poetry, and theater. Generally, he talked and I listened, enthralled. My confidence gradually improved enough for me to begin voicing my opinions, which he seemed to enjoy.

I was in love with him, even more so, but I didn't show it, except perhaps through my absolutely devoted attention to everything he said or did. Was I fooling anyone but myself?

I think he knew. Although he rarely talked about his family and personal life to me, he encouraged me to talk about mine. He was fascinated by my stories of my Japanese mother and my Welsh-American father. It was at this time that I started writing my stories down for him to read. He found it hard to picture me in the coalfields of Appalachia, and once embarrassed me by saying I was like an exotic flower found growing by a strip mine.

I worked for him for two and a half years. During this time, I dated on and off in an attempt to persuade myself that this was just an infatuation I had with him—one that would evaporate if I found someone else. My junior year, I did find someone I was attracted to and enjoyed being with. His name was John Ransome. We dated for about a year, and everyone on campus considered us a couple. No one knew there was a third someone in the picture.

I was actually relieved in a way when Dr. Akers informed me that he was taking a teaching position in another college. He had never reciprocated my love for him; strain as I might to interpret his actions or his comments as indicators of romantic interest, I couldn't gauge any such feeling...unless he was as good as I was at suppressing emotions. There was no hope for me.

My chance to tell him how I felt came and went. He left our college and went off to bigger, better things. John Ransome and I married at the end of my senior year.

You asked how college went for me. I started to tell you the usual empty, meaningless things that people sometimes write in letters, but I found myself writing maybe more than you ever wanted to know. If so, I'm sorry. It was as if someone else had taken hold of my hand and pushed my pen across the paper.

Your friend,

Kinu

❧ *Chapter Eight* ❧

Showers of Blessings
Gracie

G racie kept an eye on the dark clouds streaming through the sunlight behind her Appalachian Mountains. The sunlight, diffused by the leaves on the trees, cast eerie shadows on the grass. Thunder came in large claps. Gracie rushed to pull sheets, towels, and a denim quilt from the clothesline and pile them in the basket as raindrops wet her hair and dress. She stooped, raking up clothespins scattered on the ground. Patsy Cline's song, *I Fall to Pieces,* kept her attentive to the sound coming from the open kitchen window. The music stopped midway through the song. Gracie gasped. She wouldn't admit to this, but she was waiting for the announcement of the contest winner who would go to New York and appear on the *Andrew De Soto Medium Show.* She didn't want to admit that she was willing to put the search for her emotional well-being in the hands of someone who hobnobbed with ghosts and spirits. Someone who spent their time channeling. Besides, this was only a silly contest. *Why is my heart beating so fast?*

When she heard her name, Gracie Justice, announced as the winner, she grabbed the clothes basket, full and rain-dampened, and swung it in deep waltz steps around the kitchen with clothespins tumbling to the floor. She felt like a kid in a happy moment. She'd have her dream about her sister interpreted. That would be her request; and she wanted to know If Kinu Raines had a role in her life. She wondered if he would be able to tell if her sister in spirit form was following her.

What a day! Winner of a big contest to go to New York City to appear on a medium's show and she couldn't get over Kinu's last letter. She read and reread the letter. Kinu caught up in a taboo relationship in college. That was shocking. Kinu had the beauty and confidence every girl on campus wanted. Gracie had carried the burden as if she were the only one who'd been led into a world of grownups before she was ready. She felt even closer to Kinu now, as if they were sisters, at least in spirit.

They had things in common and things to share. Gracie couldn't wait to write with the news of her forthcoming trip to New York City.

Hi Kinu,

Thank you for writing. I was so happy to hear from you.

It is hard to believe we both shared a taboo relationship in college. Those relationships, fantasy or real, twisted and lopsided in a dozen different ways, impact the heart for years, forever making it difficult for others to break through or gain our trust.

I'm so happy connecting with a long-lost friend. It seems we saw each other only yesterday. The two of us have our Appalachian coalfield heritage and our college experiences already in common, and it seems much more.

First, let me say I'm sorry over the loss of your husband, John. I know I didn't say that in my previous letter. I do remember him, tall, blonde, and handsome. What a striking couple. I don't know many married couples who haven't struggled. Some marriages, like mine, failed.

You said it has been three years since you lost John—my cousin who lost her husband about five years ago tells me grief has no time constraints. Her heartache and sense of loss is as strong today as the day she came home from a neighbor's funeral to find her own husband slumped over dead in a chair.

Kinu, you—suffering from diabetes? Why haven't they found a cure? One can't help but question where all the research money is going? I have relatives who are diabetic—they cannot hold down a full-time job and rely on disability checks for a living. What a shame for both you and your students you had to give up teaching. You were such a good student in college—I'm sure your teaching was a reflection of that. I'm glad you have your daughter and her family nearby. I know that's a comfort.

I can't give you a sound reason but I feel an urgency to talk to you—tell you things that are troubling me and things I'm hopeful for. I don't even feel as though I need to go through the regular protocol or formality generally expected in a new friendship. Perhaps it's because of our similar backgrounds growing up in the coalfields. I don't know why it's taken this long to reconnect. We all make acquaintances, but it's a rarity to connect or reconnect with someone and feel that instantaneous bond like I do with you—almost like a kindred spirit.

Kinu, I'll get right to the point and then you can decide if you want to continue to renew our friendship, because I know you're a religious person. I'm getting ready to take a journey into the world of the supernatural—a world I'm not comfortable or familiar with. This past week's events have my head spinning. I'm trying every way possible to fix things in my life. If I only live one more day on this earth, or I'm granted many, many more, I would like to be truly happy. Like so many others searching for something money can't buy—I'm hoping for peace, and reassurance that I didn't let down those who depended on me. But that's not easily attainable because that reassurance has to come not from our world, but the world beyond—from the grave. I've just learned I'm the winner of a contest, a trip to New York City to appear on the Andrew De Soto Medium Show. This could be a sign.

Do you believe we can talk to the dead? I've never thought about it myself, but now, faced with that option, I'm conflicted. I don't think my church or my religious upbringing view the world of supernatural phenomena as part of our doctrine, so I'll not go to Preacher Paul, Jr. for an opinion or blessing. I don't consider myself an expert on religion or relationships, not even with family, so pressing, unresolved issues in my life are stronger than the religious belief I am holding on to and which is telling me not to go.

Do you sometimes feel John is trying to communicate with you? Do you feel his presence or hear his voice? The visions I have lead me to believe my deceased sister wants me to know something, but I can't be sure. This medium may tell me what I'm waiting to hear.

The reason I'm asking if you see a vision of John or hear his voice is because of my dream where you were dressed in your Japanese kimono and kneeling beside someone's bed. Do you think it was John on the bed? The fact you were in my dream with your arms outstretched as if you wanted to comfort me makes me think we are connected someway spiritually. Pray for me and pray that my church will not condemn me for my actions. I'll write all the details when I get home.

Talk to you soon, honey,

Gracie

❧ *Chapter Nine* ☙

Delores Lee
Kinu

Delores Lee's studio was discreet. Located on a narrow street next to a quiet coffee shop, it identified itself only by the etched words *Medium Consultations* on the brass plaque above the leaded glass and mahogany entrance door.

Maggie parked the car in the back parking lot; she remained seated while Kinu, after a moment's hesitation, picked up her cane and awkwardly got out of the car. She gave Maggie a small smile and resolutely made her way to the plain back entrance provided for clients like her, clients who wanted to hide their visits from the world.

The private back room was small, cluttered, dimly lit, and filled with the smell of incense. Common sense and her religion told her not to make this trip. Her heart told her otherwise. She had seen Sylvia Brown a couple of times on national TV, but shrugged off the idea that someone on this side could actually talk to the dead. For nearly a month now, thirty days and thirty nights, seven hundred and twenty hours, an undeniable force in her breast, her heart, would not let this go. The poem came late one night when she was missing him so terribly bad. She rushed to scribble the words down before they left. Now she needed only a moment to convey her love for him. That was why she was here, she thought.

As she stood there in the darkened room, clutching her poem in her left hand and leaning heavily on her cane, she heard the unmistakable whirring sound of an electric wheelchair coming through the door behind her. Startled and nearly ready to bolt, she turned around. The medium was looking at her silently; Kinu, in turn, studied the figure in the chair. Delores Lee didn't look anything like she did on her local television show. She was dressed plainly in black, no accessories, no makeup, and her sparse hair was covered with a scarf. Had she worn a wig for the show? Her eyes were implacably compelling. She indicated for Kinu to sit with a curt nod at the table and Kinu, her heart thudding, moved to the only chair there.

"I know why you're here…what you want." Her voice was as remembered, deep and rich. "Lay that cane on the floor and put both hands on the table. I can help you find what you are seeking."

Kinu didn't respond at first, but finally releasing her grip on the cane, she placed the piece of paper face down in front of her and spoke for the first time. "My husband…" she began. She was surprised to see a slight smile play across Delores Lee's face. The cloying smell of incense and the closeness of the cramped room were suffocating and she blurted out, "I have something I want to tell him!"

Looking straight into her eyes, Delores asked softly, "How long has your love been dead?" *My love?* Kinu thought and continued, "I didn't say my love. I said my husband."

"I know you are conflicted about your true love. There were two men…only two," Delores said. "What did you bring for me to look at?"

Silently and without hesitation, Kinu slid the paper across the table. The medium did not turn it over; she placed her hands on it and closed her eyes. When she opened them again she said, "There is someone on the other side with whom you wish to connect. He is aware of the confusion in your heart and wishes for you to find peace, as he has."

Peace, Kinu thought. For many years that certainty had eluded her. She was now a mature woman, alone after long years of marriage, and still yearning for peace of mind, peace of soul, peace of heart. Would she grow old without the culmination of her search?

"You'll find what you are looking for if you go back to your heritage. Go back to your roots, Kinu. Open the closed doors and let nothing color your memory but truth. With truth comes ultimate peace and understanding." With those words, Delores Lee maneuvered her wheelchair back from the table and motioned Kinu to take her leave.

Kinu whispered, "But, you didn't read him my poem!"

"You'll read it to him, with true feeling, but not now. Begin your journey. Later will be the time for your love song."

Dangerous Journey

It was raining. The rains had started as she was leaving the meeting with Delores Lee and they hadn't relented. They suited Kinu's mood.

Kinu's visit to the medium left her feeling unsettled. She had the nagging conviction that she was about to embark on a dangerous journey. But was she prepared to reopen old wounds, to face her past mistakes, and to dig for answers to questions better left alone?

On the way home from the consultation, Kinu had fended off Maggie's rapid-fire queries, finally silencing her daughter by telling her it had been painful and to please not ask yet.

"I really need some time to think," she said in response to Maggie's look of hurt and frustration.

That evening, after padding aimlessly around the house for an hour or so, Kinu settled in her designated "beading" chair. She began to work on an intricately designed necklace, a custom order she'd started weeks ago. Kinu often turned to beading when she wanted to think, knowing from past experience that the rhythm of a loved and familiar routine would help to straighten convoluted thoughts and ease anxieties.

As she worked, Kinu rehashed everything, returning over and over again to the words of Delores Lee had spoken to her. She was unable to explain away the uncanny accuracy of the medium's observations. Two loves? Only Kinu, John Henry and Gracie Justice knew about Dr. Akers and her secret feelings for him.

When the rain stopped late that night and she'd strung the last bead, Kinu knew her path. She would follow this through. Although the truths, once unearthed, could never be reburied, it would be worth the trial by fire. She and Gracie would get their answers.

Now, if she could round up and corral her thoughts on paper, the two of them together could begin this road trip through their lives. Perhaps all they each needed was an open ear. She saw this as a way for two friends in need to unburden their hearts. They both had stories to tell.

Dear Gracie,

Oh my goodness, yes! I think I hear John's voice sometimes, and I sense his spiritual presence too. How odd that you would ask me. Just the other day when I was writing you a response to your first letter, John's favorite John Deere coffee cup appeared out of nowhere. I keep telling my daughter I think he's trying to reach me.

Your dream about a man in a hospital bed? John's last days were spent in a hospice center... in a hospital bed. I was by his side. And the blue kimono in your dream? I don't own one, but my mother used to tell me stories about her mother's beautiful blue silk kimono, embroidered with cherry blossoms. I don't know how to explain why your dream would tie into my life. Coincidence? I'm thinking something other than coincidence is at play here.

Now, this is odd also. I never listen to the radio, except the other day, I did. We had a big sudden rainstorm here, and I turned on the radio station to see if I could catch the weather. When I heard them say your name, announcing you won that contest and a trip to New York City, the strangest feeling of déjà-vu came over me.

I went to see a medium too—just recently, after getting your first letter, in fact. I'm a life-long Christian, since age thirteen when my mother and I both got baptized together in a summer revival, and ordinarily I wouldn't even consider going anywhere near a medium. I can't stand to watch the show Medium because it's kind of spooky and hokey at the same time; it makes me uncomfortable. But, for some reason, I felt almost compelled to go to this woman, this Delores Lee. You might have heard of her? She's a local television medium here at this end of the county; she's got her own little show. She only had a few words to tell me. First she said something about "two men in your life," which was eerily true, and then she said, "Go back to your roots, retell your story, and you'll get your answer." I wasn't even sure what my question was.

I don't think mediums as such have an ability to speak to the dead, unless God chooses to use them for that purpose. I talk to John through God, in prayer. I think John answers me in little ways; many mornings, early, I've wakened myself answering to his voice as he calls my name. Sometimes I'll run across something he scribbled in his Bible;

when I read that familiar handwriting now, three years after his death, it seems like a personal message to me. And, of course, I see his spirit shining out of my daughter's eyes, or I hear his voice in my son's phone calls home.

John suffered so much in those final weeks; your dream is definitely meaningful to me in that respect. I stayed by his hospital bed and comforted as much as I could. On that last day, it was as if a calm and peaceful light suffused the room. John was a man of faith; his cancer would take his mortal life but it could not take his faith. Standing there, watching him fade away, I saw the faintest of smiles cross his ashen lips. Just before he died, I think he saw a glimpse of God.

John and I left many things unsaid. It's been a recurring theme in my life; I keep my deepest feelings to myself and it is hard for me to talk of love sometimes. Perhaps I, too, am on a road of redemption and reconciliation, as are you. Could I perhaps enlist you to help me? I need a willing ear...I cannot easily talk about these things, but if I could write them down to be read only by an empathetic friend, I think I could maybe follow the path Delores Lee told me to take. You and I have reconnected for a purpose. I feel it too.

I also want to offer my condolences to you; losing your sister is bad enough, but when you have questions about whether you did enough—believe me, I understand. Anything we share will be confidential. Together, maybe we can get to the roots of our connection.

Your friend,

Kinu

Out-Child

Leaving her letter to Gracie both finished and folded on her desk, Kinu felt a familiar urge. Grabbing her dark glasses and car keys from the top of the oriental chest next to the front door, she headed for her car, knowing ahead of time where this drive would take her. She had been there twice before in the years since John's passing.

Twenty miles down the road, as she came to a small clearing in an otherwise wooded area bordering the old country road. Kinu slowed her car almost to a stop. There, set on a slight hill, was a log and plaster cabin. It was as she remembered: small, ramshackle and with no pretensions to rustic charm or glamour. A narrow front stoop and a sparsely graveled driveway were its only adornments. As Kinu looked, a little black dog came running around the corner of the cabin, chased by two laughing little girls. A young woman stepped out on the porch, shading her eyes to peer at the slow-moving car.

Kinu and John Henry had started their married life in this very cabin. The lilac cuttings she'd once planted on either side of the porch were mature bushes now. She thought she could smell their sweet scent wafting through her car window. She briefly contemplated stopping and introducing herself to the young family living there. She wanted to see, once again, those four cramped rooms where so many memories were housed. But she didn't stop. Not this time; not yet.

When she got in from her drive, she ate a light supper of cottage cheese and fresh fruit. Maggie came in to check on her and to offer her a hot meal, but Kinu pointed to her empty plate and said she was fine. Maggie looked at the folded letter on the table and nodded knowingly. She knew her mother was focused on something other than supper and everyday small talk. She kissed her mom on the cheek and left Kinu sitting at the table.

Smiling ruefully, Kinu began writing her second letter of the day to her "dear listener." Gracie would have some heavy reading to do when she got back from her trip to the big city lights. And she had the feeling that Gracie's medium visit would spark some interesting revelations of her own in future correspondences.

Dear Gracie,

I knew when I married John that my heart wasn't in it. In the early years of our marriage, my dreams were haunted by the face of another man, but during the day I lived out the life I'd chosen. John tried hard those first few years to be the man of my dreams, but I think he realized that I left a piece of my heart behind me.

We were in the small bedroom of our rented four-room log cabin. John Henry was partially dressed, lying on our double bed, drinking beer and smoking. My white chenille spread bore witness to his habit of smoking in bed. I fought my resentment, knowing he was baiting me. He was geared up for another argument. The room was drafty; I felt cold shivers race up my arms as I sat at my small vanity table brushing my hair. I sensed his mood and braced myself.

When the confrontation came, it was nasty. He asked the question I dreaded, "Did you ever love someone other than me?"

A moment of decision. Should I tell him? The truth may not be what he wanted to hear, but my face answered for me. Unforgotten feelings for a man not my husband flooded my mind, flushing my face with a rush of suppressed emotion.

John watched me struggle to compose myself. His face was impassive, but his hands were tightly clenched and his bright blue eyes clouded as he waited for my answer.

A moment in time—crystallized, hard as ice, as inevitable as death.

I decided to be truthful. When I tried to explain and tell him it was my first love, and a hopelessly futile one, with my professor at college, he was first hurt, then enraged.

"The rumors were true," he said. "There were rumors about you and him…"

I interrupted, "But nothing happened between us. I just fell in love!"

"Why can't you forget him?" he said.

"I will, I'm trying," I answered. I stood up and got into the bed, turning away from my husband; he turned his back to me, rolling as far away as he could get. There was nothing else to say. The hole in my heart was as obvious as the burn marks on the bedspread. The next morning, John left and stayed gone for a week. I was actually relieved that he left me and secretly hoped he would ask for a divorce. It wasn't that I wanted another man, but the realization was dawning that I needed time to nurse my broken heart, because that was what I was suffering from, and it wasn't fair to John.

But he did come back, and we decided to try and make it work. I got pregnant with Maggie. After Maggie came, my dreams were less troubled. Oh, I dreamed of Dr. Akers still, but his features were blurred, as if he was fading away. My heart still knew who he was, though. But between teaching and caring for my child, I had little time for old memories. John began drinking and staying out with the boys; I hated the drinking and had my suspicions that he had other women on the side. Those suspicions turned out to be true, and that brings me to the purpose of my letter.

When Delores Lee told me to search for answers through my heritage, I thought only to look back at my history and that of my parents. I've been staying up at night writing down the old stories and trying to recapture memories and impressions of certain events in my life. Then the other night, when I was again having trouble getting to sleep, the thought came to me to read John's Bible. I told you sometimes I have found messages and notes written here and there in the margins; I found a name and a date that night.

Her name is Allison Rene and she's twenty-seven years old. I searched some school records and found a number and address.

Twenty-seven years ago, around the time John and I were going through that dry spell in our marriage—his drinking, my detachment—it all blew up and we had our one and only violent confrontation. Well, I was the violent one. My worst nightmare came true. I heard the same harsh, abusive words come out of my mouth I had so hated to hear from my father years ago. I was trembling with the effort to not do something physically violent once again, and if my children hadn't been there in the house, I don't know if I could have controlled myself.

He left and stayed gone for several weeks with no word. When he did come home, he asked, "Do you want me to stay? Because if you don't, there are others who want me."

I knew then for sure that he'd been with someone; even so, I overcame my pride.

"Yes, come back for the children. And for me, too," It wasn't what I had planned to say when and if he returned, but the words came surprisingly easy and they were from the heart.

Shortly after that, John joined the church. He quit drinking. He stayed home, and he and I made a real effort to repair a relationship that had never been strong.

I know what he has been trying to tell me, what his message is: he fathered a child and kept a secret from me. One good secret deserved another? I don't know. Maybe he thought I wouldn't understand, but I do now. You see, I wasn't there in our early years of marriage and someone else made him feel wanted. Wasn't that why I married John in the first place? I'd wanted to feel wanted, too.

Kinu

❧ *Chapter Ten* ❧

The Chase
Kinu

Kinu picked up the notebook labeled Mom's Stories of Hawaii. Years ago, while she was still in college, Dr. Akers suggested she write down her remembrances of tales of a different life—a world before Appalachia. Turning to the first of several stories, Kinu began reading aloud; as she read, she heard her mother's voice telling the story instead of her own:

I was a spoiled brat—the youngest of the family. I demanded my way and usually got it easily, but not today.

I was lying face down on my double rattan bed which I shared with my sister. I was fake-crying monotonously, no tears, just making myself heard and being a brat. Mother repeatedly warned me, "Yoshi, be quiet. Your father is resting." But I was bored and mad because we were having fish again for dinner. I had asked for hamburger pie and coconut cake, but my mother decided to prepare the fresh fish Dad brought in that morning. I told her crossly that I hated fish, even though it wasn't true.

One more time, I thought to myself, and opened my mouth for a big, long, drawn-out wail, when I heard heavy footsteps in the hall.

He gave me no admonishment, but I could tell from the slamming of the door behind him and the thud of his feet on the wooden floor that my father was mad. I'd witnessed him mad at my brothers, but not at me—I was his little pet.

Shocked, I sat up straight in my rumpled bed and listened hard. I thought I heard my mother's voice urging me to run, so I did. My room had a screened door that opened out to the broad wooden veranda. I jumped barefoot from my bed and shot across the room and through the door. I could hear my father coming fast right behind me. He had still not spoken a word.

I leaped off the veranda, skipping the steps altogether, and landing agilely on both feet, took off running. Our house was partially

70

fenced so I just ran around the house, past the koi pond and the mango tree, through the vegetable garden in back and the small grape arbor, past the chicken coop and my father's workshop and the bathhouse. After running a complete circle around the house, I dared to look over my shoulder.

I could see my father, also barefoot, fifteen steps behind me and closing fast. His iron-gray, bristly hair was sticking straight up with anger and his prominent jaw was clenched with the effort of running. I was shocked to see him in his underwear and t-shirt.

We ran around the house three times, scattering chickens and dogs, my mother imploring us to stop. I was fast and slim and nine years old; my father was fifty and amazingly fit for his age.

Finally, I realized he would never quit chasing me in circles, so I changed my tactic and ducked between some tight bushes and pushed my way into the neighbor's back yard. He didn't follow me, only because his dignity would not allow him to be seen by the neighbors in his underwear, but he finally spoke, yelling in Japanese for me to come home now! Fat chance.

I pouted the rest of the afternoon at the neighbor's house. They'd heard the ruckus and allowed me to stay. I told their two daughters I would never go home. But close to dark, I heard my mother calling my name, so I cautiously snuck back into our yard.

The lights in the kitchen gleamed invitingly, and even the smell of cooked fish was secretly delicious to me. I decided to take my chances, and walked into the kitchen

Everyone was sitting around the large, circular table. My mother and brothers and older sister all looked at me closely when I walked in. The table was loaded down with freshly cooked rice and steaming plates of vegetable stir-fry. A huge platter of fried fish was sitting directly in front of my place at the table. It seemed like everyone had been waiting for me.

I told you I was a spoiled brat and I couldn't help but act that way now. I stalked sulkily by everyone. My father was sitting at his usual place at the table. His hot sake had been placed before him, and he took a slow sip of it as I walked by him.

I would not look at anyone and kept my eyes on my bare, dusty feet. My expression was sour and I pushed my lower lip out as far as I could to show my displeasure.

As soon as I sat down, everyone began eating and talking among themselves. No one addressed me or even looked my way again. I determined I wouldn't eat—that would make them feel bad. But my stomach was growling and my sister started sniggering beside me.

Finally my father said, "Do you want some of this good fish, Yoshiko?"

This was a deciding moment. I squirmed, then put my thumb and forefinger against my nose, pinching it shut and said haughtily, "Yes, I will try to eat some stinky fish tonight."

Dad's expression did not change. He gave me a large portion of golden fish. I tried not to eat it too rapidly, but I had eaten nothing all day, so that piece quickly disappeared. He placed another on my plate, and this time I detected a small twitch at the corner of his mouth.

"You must eat a lot so you can run fast, little Yoshi," he said. Then, to my surprise, he stood up from the table and made a rapid pumping motion with his arms and legs and ran around in a tight little circle.

By this time, everyone was laughing, except for me. Then he stopped and said, "The next time, little one, I will run faster, and I will have my pants on." Then he smiled a little again and drank his sake.

I thought about it that night before I went to sleep. I decided I was too old to be chased by my father; therefore I would perhaps adjust my behavior accordingly. And the fish wasn't that bad.

Shark Race

"Yoshi, your father said, 'Don't swim by the Old Maui Pier…too dangerous.'" My mother's voice called out as I was sprinting through the front gate toward the inviting turquoise waters and the white beach before me. She called out something else, but I didn't stop or even slow down to try and listen. I was intent on meeting my friends, who were gathering ahead for our usual afterschool swim.

I was the best swimmer in the group, and that day we'd have a race between me and the big Hawaiian girl who had challenged me at school.

As I was running as fast as my skinny brown legs would take me, I reached into my pocket for a handful of eliko, the dried minnows I loved to snack on. The salty taste and chewy texture filled my mouth with a flood of satisfying flavor. I was hungry, having just gotten home from afternoon American school, but I hadn't taken the time to eat the warm rice and pickled cabbage ko-ko my mother had set out for me. The race was on my mind.

I stuffed all the rest of the fish in my mouth, chewing rapidly and wishing for a drink of water to wash the dry eliko down.

"Yoshi, you're late! Everyone is here and waiting for you. Are you ready to win?" That was Gladys. Her Japanese name is Meichan, but she wanted to go by the American name she had picked out at American school, so I no longer called her Mei.

"Yes, I am ready, Gladys. Where is the big, fat Hawaiian? Did she chicken out? Hah, I knew she…"

"You knew what, little skinny Jappo?" There she was. At age ten she was taller than my father; her legs were thick and sturdy—swimmer's legs.

I tossed my head in my characteristic gesture and blew out my cheeks to imitate her round, full face. I quickly took off my overalls and stood waiting in my old red swimsuit.

"Let's go!" someone in the small crowd of kids said, so we all took off running the short distance down the beach to the old pier.

The pier was no longer in use by the fishermen of our town of Lahaina. It was rotten and dangerous to stand on. We had been told many times by our parents not to swim there because of the deep drop-off and jagged pieces of timber embedded in the sand beneath the crumbling structure, but none of us listened to the warnings. We all swam like fish; we were afraid of nothing. Besides, sometimes we would find and catch the little octopus that were such a delicacy; we would dive and find them hidden under the rocks and sunken timbers of the pier.

So we scrambled to the edge of the wooden structure. I threw the big girl poised next to me one more taunting look as we got ready to dive in. "Can you swim to the buoy and back without drowning, little one?" I asked sarcastically. I had just learned what sarcasm was from my older brothers and practiced it as often as I could.

She hitched her suit up at the shoulders and smiled down at me. Looking at her big muscles, I had a small twinge of doubt, but I wouldn't let anyone see it.

"Get ready, set, go!" We dove off the pier at the same time and the push of her legs drove her a good head and shoulders out in front of me as we hit the water. Everyone was cheering us on and jumping up and down excitedly. As for me, I heard little. For the first time, I was swimming in someone's wake, astonished at how fast and strong she swam. My one hope was that maybe she would get tired.

She reached the marker first and turned for the return lap of the race. I was closing on her now, and imagined that she was slowing down a little.

I could hear my friends yelling my name. Was there a difference in the pitch and tone of their entreaties? What were they screaming? They were telling us to "Swim harder, swim faster!" Something about the urgency of their yells caused me to kick fast and hard in a sudden spurt of energy, although I also was getting tired.

The big girl glanced at me when I pulled up to her and she said, "I'll give you a head start next time." But then, her eyes focused on something in the water. "Behind us...twenty feet...shark!"

Heads down, we both swam furiously; we were no longer racing each other.

My friends began throwing sticks and rocks in the water; they were trying to distract the shark that was gaining on us despite our frantic efforts. It was nearly on us when, for no apparent reason, it suddenly veered off and began swimming in somewhat erratic circles, finally moving back out to sea.

Somehow, I clambered out of the water to collapse on the beach. My friends were trying to pull the Hawaiian up out of the water; she was limp and heavily exhausted. Finally, after much heaving and pulling, she too lay safely out of reach. The shark had now come back and was swimming slowly in and out around the supports of the pier. We watched its fin for a while, and finally it turned back out to sea.

That evening, having fled to our various homes and told our parents about the shark, we were questioned closely as to where we had been swimming. Everyone told a different story, but the truth was finally revealed. I expected a severe and immediate punishment.

My father briskly checked me for injuries against my protests, and my mother gave me a bowl of hot tea and rice. I noted that she'd forgotten to give me my customary saucer of pickled plum to eat with my rice and tea, but she seemed distracted, so for once I didn't complain. After I'd eaten, they told me to go to the room I shared with my sister. I waited for my punishment, but finally sank into a tired, fitful sleep, broken through the night by many sudden starts and shudders.

Early the next morning there was a crowd at the pier. They were examining the dead body of a seven-foot shark. It had been killed that morning by some fishermen who said they spotted it swimming in a disoriented manner around and about the pier. My brother told me later, minus his usual sarcasm, that it was a sick shark. They'd cut open its belly and found large pieces of tin the shark had somehow ingested; the metal had cut its way through vital organs, inflicting much internal damage. My brother said, "That is the reason you were able to get away, not because of your great swimming skills!" He had reverted back to sarcasm. My ego was somewhat deflated.

But nevertheless, both my reputation and that of my new Hawaiian friend became greatly enhanced by this incident. Our friends proclaimed us equally fast—champion swimmers. Also, we were asked to tell the story of our race over and over again at school.

We were also both punished. My mother had been trying to tell me that a shark had been spotted in the area and I hadn't listened. They tore the pier down.

My father was stern and strict with me for weeks, and worse, I was forbidden to go swimming after school with my friends. However, none of them went swimming for a while either, and no one complained much.

Kinu sat for a minute after reading her mother's stories. What a wonderful childhood her little Mama-san had growing up in Maui, Hawaii! She smiled when thinking about the young, spunky, racer of sharks and irate fathers. The spoiled-rotten apple of her parents' eyes, her mother left family and the white sands of Maui behind when she married her Marine captain. There was a certain sadness in that, but her old stories of growing up in a fairytale land of beaches and sharks never failed to invoke smiles and laughter among her children and grandchildren. Kinu resolved to write down more of her mother's stories; a testimony to life's shining moments.

Country Boy

Maggie came in from the front porch; she'd been watering her mother's potted plants and witnessed her sudden smile. *She looks so much better when she smiles and has happy thoughts,* Maggie said to herself. Her mother's smiles had been rare lately. Maybe the trip to the medium had helped?

Maggie was Kinu's oldest child; she had her father's reddish blond hair and beautiful blue eyes, and also his practical nature. She shunned make-up and jewelry, preferring to get up and go about her day's work without bowing to fashion or vanity. With her toned figure and fresh face, she could get by with it. She ran her small greenhouse business efficiently and did everything at a quick trot, much to the dismay of anyone else who was hard put to keep up with her. Again, like her dad.

"Did you have a good night, Mom? No low sugars or getting up because you can't sleep?" she asked, her observant eyes taking in Kinu's pale face and tired air in one practiced, piercing glance. Maggie had been a registered nurse before becoming disabled with an on-the-job injury. While working in the Intensive Care Unit at University of Kentucky Hospital, she'd suffered a devastating back injury; a bed occupied by a three-hundred-fifty pound woman collapsed. Maggie instinctively tried to keep the woman stable by holding up the bed. She tore loose the muscles of her back in her Herculean effort. Repair surgery had not been totally successful; she filed for benefits. She received a small settlement from workman's compensation, but was denied disability under Social Security. The reason they gave for the denial was her college education.

She would never work as a nurse again because she could no longer pass her nursing physical. Ever the nurse, she was always alerted to Kinu's health issues.

"You worry too much about me honey…I slept just fine," Kinu said, a little too brightly, sipping her steaming tea. "What do you have to do today? Delivering more flowers from the greenhouse?"

"Yeah, I thought I'd grab something to eat first, then load the truck and go up Old Salt Lick way; I've got a lot of orders to deliver there. Do you want to come with me, Mom? Joe's going too."

"No sweetie…thanks, but I'm going to the graveyard this morning. It looks like it's going to be a beautiful day."

When Maggie left, Kinu had a second cup of tea as she took a quick survey of her living quarters; everything was neat and orderly, the way she liked it. The richly-hued oriental rugs warmed the polished hardwood floors John had insisted on, and her four rooms were well-decorated in an eclectic combination of classic and traditional furniture highlighted with oriental accent pieces. Many of her prized possessions had been handed down to her from her mother and grandmother, and others had been carefully selected from the antique stores she loved to frequent.

"Not a bad living arrangement…not at all," Kinu mused as she rinsed out her teapot and cup. She was satisfied and comfortable with her well-planned space; sharing her daughter's home gave her the additional pleasure of sharing in Maggie's everyday life also.

When she and John found out he had cancer, they quickly sold the hundred-acre farm at Old Salt Lick. John knew she couldn't take care of it herself, if things came to that. Maggie offered to let them build a smaller, more manageable house on her twenty-six acre farm, or better yet, she suggested, "Just come and live with me." She lived in a large farmhouse with her two children, new husband, and stepdaughter.

"My Maggie, always generous and loving," Kinu smiled as she began to get ready for the morning. Thinking about the touching offer of her oldest child moved her. John had agreed, asking Maggie to allow him to build on to one side of her place, adding another nine hundred square feet to her farmhouse and creating a separate driveway and entrance.

Kinu had come to think of these nine hundred feet as her side of the house. Her area consisted of a spacious living room, a combined kitchen-dining area, a large bathroom, and one bedroom. There was a door in the shared living room wall separating her side from Maggie's side; they kept this door closed most of the time and it was mutually agreeable that a standard procedure would be to knock once or twice before entering each other's domain. Usually, it was only a perfunctory knock, but still always the courtesy of a knock.

As she finished applying her makeup, Kinu looked once more at her magnified reflection. "Not as bad," she decided, comparing her polished face to her early morning reflection. Her usual fifteen-minute regime of putting on cosmetics had been slightly compounded by the time it took her to carefully apply the expensive Estee Lauder concealer she had splurged on to the dark circles under her eyes. Unlike Maggie, Kinu couldn't start the day without first doing her morning routine of hair and makeup. Her own mother had been the same way, she remembered.

She chose one of her Bohemian tops and added some of her own handcrafted turquoise jewelry; jeans, sandals, her favorite large, slouchy bag and she was ready to face the world. She had a few errands to run, but first she would visit, as she did once a week, the small country cemetery located by the church John had attended.

Grabbing the beautiful dragonfly cane her sister Sharon gave her for Christmas, Kinu stepped out onto her sunlit porch and stopped for a minute to survey the breathtaking view. The beauty of the valley foothills of Mercy Mountain always took her breath away, but this was especially true in the mornings when fog was dissipating and the sunlight filtered over the woodland of their mountain farm. Her heart lifted, Kinu turned to begin her day.

Driving down the graveled and deeply trenched driveway, Kinu raised her hand in farewell to Maggie and her husband Joe, who were in the mum field. Joe straightened to his six-three height and threw up his hand in salute. He towered over Maggie by nearly a foot; a gentle giant, he treated Maggie with love and respect, like she deserved. Her first marriage had been a difficult one—this one had all the makings of a perfect match.

Turning onto US Highway 421, Kinu slipped her old favorite Bob Dylan CD in the player and let the music wash over her. *I'm a child of the sixties, for sure*, she thought as she sang along with Dylan.

Driving her silver Corolla Sport swiftly around the familiar stiff curves, she let herself drift into a relaxed state; she was startled by a vivid personal memory of a late afternoon grading papers in a dusty college office. The clear soprano of Joan Baez filled the room.

That was years ago, she realized with disbelieving shock. Why was that memory, seemingly harmless, so emotionally loaded for her? Yes, she remembered. She'd been in love. But she'd long ago let those memories of him fade into dust, hadn't she? After all, he had never been for her. She turned off the CD.

She was passing the high school now. *There's a more recent, safer memory*, she thought as she drove by the building where she'd taught for nearly fourteen years. One of several high schools in the county, it was built solidly from red brick and creek rock and set on a hill. A concrete bridge afforded crossing of Salt Lick Creek, which ran parallel to the road and school grounds at this point. Salt Lick sometimes flooded in the spring, but like the school, the bridge was sturdy.

Hours spent grading papers in that classroom too, she sighed. She missed teaching. No one had ever called her an easy teacher, but teaching had come naturally and her students had loved her. She was genuinely interested in getting them to do their best, and in return they worked hard for her. It was so rewarding when students hugged her neck when they saw her and told her about their lives and families.

Kinu came out of her reverie as she approached the big curve just past the school. Around the curve and on the right was the Pentecostal Church of God, John's church. Behind it, fenced in by a white picket fence, was the cemetery where he was buried. She had accompanied him to this church several times, but felt out of place there. Her makeup, jewelry—both scaled back for the occasion—and loose shoulder-length hair made her stand out in the congregation; although she'd known many of the people in this church for years, she was aware she still didn't fit in.

It was especially evident the last time she'd attended, when the new visiting preacher, Tommy Melton, preached against makeup, pants worn by women, and finally, "women cutting off their crown of glory." Wasn't it "crowning head of glory," she'd wondered? She knew his message was directed at her. He could just as well have used her name to single her out—he was looking right at her. John whispered, "Don't pay him any mind." She told herself she didn't care what this preacher's opinion of her was, but that was the last time she went to John's church with him, except for the funeral service.

Now, putting all that out of her mind, she parked in the church parking lot and sat for a moment, appreciating the new landscaping of flowers the women of the congregation had planted. Before she got out of the car, she fished out several carefully folded pieces of lined notebook paper from her purse, and sat for yet another moment rereading what was written there.

Kinu suddenly heard her name called out. "Hey, Ms. Ransome!" She recognized the friendly voice as that of Mike Mullins, the caretaker of the little cemetery.

Looking up from her reading, she waved and answered, "Mike! How are you?" She'd taught Mike in school when she first started teaching, and he never failed to greet her.

Watching him as he hurried over, she noted that the years had been kind to Mike. He still had the innocent, trusting face she remembered and looked physically fit. She'd heard he had a problem with alcohol after getting out of the Army, but the church had taken him on as a caretaker and that gave him a chance to get himself under control. He seemed fine now.

"I'm good, Ms. Ransome. I'm glad I caught you. I've been meaning to tell you about a strange dream I had about Mr. Ransome. I keep having the same dream; it keeps pecking at me and I've been waiting for you to come so I could tell you about it." He shifted from foot to foot, holding his old high school ball cap in his hands.

Kinu smiled reassuringly at Mike. Some at school had thought Mike was almost simpleminded because of his complete disregard of people's opinions of him. *Simple and as honest as they come,* she thought. He would tell you whatever was on his mind.

"I'm listening."

"I've been dreaming about your old man. He looks healthy in my dream, not like he did when he died." Mike blurted. "He wants me to give you this." From his back pocket, Mike withdrew a folded handkerchief. Opening it, he proffered a gold wedding band, heavily scratched and slightly bent out of shape.

Kinu recognized it immediately. It was her husband's old ring. John used to wear it every day until five years ago when a piece of farm machinery caught on the ring, nearly ripping off his finger. After that he'd always carried the ring in his pocket, tucked away in his wallet. She'd bought him a new one. When John passed away, she looked for this old ring, hoping to bury it with him, but to no avail. She'd never been able to find it.

"Mike," she whispered, "how did you come to get this?"

"In my dream he was standing by his grave holding it in his hand, so after I dreamed it the third time, I went to his site out here in the cemetery. It was lying right in plain sight next to his headstone. Did I do right by telling you?"

"You did right, Mike. Thank you."

Mike smiled and offered, "Some people don't want to hear about dreams…maybe they think I've been drinking again, but I haven't. I dream a lot, but this dream was important; it must have been, I figured, since it kept coming back." After Mike turned and left her alone in the cemetery, Kinu walked carefully to John's grave.

When she reached it, she extended the ring in her hand and said, "Are you trying to tell me something, John Henry Ransome? What is it? Do you want me to do something…what?"

She stood there for a long moment in silent thought before finally whispering, "I have something for you too, John." She unfolded the papers she had been clutching and began to read to her husband…

"'Hi, sweet thing.' The first time I heard you say those words to me, I tried not to laugh out loud. Most obvious pick-up line I'd heard yet, but then I realized I liked it, maybe because somehow those corny words made me feel sweet. Blue-green eyes and a dimple did the rest. I knew you were going to be trouble.

"So, Hi, sweet thing. You're gone now, but I'm thinking of you as usual. Do you know that today is the twenty-eighth of May, our boy's thirtieth birthday? How clearly I remember your reaction the day he was born; I remember it like it was yesterday. Remember how the pregnancy was so full of problems? It was touch and go, and we wanted this child so badly. I stayed in and out of the hospital on bed rest while you and little Maggie did your best to carry on at home. We didn't know what the baby would be, but in the recovery room when they said I had a big nine-pound, eight-ounce boy, I knew you'd be jumping for joy. And you were. You kissed the doctor! Today Luke's still living in Connecticut, like he was when you passed, but I'll call him tonight for both of us. On days like today, I miss you the most...landmarks of our life together. Ours was not a bed of roses, but we worked it out, didn't we?

"You know now what I couldn't always tell you, not even on your deathbed; but then, I think you always knew my struggling heart, my inner feelings. I think you always knew that my love words came easier on paper. You loved my poetry, so I'm writing to you now, and I know you're hearing me and smiling that dimpled smile. I'd like to hear you call me sweet thing again. Sometimes, in the early morning before I quite wake up, I think I do hear your voice and it's a blessing to me. You'd be proud of our children and grandchildren; they're proud of you. You were a good man, the love of my life.

"This poem is for you."

My Country Boy

When I was young and girlish
Many a year ago
I gave my heart to a country boy
One whom you may know

Tall and blond and dimpled
Eyes of a sparkling blue
Your way of speech was simple
Your heart was mine, I knew

We had our share of troubles
Laughter and joys too
Me and my country boy
I grew in love with you

Over thirty years together
We worked for our due
And although your face did weather
Your eyes stayed sparkling blue

A Christian man, you say God's plan
Yet you were taken from me too soon
My country boy, my biggest fan
A gift to me, a boon

Yes, you are gone, but I'm not alone
I have sweet memories of me and you
And so my heart will never roam
This, my country boy, you know is true

The breeze rustled softly through the poplar trees lining the graveyard. Kinu felt the filtered sunshine on her upraised face. She wondered how long she'd been standing at John's gravesite. At some point during her time of prayer and contemplation, a revelation had come to her. No, she wasn't hearing voices, but she'd felt a deep certainty that the same unease troubling her recently was troubling John's spirit also. The ring was his way of giving her a message, and now it was up to her to figure out what was meant by it.

She felt strangely invigorated by this concept. If this were true, then she hadn't been just feeling her age, her tiredness, her loneliness this last little while. John was trying to reach her. If she could figure this message out, she could find a measure of comfort. No longer feeling heavy-hearted and weary, but filled with a sense of hope and determination, Kinu walked back to her car. The morning sun was stronger and brighter today than it had been in a long time.

❧ *Chapter Eleven* ❧

The "Frenchies"
Kinu

For the next several hours she ran her errands, including a stop at Ratliff's Jewelry Store located in Old Town Square. Ratliff's Jewelry had first been owned and operated by Gilles Ratliff's father, a distinguished-looking gentleman who moved into Mercy Mountain forty years ago with his family. They were promptly labeled as "Frenchies" in the typically derogatory and prejudicial way that Kinu was familiar with. Gilles, his son, was an only child and took over the shop after his father died.

Kinu didn't know Gilles well; he was eight or ten years older and he always kept to himself. She knew he married late in life and that his wife became an invalid over the past several years; she died a little more than a year ago. They had no children.

She concealed a brief moment of surprise when she first stepped into the shop; she hadn't seen Gilles for at least a year and he looked totally different than she remembered him. He'd lost weight and was dressed casually in jeans and a pullover. She'd never seen him in anything but a suit when he was working in the store. And the last time she'd seen him, at his wife's funeral, he was pale and drawn. She almost didn't recognize him; he looked tanned, healthy, and younger than his age.

"Gilles, how have you been?" she greeted him as she looked around the elegant little store. There was an air of quality about the shop, in stark contrast to the other stores on the Square.

She showed him the ring and asked if he could restore it; as he examined it, she looked at some of the jewelry in the display cases. He appeared to have expanded his selection since she had last been here, she noted.

"I can have this as good as new for you, no problem. It won't take long. Is there anything else I can help you with?"

"Yes, I want to wear the ring on a chain, something thin and delicate in 14 carat gold." she replied. He showed her a tray of finely-wrought chains and she carefully selected one of the nicer ones. She would wear this close to her heart.

Gilles gave a small nod, as if he understood her desire to keep a part of John close to her, and she wondered if he was thinking of his wife. She thought his smile was slightly sad and lonely. She understood lonely too. She was suddenly close to tears.

Never one to show her emotions, she averted her eyes. After she paid him for the chain, she smiled briefly and turned away.

"How's your handcrafted jewelry business doing?" he asked. "The piece you're wearing is beautiful."

She turned once again to face him, pleased that he had noted her necklace; it was one of her favorite pieces.

"The ones who buy my jewelry are mostly ol' hippie types," she joked. That brought a little smile to his face as he eyed her chunky turquoise necklace and then her distinctly hippie shirt. "It's really just a hobby, something I can do out of my living room."

"Hobbies are good...I like mountain biking. Just took it up a few months ago." She suddenly noticed he had dark green eyes behind his wire-rimmed glasses; the color reminded her of someone else's.

"I'll have your ring as good as new," he called after her as she went out the door. She could hear a smile in his voice.

Outside, Kinu was surprised to see that a sudden storm was brewing by the looks of some rapidly darkening clouds and the feeling of a brisk wind coming out of nowhere.

She hurried to cover her motorized scooter, which was mounted on the back of her car. The scooter had been a drain on her funds, but it was worth it; it made her mobile. Even after the surgery on her feet, she still couldn't walk for extended periods. In fact, she'd been on her feet too long today, and her ankles were stiffening up, causing her to stumble several times while walking around the car. After she finally managed to secure the cover, she looked up to see Gilles standing at the storefront window. Oddly, she was not embarrassed that he witnessed her maneuvering on her clumsy feet; she gave him a little wave and quickly drove off.

Yellar Dress

Kinu remembered she had one final errand to take care of before she went home. She stopped at Wal-Mart, got in her scooter and went straight to the greeting card section of the store. John's mother's eighty-eighth birthday was in three days, and she had to get her a flowery card. She loved the flowers on a card more than the words, since she could barely read.

Mrs. Ransome had to quit school in the third grade; her pappy, as she called her father, needed her to work in the fields; he had no sons to do the hard farm work, so growing up, she and her sisters worked like boys. Even though she hadn't finished grade school, Mrs. Ransome learned enough to be able to do some reading, writing, and figuring. She was smart in ways that counted.

As she was paying for the Hallmark card at the checkout, Kinu thought, *I'll just drive up to Mrs. Ransome's tomorrow; it's four hours over and back, but she'll be tickled to see me and we can spend some time together talking. Maybe she can help me or give me a clue.*

His mother had been always close to John and was one of the last people to talk to him on his deathbed. Had he said anything to her?

When Kinu got home from her trip to Mrs. Ransome's, she felt exhausted and emotionally drained. She'd left home hoping to find out something that would alleviate her sense of unease. What she'd learned only gave new dimension to her disquiet.

Emma Ransome was a woman who didn't lie. Yet she'd confided to Kinu a story that was hard to believe—a story of physical and emotional abuse endured by Emma and her sons; abuse administered at the hands of John's father, Robert.

John had never spoken about the violence in his home. But, in fact, he rarely talked about his youth and he always avoided talking about his father, period. She accepted that John and his father didn't get along and they had nothing to say to each other.

Actually, Kinu understood this relationship, or lack of one; it was similar to hers with her own father. She hadn't dug too deeply, respecting her husband's desire to not share the reason for his detachment toward his father. She hadn't shared, either.

She'd only met Robert Ransome once or twice, early in her marriage. Although he and Emma had never divorced, they didn't live together. Robert simply left one day. He moved in with his brother Emmett, a widower, and left Emma to raise their children herself. He'd spent the rest of his days drinking moonshine whiskey, and his nights coon hunting.

This was all Kinu knew, until the previous day.

Mrs. Ransome had been happy to see her. Kinu noted almost immediately, though, that Emma seemed not quite herself. She was a little disoriented, asking Kinu how her three children were—Kinu had given birth to three children, but the middle child had died within a few minutes of being born.

And even more disturbing was that while talking, Emma was focusing on a point beyond Kinu's left shoulder, as if talking to someone standing behind her. Kinu wondered if Emma had suffered a mild stroke.

Finally, after eating supper and cleaning up the dishes together, Kinu sat down with her eighty-eight year old mother-in-law. And Emma began to talk. "My mammy and pappy had eleven young'uns. I was the oldest. All of us were girls except the least one and he died afore he turned three. Whooping cough. There weren't nothing no one could do fer him. Pappy raised us on a farm up Big Shady Holler, a hardscrabble mountain farm.

"I was little but stout as a horse; I weren't afraid of work. So I worked side by side with Paps in the fields, planting and hoeing, as there weren't no boys to do the work. Later, my sisters helped, but hit was mostly me.

"Mammy didn't work in the fields much. She was allus carrying a baby in her belly or nursing two at a time. My mammy was a granny-woman too. She was called on many a time to come catch a baby about to be borned. What time she weren't out on a granny run or taking care of the least 'uns, she was roaming the woods, looking fer particular bark and roots and such. She used them in her doctoring.

"I never had time to go to school much, but I learned me a little figuring and writing and I could read right good. Pappy made me quit school. My teacher, Miz Smith, said hit was a shame, but times were hard and Pappy, he needed me on the farm.

"Our farm was eighty acres, mostly timbered, but we had five big clearings planted. It was day in and day out taking care of them clearings. Many a time I remember standing in the field with Paps thinking my back would surely break afore the day was done. But when I'd look and see how our clearings were all planted and hoed, and how our farm was snug and protected by the tall hardwoods and pines surrounding our valley...then I was settled and happy. At those times, my Pappy and me, we'd just look at each other and smile.

"Paps had butted up our house against the slope of mountain which rose up into the ridge. He claimed there was coal seams in the mountain. There was a little one back behind our house near the spring; we dug coal fer the winter there.

"I met Robert Lee Ransome at a church revival the summer I turned fifteen. Though I rarely had time to go to church, I went that day; hit had poured the rain so we couldn't work in the fields much. I begged Pap to let me go with my cousin Becca and he finally agreed.

"Mammy gave me one of her old dresses to wear. I recollect hit was yellar with purty blue flowers. Blue to match my eyes, she said. I had hair as black as a raven's wing back then and my eyes was the color of a robin's egg. I had grown some that summer and her dress fit me good through my bosoms and hips.

"They'd set the big revival tent up in the next holler over, and when me and Becca got there, the meeting was commenced. Robert was setting up front with some of the men who played music.

"I never did like Robert's looks. His hair was slicked down and shiny black with grease. He had a big ole hook nose and eyes the color of dirty dishwater, but he could surely sing a fine tune. I purely did love to hear him sing and pick the banjer. He was singing at the revival that night. I stood in the back of the tent letting my ears fill up with the purty music coming from that banjer.

"Becca said he was giving me the eye, but I was shy and wouldn't look his way. Later, when I went outside the tent to get me some fresh air, there he was, waiting fer me. He told me I was purty in my yellar dress and I guess it went to my head cuz I started smiling and talking.

"Wish I'd never wore that yellar dress…hit was the end of me.

"Robert walked me and Becca home that night and asked my Pap if he could come calling. I thought Pappy would surely say no, but he must of figgered a big man could work a sight harder than a little ole girl and could be a help to him, so he said it would be awright. You could'a knocked me over with a flyflap.

"I knew Robert Lee Ransome was wild. I'd heard tell he'd gotten Lily Deel pregnant last year but wouldn't own up to it. So I had my hold backs, but when he begged me to marry him, I looked at his black hair and his straight, strong back and I said yes. I got married in that yellar dress, too.

"Three months after we got married, I tried to run away. My plans were to slip off whilst he was at work at the lumberyard. I was gonna ask my Pappy if I could come home. Robert must of gotten wind of hit somehow cuz he was waiting for me at the end of our holler. When I tried to get by him, he turned mad and gave me a whipping with his belt. He tied a rope around my waist. "In case you take a notion to do hit again," he said. Then he half-walked, half-dragged me home with him. I never cried much, nor begged, but I figgered there would come a day that I would get away.

"Every time I tried, the whippings got harder. He started tying me to the bed at night, and finally, to get away, I just went to another place in my mind, a place where he couldn't hurt me. For about a year I didn't talk much or feel much. I guess I was like a young horse that had gotten broke too hard. I lost my spirit. Some said I was acting quare; Mammy treated me with her herbs and worried over what she called, "my puny spell.""

"What saved me was the birth of my first child. I named him William after a story I remembered reading in school about a feller named William Tell. I nursed him good and in the taking care of him, I came back slowly to myself. I never tried to leave Robert after that. When he first heard of my situation, my "puny spell," my own Pap declared he wouldn't allow me back home and that a woman's place was with her man. I had nowheres to go.

"The good thing was that for a time of about two years, Robert quit beating me and he settled down some. He slowed down his drinking and came home from the lumberyard with a full paycheck. I praised God that he had stopped drinking, which was why I wanted to quit him in the first place. I never could abide a drunken man.

"But after my second son, John Henry, came along, Robert took a wild spell again, and the drinking and beatings commenced all over. He'd whip the boys too, over nothing. Many a time he'd raise big red welts on William's back with his belt, or stripe the baby's legs with a keen willow switch. I got so I'd lay awake at night planning on how to kill him just to make him stop. Finally, I knew I had to lay hit in God's hands.

"I began to go to church regular; I'd get on my knees and pray for Jesus to help us. Then one day, when the boys were thirteen and fifteen years old, He did.

"Robert come home from a long coon hunt. He'd lost his best hunting dog, a red-tick named Ole Wheeler, and he was boiling over mad and drunk on moonshine. He started on me and when William tried to step in, he swung around on him with his fists balled up. William was near a grown man in size and this time, my boy didn't step back. John came up to stand beside him; he had a piece of stove wood in his hand. Robert staggered around some, trying to get his belt off, and yelled at William to, "Come on if you're big enough!" Well, William and John both came on. They gave their dad the beating he deserved and I threw in a lick with the iron skillet for good measure. We all three stood up to the drunken bully who'd ruled the roost with his belt and fists for too long. This time, he took the whipping. When he stumbled out the house, I barred the door against him and told him I didn't want to see hide nor hair of him again.

"I burnt that yellar dress with the purty blue flowers. I knew I was finished with Robert Lee Ransome.

"My Pap left me the farm when he died later that same year. He said I was like the son he never had. Maybe he felt sorry for leaving me with Robert Lee, I don't rightly know.

"Later, I had to sell the land to the Clinchfield Coal Company. They was buying up property. Paps had been right. Our place had all them seams of coal on it. I needed money for a living as I never took nothing from Robert. I was dead set on sending John to college. My John was the smartest boy in school, according to what his teachers said, and I wanted this for him so bad. His brother wanted it for him too. He told me I did right. That was jest before he got kilt in the mine that was on what used to be my Pappy's farm. My brave William.

"I did what I had to. I sold that land and gave one of my boys a better life than what I had. Hard for some to understand, I reckon; hard to sell the land you grew up on and worked on. But then, life's hard for a woman here, especially if she didn't have much of a man to take care of her. I did what I had to."

Kinu was in shock. The phone was still clutched in her hand, although the caller had hung up. Mrs. Ransome was dead. On the kitchen table, a copy of the "Yellar Dress" story was ready to be sent, along with a batch of other stories and letters, to Gracie. She added a tear-stained postscript to the last letter and hurried to the mailbox.

❧ Chapter Twelve ❧

Regrets
Kinu

Dear Gracie,

I wrote you that John's mother died; she had a stroke the morning after the day I visited her for her birthday. They found this message by her bedside. So saddened by her death. She was such a wonderful, strong woman. She took me under her wing from the day I first met her. Here is her dear message and a story about the out-child she thought was hidden.

Deathbed Message

Kinu, i should have tolt you. Hit's a secret i bin keeping ever since John passed. He has a out-child, a girl. He said you never knew it. He never did know it hisself till just afore he died when he heard from her. He couldn't bear to tell you. A-laying in his bed, he begged me to tell you. Reckon he didn't want to die with such a burden on his heart, but i couldn't bear to do hit neither til now. I'm tired, Kinu. He ran out of time and i am too. Tolt you that story about me cause i wanted to show why John needed so much love. See, he never got enuff as a young'un what with his daddy beating on him and all. Not that i am trying to take up for him. You was a good and faithful woman. He just needed more back in his drinking days. He was some like his daddy, I reckon.

Sorry, i'm sorry for keeping this from you dotter. Pray to my Lord...forgive.

Emma Ransome

Gracie,

When I first saw Allison, I was stunned to see John's sparkling blue-green eyes looking at me from a feminine version of his face. The resemblance was so strong I knew she was truly his child.

We talked, and she told me her mother died four years ago. About a year before John passed, I noted. It was only on her deathbed that her mother confessed to Allison who her father was. She said she'd never even told John she was pregnant and everyone assumed the baby belonged to her husband. Her husband never questioned it either.

Allison told me she actually realized while in nursing school that the man she called her daddy was not her biological father. When her blood was typed, she was a Type A; both her parents were Type B. But she'd never questioned her mother about it, preferring to let matters go and even afraid to hear the real story. She'd listened quietly to her mother's deathbed confession of her affair with a man named John Henry Ransome from over Mercy Mountain more than twenty-five years ago. After her mother's funeral, she sent John a letter explaining who she was. She didn't want anything from him, just wanted him to know she existed. He wrote back and apologized for not being in her life. Several months later, they finally met. By this time, John's cancer was beginning to take over his body and he told her he was dying.

During their conversation, she learned that he and her mother had been in lonely marriages at the time they met. The affair was short-lived, he said, and after they quit seeing each other both marriages improved. They never contacted each other afterward and he had no idea that she'd gotten pregnant.

"He told me he didn't want to die seeing you hurting over this," Allison said. She had promised she wouldn't tell. When he left, she found a gold ring on the ground; she thought it must have fallen from his pocket. She picked it up, planning to get it to him later. When she heard he'd died, she went to his grave and placed the ring on his tombstone, hoping someone would find it and return it to me.

When we parted, she said to me, "Mrs. Ransome, your husband, my father, must have loved you very much; he was so concerned that you not be hurt or disappointed by this."

I showed her the ring I wore on its chain around my neck, and thanked her for it. I explained that I thought it was a message of sorts from John to me.

The tears on my face were for many things—for me, because I was so closed off I couldn't love this man until it was almost too late. And for the revelation that even in his extremity, my poor John was concerned with not wanting to disappoint me. He was always trying not to disappoint me.

My regretful tears came hot and hard on the way back home to Mercy Mountain.

I wrote this poem late that night. Maybe it can help me explain to you, and to John, my heartfelt regret and remorse for broken hearts.

Regrets

Silent serpent that coils so smooth
Around my heart you make your move
Again the flair of yearning pain
Again the longing, all in vain
You harden my heart and turn me cruel
You fire my memory of playing the fool
Silent serpent from times long past
You poison my tears, make sorrow last
Regretted deeds come back at night
Remorseful sighs can't make them right
Around my heart are aches and blames
Cold whispers say, no time regained
Nothing gained and innocence lost
Such sacrifice is life's high cost

Choices were made and hands were played
Now loosen your grip from my heart of clay

Your friend,

Kinu

❧ *Chapter Thirteen* ❧

Channeling
Gracie

On the day of the trip to New York, Gracie took her blue cotton dress from its hanger and pulled it over her head. She looked at herself in the mirror. Trim and tan, she smoothed her wavy hair, applied pink lipstick and put on her best high heels. She picked up Cali and whispered, "I love you. Stay out away from my birds."

Gracie felt apprehensive, nervous, and wanting this both to happen and be over with. She offered up a prayer of Christian discernment. She'd always felt so alone in her misery, but the letters from Kinu proved differently. There were others out there suffering from failed relationships and broken hearts. Gracie remembered Kinu in college as a girl reserved and private, but the letters Gracie received from her were revealing. She, like Gracie, had a life filled with trouble, disappointments and struggles. Her letters were open and straightforward. She didn't hold back. Earlier in the week Gracie mailed Kinu a pencil drawing of a farm scene—a two-story farmhouse on a hill with pastures and cornfields. A coal tipple was sketched in the distance. She wanted to comfort Kinu.

Reservations were at the Crowne Plaza, a ritzy hotel in New York within walking distance of the television studio. Her head was spinning, not from the trip to New York, but from the prospect of venturing into the world of the supernatural.

The first night was fitful. The busy street twenty-five floors below was noisy. The night inched by slowly. She watched for the first sign of daybreak, giving her permission to begin the ritual of day—bathing and dressing, applying a heavy coat of foundation, mascara, lipstick, and blush. Two hours later she walked to the studio and found her seat in the second row.

The show began. Andrew shared personal experiences in contacting the dead. His voice was deep and soft. A chill and fever rushed over Gracie.

Halfway through the show, Andrew called out, "Gracie Justice! Gracie Justice!" Her knees locked when she tried to get up from her seat. She held up her hand and he came to her. Their eyes locked. They connected. Gracie's eyes filled with tears.

"You've carried your burden for a long time." Mentally they were alone in the crowded studio. He picked up her left hand and touched the single charm, half a heart, dangling from a small gold charm bracelet given to Gracie by her deceased sister on her thirteenth birthday.

He continued, "A family member on the other side has a message for you. Someone you feel you abandoned and neglected in their greatest time of need. That's what's troubling you, Gracie? You've carried heavy responsibilities since you were a young girl. You still carry the guilt and pain associated with those family members. Gracie, you need support and understanding but ultimately it's up to you...you've got the power within your grasp, but it's going to take work on your part to unravel the ravages of your life. I can tell you where to start, and I'll be here for you for the duration.

"The first thing to do is to help you sort things out; take your life apart bit by bit so you can rebuild it and get an understanding of where your feelings and deep sense of responsibility comes from. Is it part of your mountain heritage? What about your parents? Why did they feel and act as they did? And their parents and their parents. Trace your ancestral roots. Go back to where you parents and grandparents came from. Ask those who knew your people what they remember about them. How did they handle their feelings toward each other? Were they abusive? What were their religious beliefs and how did they rear their children? This information will give insight into yourself. That will put you on a path of healing. The message you are so desperately seeking will unfold when the time is right."

The Long Road Home

Winter passed and summer was half gone since Gracie's return to this coal mining community. Physically she was settled in a safe and familiar setting, but her mental faculties were still at war with each other. The trip to New York City and her meeting with Andrew De Soto only stirred up feelings better left repressed. Those thoughts came during the day, but when the shadows fell and night surrounded Gracie, she was ready to surrender, especially when visited by the dead walking through one dream—the dream of her sister. Gracie's subconscious mind was telling her conscious mind to move forward.

Dear Kinu,

I thought I would be sending you a letter by express mail the moment I returned from New York City telling you of a productive meeting with Andrew De Soto, but it wasn't what I expected. In fact, I feel disappointed. I thought when I agreed to appear on his show he'd use his special gift to communicate with my sister right there while we were on the stage before God, a live studio audience, and television land. I thought he would read my heart. I thought he would ask about my dreams and tell me about my spiritual guest. I thought he would tell me about you. I thought he would talk about spiritual redemption. That didn't happen. Instead, he looked into my eyes. He knows about my troubles, he could read that, but instead of using his power of communicating with the dead he gave me instructions—instructions you might find in a textbook or a Psychology Today magazine. I expected more and different. He wants to teach me how to reclaim my life by fixing one broken piece at a time.

I was secretly hoping he would set up a three-way communication line between myself, my dead sister, and him. Instead, I was told to trace my ancestral roots for answers. That process could take forever. The one thing I wanted so badly: the message from the other side, a word of anger or bitter disappointment, an admonishment, or a chance that I could ask for redemption from my sister—he said that could wait and would come when the time was right.

I'll just have to deal with it. Thank you for listening. I would never share all these deep, dark secrets, failings and problems with anyone else I know. The thought came to me the other day: could this self-revelation through my letters to you be part of my healing process? Because I always feel so much better after writing to you about my life or receiving a letter from you about your life. I feel as if I've been to therapy.

Thank you,

Gracie

Gracie mused—were the stories in the letters Kinu was sending acting as a catalyst? The trip to New York City to meet with Andrew De Soto had some good points. She chastised herself: had she not wanted De Soto's help? It wasn't up to her to tell him how to go about that. Now she felt badly she'd written such a negative letter to Kinu, but it was already on its way. Her nerves and temper were settling. The outpouring to Kinu helped. She thought about what De Soto said—it made sense. She was hoping for a faster cure but now she was ready—ready to take the long road home—a journey back in time—a journey of her life. She was ready to bring out all the skeletons hanging around in her families' closets— trace her coalfield bloodlines and find the person she never knew: herself.

She found an old blue spiral notebook, creamed her Eight O'clock coffee, and pinned back the old-fashioned curtains on the window behind her chair. Coal dust fell to the bare floor, but the natural light was easier on her eyes. She made a quick trip to the kitchen to turn up the volume on Patty Loveless, *You'll Never Leave Harlan Alive*. That song made her cry. She didn't know why, exactly—perhaps a reminder of her ancestors—a story that hit home about her own family's hard life, her grandparents' struggles.

You'll Never Leave Harlan Alive

Written by Darrell Scott

In the deep dark hills of eastern Kentucky
That's the place where I traced my bloodline
And it's there I read on a hillside gravestone
"You'll never leave Harlan alive"
Oh my grandfather's dad crossed the Cumberland Mountains
Where he took a pretty girl to be his bride
Said "Won't you walk with me out the mouth of this holler.
Or we'll never leave Harlan alive"
Where the sun comes up about ten in the mornin'
And the sun goes down about three in the day
And you'll fill your cup with whatever bitter brew you're drinkin'
And you spend your life just thinkin' of how to get away
No one ever knew there was coal in them mountains
Till a man from the northeast arrived
Waving hundred dollar bills
Said "I'll pay you for your minerals"
But he never left Harlan alive...

Gracie's memories of her mother's people came to her first, her maternal grandparents. The memories were plentiful and painful. She felt as if a floodgate had opened. Had De Soto given her a truth serum? She was ready to be led from Babylon. She, like so many of the Israelites, had learned to survive a life of exile. She'd become so proficient in making up details about her own family, using what she'd heard from the "good families" stories, she had difficulty distinguishing fact from fiction. But that was over with—"Then you will know the truth and the truth shall set you free." Where had she heard that?

Gracie pictured her formidable grandfather on her mother's side. The image was from childhood:

I remember one hot summer day. The low-hanging air was almost too thick to breathe as it hovered between the close mountains. I could see my grandfather veering off the one-lane road onto the path towards our house. He would take a step, wait for his foot to settle, and then step again. His shirt was open and drenched in sweat. He was drunk.

I slipped behind a tree when I saw him coming. Shading my eyes, I could see his face. His eyes were as blue as the bluest patch of sky. The irises were swimming between red lines. He didn't see me because he'd already spotted two of our boys. He yelled that he was going to give them a haircut—cut off those red and blonde curls so they would not look like little girlies. When he reached out to grab the boys they both lunged for protection underneath the house. With arms as long as tree limbs he reached under for an arm or leg but couldn't find one. He found a stick and began gouging at intervals. He even got on the porch and poked the stick through openings. Finally, my dad came out of the house and my grandfather went up the road.

My grandfather's violent behavior was accepted by his followers—union coal miners up and down the hollers looked up to him as a leader—and my grandfather had a hero of his own: John L. Lewis, President of the United Mine Workers of America. My grandfather held John L. Lewis and the United Mine Workers Union in reverence. That was the only thing sacred in his life. My grandfather and my grandmother were total and complete victims of the coal culture, living below the poverty level. Feeling inferior and like they didn't deserve any better. Feeling subservient to others—almost like slaves. For my grandfather that was only outside his job; on the job, he was the one with power over others. The coal culture created horrible family crises.

The Beautiful People of Stretchneck Holler

Gracie wrote and rewrote; evening turned to early night, and early night to late night. The country countdown was over and finally she was halfway satisfied with what she'd written. The intent was to begin tracing back to her beginning. She'd done the best she could for starters. Gracie switched off the light and carried the first piece of the puzzle of her life, scrawled down in black and white in a used blue spiral notebook, from the dining room to the kitchen. Large tears rolled down her face. Carefully she felt on top of the old-fashioned kitchen cabinet to make sure a piece of wood separated the top from the flour sifter; after feeling the hard, slick wood, she carefully placed the notebook as close to the back of the cabinet as possible for safekeeping until she was ready to share this diary of intimate details of her people's lives with the rest of the world. She'd written about her mother's family. She wanted it up high and out of sight in case of an emergency during the night. What if she became sick and had to call someone to come and take her to the hospital? While she was getting her purse out of the bedroom, that person could read portions of the paper if left lying out in the open. What if someone in her family became ill and the police or Preacher Paul, Jr. came to tell her? They would see the notebook on the table and while she went to get a glass of water to calm down, they could read bits and pieces of how her grandfather was drunk every payday. What if her kitchen caught on fire from the old and outdated electrical system serving all the outlets and the new refrigerator? One of the local firemen she knew might see the paper and read bits about her how her grandmother suffered so much abuse. Mostly, Gracie wanted to hide the notebook from herself. What she'd heard and imagined as she grew up, fantasy and fiction, suddenly became reality. It was detailed in black and white. She would be embarrassed for people to know; even though they did know the details of her rough, poor life, everyone pretended it didn't happen. Would she have the courage to share these secrets?

She made a mental note to wake up early to read over what she'd written one more time before handing a big piece of her life over to Andrew De Soto, the famous medium who was coming to a once-thriving nearby coal mining community. He'd called to ask her what she'd done as far as researching her family's history, and could she have something written to share with him?

Gracie straightened up her cozy, artsy living room. She had pulled colors from nature for the quilt she stitched and hung above the couch on the long wall. The quilt alone—one single item—made this room. The corner fireplace opening was covered with a handmade screen. Her grandmother's clock sat on the mantle. Every strike reminded her of her grandmother, her mother's mother and Gracie's favorite person in the world. Odd chairs dressed up with fluffy handmade pillows on either side of the fireplace beckoned visitors. A hand-braided rug purchased from the deacons' wives' group at the church covered a large portion of the wide plank floor. Andrew wasn't coming to her house, or even to Stretchneck Holler, why the fuss? She had to drive to a coal mining community across the mountain to meet him. Exhausted and flustered, she was almost ready for bed.

For the first time in a long time, she moved her radio out of the kitchen window into her bedroom. Still dressed, Gracie lay crosswise on her bed with her athletic shoes, green around the soles from grass cuttings, dangling over the edge. Gracie drifted off listening to Crystal Gayle, *Somebody Loves You.*

It seemed she'd barely dozed off when coal trucks running up and down Stretchneck Holler woke her. Still dressed from the day before, she hurried to the kitchen, but before fixing her morning coffee she reached up and felt along the top edge of the kitchen cabinet. The notebook was still there. No ghosts in the night had stolen the first piece of her life. She poured cup number two before she began to read out loud about her mother's people.

I remember seeing my grandfather on my mother's side. I was scared to death of him. I saw him a few times when I went with my mother back to visit after we moved across the mountain. His image remains vivid even today. I may have gotten my height and coloring from him.

He was tall, big and blond, with white and pink baby-looking skin. He was a violent man. His work: a union organizer. He called men out on strike by shooting a pistol in the air near the mouth of the mine.

He carried his money in a large leather wallet chained to his belt. His job afforded him good money. He drank heavily and everyone up and down Knox Creek, where he lived, knew he had another woman. She was young and beautiful with fair skin, red hair, and pretty clothes. That's where he spent his time off from work. She got his money—what he did not spend on moonshine. He would walk up the road, staggering back and forth, on payday. Sometimes falling down by the road and lying there until he came to, then back up to stagger towards home and my waiting grandmother. Once he made it home to his tarpaper shack, he hung up his wide-brim hat on the wooden peg by the front door. After making sure his white shirt was open down almost to his waist and adjusting his shoulder holster, he sprawled out on the feather tick bed after he checked the chambers, making sure the Smith & Wesson pistol was fully loaded. When he was roused up by cars and trucks speeding up and down the road and blowing their horns as they passed his house, he'd get out of bed, pull his pistol out of his holster, throw the door open and shoot up in the air yelling, "You scabs, damn you. You sons-of-bitches. Go to Hell." Then he would slam the door shut and sprawl back down on the feather tick bed until the cars and trucks came again. He guarded the United Mine Workers of America on Knox Creek with his very life. His allegiance belonged to the miners' union, and anyone who did not swear by John L. Lewis was in danger of my grandfather's wrath.

His wife, my grandmother on my mom's side, was my favorite person in the world. I knew her best because my mom talked about her constantly. A battered and abused woman, she fought off my grandfather with a hot poker when he tried to beat her while he was drunk. He cursed my grandmother and left her mostly penniless except for what little bit she could lift from his wallet while he was in a drunken stupor.

Often I wrote about my grandmother so I did not lose my memory of her.

I remember my grandmother:

I thought she was the most beautiful woman in the world. She was small built. I'd say about five-two or five-three. Her weight was comparable. Her skin was soft and white. She wore cotton dresses made out of flour sacks as long as she could get them. They were all homemade using the same pattern. The dresses were blue or purple with tiny pink or yellow wildflowers on the cloth. They had long sleeves with a cuff and a button. The dress had four or five white buttons from the waist up and was slightly gathered. She wore an apron made from contrasting fabric over the dress. She made all her own clothes by hand for as long as she could until her fingers would no longer cooperate. I can see her now, unfolding a cotton scarf, shaking it out, folding it into a triangle and covering her soft white hair after she combed it with a fine tooth comb and pinned it at the nape of her neck. She wore brown cotton socks pulled up over her knees, twisted tight and turned under. I can't remember her shoes, but I believe they were black or brown with a square heel. She made her own underwear. I have one of her handmade cotton slips, which I treasure. She dressed the same every day. Her eyes were bright blue and they twinkled. She never wore glasses. Her four-room tarpaper shack was immaculate. In what she called her front room or parlor was a big brass featherbed covered with handmade quilts. There were no lumps or wrinkles in her bed. Big feather pillows were at the top of the bed. No one was allowed to lie or sit on her bed during the day.

On the left against the papered wall, which was held up with homemade wall paste and tacks, sat a large wooden wardrobe. This held my grandmother's clothes and sheets and towels. She kept cigar boxes there as well, with dollar bills carefully folded and kept there to make purchases from the Blair lady, who rode a mule up and down the holler selling red salve, flavorings, body powder, and other Blair products. She got the dollar bills from my grandfather's wallet while he was drunk and sleeping. The Blair lady also had tobacco products in her leather saddlebags, which hung on either side of her mule. She carried a Bible and a pistol.

Two rocking chairs sat in front of the low fireplace in my grandmother's house, where a fire was going spring, summer, fall and winter. After a four o'clock supper, the dishes washed and dried, my grandmother sat in front of the fireplace each day, rocking. She often talked to herself. She had a large yellow Shepherd dog who sat by her side and followed her every footstep, and a big cat rested on her lap when she sat down. She cared for her animals faithfully and tenderly. She had a large cedar chest in this room. I don't remember her opening it while I was there. Later, I learned she'd kept my mother's love letters in that chest. A single light bulb hung from the ceiling with a cord to turn it on and off. She had pictures on the wall. She had a picture of Jesus with a little lamb and Jesus at the Last Supper. I don't remember my grandmother going to church, but in my mind she was perfect. People tell me a picture of John L. Lewis, United Mine Workers of America President, hung on the wall above my grandfather's chair in the dining room where he took his meals.

Gracie, wiping away tears, closed the blue spiral notebook. She would not forget it on top of the old-fashioned kitchen cabinet when she went to meet Andrew.

Dew Drop Inn

After reading the first piece she'd written about her family, *The Beautiful People of Stretchneck Holler*, for the last time before giving it to Andrew De Soto, Gracie walked outside to get her blood stirring and shake off the nerves. She loved the outdoors. The blue birdhouse was tilting and needed fixed. She stopped halfway through making the repairs—it was time to get ready to drive the twenty-five miles across the mountain to meet Andrew De Soto, the medium. She couldn't believe he was actually following through with his promise of staying in touch and being there for her. Her nerves were in control of this trip.

What should I wear today? she thought, as she opened every closet door and dresser drawer. She regretted she hadn't bought anything new since returning to the mountain. Finally she pulled out a pair of her favorite faded blue jeans and a white blouse, hoop earrings and a twisted fabric, multi-colored belt. She was more slender than usual because of all the outside work. Her blonde hair had grown longer, so she brushed it to one side and tucked a few strands behind her right ear. Brown leather sandals finished out her look. She was confident as possible under the circumstances with this country-casual look.

The Community Action Center was the designated meeting place. Gracie was there when Andrew arrived. They walked up the narrow street towards the Dew Drop Inn. At one time the town was the hub of mining activities. Now only one mining company hauled out of Big Conover. The mining companies that pulled out did so leaving tipples in disrepair and broken equipment on the site. Many of the buildings that housed mining equipment repairs, the medical building, and the old company store were now vacant. The Miner's Hotel on Main Street, which once drew coal barons from across the country, was occupied now only by the owners. A large lobby boasted of a time before with life-size photos of Hoover, Roosevelt, Truman, and John L. Lewis suspended from large golden hooks anchored into the trim around the ceiling. Thick, dirty carpet with an oriental design covered the lobby and stairways. An old-fashioned switchboard took up one-third of the wall on one side of the room. The heavy round tables with matching chairs were remnants of days when miners and mining officials swarmed the town.

Andrew, fascinated with the elements of years gone by in coal mining towns, loved the aura of the time and place. He recognized Gracie as a member of that struggling breed, for she too possessed that aura of coal culture vulnerability. He was taken with that about her.

They moved slowly up the street, looking up and down at the layout of the small, ghost-like, almost forgotten mining town. The smell of baking cornbread and the pungent odor of onion from the potato soup filled the air every time someone opened or closed the door to the Dew Drop Inn. As they approached the diner, they could see a couple of the regulars standing near the windows that flanked the wooden door, which was painted a deep forest green. Above the door a neon sign flashed "Dew Drop Inn." A bar in a semicircle took up half of the floor in the first room of the small diner. Tall barstools were pushed up against the wooden frame of the bar. The bar was for quick service, a cup of coffee and piece of pie, or a Coca-Cola and a hamburger with fries. A large glass case separated the quick-serve area from the official dining room. The case contained photos of JFK and Lyndon Johnson, and a United Mine Workers Association calendar from the sixties. Hard-shell mining hats decorated the walls. Coal picks, axes, and hard-toed boots rested on shelves above the case. An announcement for pickup dates for commodity cheese and other food items was stapled to the wall above Lyndon Johnson's photo. A long list of mining companies that had come and gone in the mining community was printed out on yellowed paper and covered a large wall area. This town told the story of many once-thriving coal mining towns abandoned by big, rich absentee coal operators who pulled out after the coal was mined, creating a welfare community, depressed and suffering. Another mark of the coal culture.

Opal, co-owner of the Dew Drop Inn, held the door open for Andrew and Gracie. Opal ushered them to the formal dining area separated from the quick bar by a rough arch doorway. The formal dining area consisted of six small tables and two double tables with straight-back chairs. A couple of regulars got up and offered the visitors the best table in the house, right beside the window next to the once bustling street. Opal appeared to have stepped out of a forties movie in complete costume. Her hair was dyed black, permed tightly, and held back with a hairnet. She wore a red flowered dress to match her nails and lips.

Opal summoned Sam, her husband, out from behind the door leading to the kitchen. Sam, wearing a fedora perched halfway back on his head, smiled. He loved to talk to anyone who'd listen about relatives left behind in Italy. A curl of smoke softly floated above Andrew and Gracie's heads as Sam smoked and passionately described his grandfather's trip to America, knotting his hand up in a fist to show how his grandfather had to fight off bullies on Ellis Island. A dark vest worn over his white shirt didn't quite conceal his snub nose pistol. He wore a narrow white bartender's apron.

When both were finished with the warm home-cooked meal, Gracie lifted her purse and pulled out the blue spiral notebook containing *The Beautiful People of Stretchneck Holler.* She handed it to Andrew, and then excused herself. She didn't want to see the shock on his face when he read of the abuse and violence contained in her family's lives.

When he laid the notebook down, Gracie returned to the table. Her blue eyes were again filled with tears. Andrew looked directly in her eyes and spoke in a matter-of-fact voice.

"Gracie, you have nothing to be ashamed of or embarrassed about. Those are your people. You cannot change that, but you can learn about yourself and get an understanding of your own thought process by learning about where you came from, and how the culture made your people the way they are. Remember what I told you when you came to New York—go back to your roots."

"Andrew, I didn't get the chance when I was on your show to tell you about my dream. You can interpret dreams, can't you? In the dream I'm in a room, a blue room, waiting for someone…my sister, I suppose. She never comes. A strange girl is in the dream. Annie Lynn, a close friend who goes to my church, helped me figure out that she's a former college classmate, Kinu Raines. We've been writing to each other. We have so much in common. She's so easy to talk to and such a comfort to me. Our life experiences are nearly parallel. Being able to open up, laying out all my hurts and transgressions to someone you were never that close to before is eerie. But I feel as if she is my closest my kin, at least my kindred spirit."

"Good, Gracie. The puzzle is coming together piece by piece." Andrew said. "This dream is part of your healing process. Connection with a spiritual friend with similar experiences will serve as support to you and you to her. This dream is another piece of the puzzle."

❧ *Chapter Fourteen* ❧

A Leap of Faith
Kinu

Gracie came to a slow roll as she approached her mailbox. She stopped to open the door. There was an envelope from Kinu. Andrew's encouragement and understanding gave her a sense of hope through this new connection to Kinu. She hurriedly opened the letter as she slouched down in one of her easy chairs in the living room. Inside was a nice thank-you note from Kinu for the drawing she'd sent.

On an early morning, Kinu sat on her porch swing, sipping her second cup of tea and musing over an open picture album. The photo that caught her attention was an old and grainy one of her son Luke standing in his Grandma Ransome's chicken yard. Mrs. Ransome stood in the background surveying her flock. Luke had an uncertain look on his three-year-old face; his chubby arms were outstretched beseechingly as if imploring someone who was just outside the camera's range. As she studied the image carefully, Kinu made out the partial silhouette of a wheelchair, its shadow captured in the lower corner of the photograph.

The memory, vivid with accompanying emotions, came back to Kinu—the heat of the afternoon sun on her bandaged legs, the high-pitched quality of her son's voice calling, "I want you, Mommy," the panicked clucking of disgruntled chickens, the hot metal of the wheelchair handles clenched in her hands. A realization that her son was truly frightened galvanized her; she lurched out of the chair to go to him, but her legs would not support her. She stumbled and fell heavily. Although his eyes widened in fear when he saw her fall, Luke was distracted by the flurry of scattering chickens. Mrs. Ransome had finished sizing up the flock and was deftly cornering a fat red hen. Sunday supper was to be chicken and dumplings. John Henry, camera in hand, stepped forward, scooping up Luke, and then turned to assist Kinu.

She knew he was trying to circumvent Luke's witnessing the impending neck-wringing of the unfortunate chicken. The image Luke did see was that of his mother, crumpled on the ground and crying in heartfelt empathy with the red hen.

The impact of the memory left Kinu shaken and thoughtful. Calming herself, she took a deep breath and finished her tea. That moment years ago, when the circumstances of her emerging disability, combined with an intense feeling of entrapment and helplessness, all culminated in a moment of defeat and collapse—that moment now served to crystallize her resolve. She would fight to get up after a fall, after being knocked down, after feeling closed off and isolated. She would be a strength to her family and friends rather than a burden, her mother's daughter, a testament to resilience.

She must write Gracie; she stood and walked steadfastly into the house.

Dear Gracie,

Can I tell you a little about my mother? She was my pride and joy; I loved to show her off. She was like a beautiful, exotic flower. When any of my friends asked where we were from, I proudly said she was born and raised in Hawaii; just that little bit of information was enough to give her movie-star status. Of course, my friends' parents promptly informed them we were Japanese—Japs was the word more commonly used. We were no strangers to racial prejudice here on Mercy Mountain; the wounds of World War II were still recent. Even so, more important to me than my friends' and their parents' opinions was my sure realization that I could always count on Mom. Unlike my father, who had a worsening drinking problem, my beautiful, steadfast mother was a stable factor in my life; she was there in all the ways a mother should be. She was there the night I made the most important decision of my life.

The summer revival was going on at the Baptist Church down the road from our house. We could hear the music: the hypnotic cadence of old-time hymns being first lined out and then sung by two hundred voices rose and echoed through Backbone Ridge. I loved to sit on the porch and listen to those old songs in the hot summer evenings.

Those who attended this church were labeled as hardshell. I didn't know what that meant, but I think maybe members were old-timey and traditional. My dad's mother went to this church; Grandma had repeatedly asked us to come to church with her, but Dad was not a believer. Mom, on the other hand, was open to going to church but hesitant to go to this one. I think she knew they considered her an outsider and would treat her as such, not only because she was Japanese, but also because she was more of a city girl with her makeup and clothing. She was definitely not old-timey or traditional. Mom was aware that not even Grandma could protect us from the covert looks, accompanied by nudges and strained silence. It had happened before in this mountain community: the stares and comments she was practiced in pretending not to see or hear. She didn't wish to subject Grandmother and us to this, yet I could tell she was considering Gran's comment that "you and the children ought to go to church."

One evening when the revival was in full swing, she said, "Let's get ready and go to church." We hurriedly got dressed in our best cotton summer shirtwaists. I was eager to go. My friends said church revivals were exciting; besides, I loved the chance to get dressed up and to sing the old hymns Grandma had taught us. Surprisingly, Dad made little more than a token protest. In fact, he gave us each a nickel for the offering plate.

As we were walking down our hill headed toward the Baptist Church, I spoke up. "Mom, the Presbyterian Church on up the road is having revival tonight, too." On Mercy Mountain, churches were found close together and there were plenty to choose from. "Do you think Grandma would get mad if we went there instead?" I knew some of my friends were going to be there, and there was comfort in that thought.

"Actually honey, I think Grandma will just be happy we're going somewhere to church." She looked at my sisters and asked, "What about it, girls?" My usual supporter in such decisions, my sister Sharon, hadn't wanted to go to church, so she wasn't there to back me up, but little sis, Sophia Rose, who was usually the shyest, took our youngest sister's hand in her own and spoke up. "Mommy, let's go where Kinu wants. My best friend goes to that church too, I think."

Mom smiled at little quiet Sophia, who was so protective of her younger sister, Jenny, the baby girl in our family. She noted that they

113

always clutched hands. "That's fine, girls. It's a longer walk, but not by much, so we have time to make it there." Was she thinking, as I was, that the veiled looks and shushed comments would be fewer if we knew some children our own age in the congregation? I know Mother knew she was the target of comments about the "yellow Japs who killed our boys in the war," and "what was he thinking, marrying one and bringing her here where she's not wanted." Outwardly, she never expressed anger or cried in frustration. I also never saw her bow her head except to pray. So she bravely led us to church.

The red brick Presbyterian Church was set up on a little knoll, and we were slightly late and out of breath by the time we got there. But when we walked in, my friends waved and we were greeted warmly by the preacher. Preacher Elihas Sutherland was old and grandfatherly, with thick white hair and a crinkly-eyed smile. He made us feel comfortable right away. People squeezed together to make room for us to sit as we settled in one of the back pews and joined the congregation in singing The Old Rugged Cross. My friend came to sit with me and Mom talked to several of the women in our row. When I saw we were no longer the center of attention, I relaxed and enjoyed the singing.

The revival was still going on when we left three hours later to walk home in the late evening. We held hands and sang pieces of hymns as we walked. Mom kept saying how friendly so-and-so was.

That night, I heard Mom and Dad talking; Mom told him she had felt a measure of acceptance at that church and she was planning on going again. When Dad started to protest, she told him firmly that she wanted us to have a Christian upbringing. For the past several years, she revealed with uncharacteristic emotion, she had been missing the fellowship of worshipping together as a family; she explained to him how her family, who were Buddhists, had worshipped together when she was growing up. She softly told him that she missed her family, being so far from home in a culture so different from what she was accustomed to. She would take comfort from church. He fell silent.

This was the strongest stand I'd ever heard my mother take against my father. She was sometimes helpless in the face of his periodic drinking, but in this instance, she must have had the Lord on her side, because she convinced Dad that we should go to church.

Mom and I attended all seven nights of the revival and at its close, when they were singing about Jesus knocking on the door to your heart, we let Him in. My mother was my support as I stood at the altar with tears washing my face. She too accepted Jesus as we held hands and stood before the preacher. Her face was glowing with her own conviction. We were baptized together the following Sunday.

If I learned nothing else about my mother, I learned that she was not just a beautiful hothouse flower, as my father sometimes affectionately called her, but that she was a woman who could stand before her husband in conviction, before a judgmental community with dignity, and before God in humility. My mother had a strong backbone, and it was sometimes needed to survive on Mercy Mountain.

In looking back, I can see the struggle my mother faced in dealing with the prejudices of the times and of the area. As I said, she handled it well. I, on the other hand, was not always so diplomatic in dealing with stressful situations. I went through my teenage years with a lot of anger—anger at my dad and his Dr. Jekyll and Mr. Hyde personality when drinking, anger at being singled out as somehow inferior because of my singular Asian features in a white culture, and anger at myself for my growing inability to show my true emotions. Other than my church experience, I was guarded in all areas. I practiced stoicism, or maybe it just came naturally to me. After all, it fit the Asian stereotype. This is painful. I'll have to write you more later.

Remember me in your prayers,

Kinu

Needing to do something to distract herself from what she'd just written to Gracie, to escape from the resurgent memories she labeled as too painful, Kinu decided to do some beading.

Her workshop was her living room; she had a comfortable leather chair positioned next to a floor lamp and a table. Her beading supplies were stored in an antique, lacquered oriental cabinet, a treasured piece of family memorabilia handed down from her grandmother. At one time, nearly a hundred years ago, the cabinet held kimonos, obi sashes, and platformed zori sandals for her Obaba. Now it housed Kinu's trays of select beads.

She settled down with her beads and her thoughts and began to work. As was her usual habit when she beaded, she found herself softly humming the Japanese songs her mother sang to her as a child; Kinu was comforted now with the warmth of good memories. As she selected antique cloisonné beads in shades of cobalt blue along with some brilliant Swarovski crystals, Kinu designed in her mind's eye a simple yet classic necklace and earrings for Gracie. It was a thank you for Gracie's taking the time to read her outpourings; the design was reminiscent of a necklace she remembered seeing as a child in her Japanese grandmother's carved ivory jewelry box. She took a few minutes to study the cloisonné—delicate flowers in pinks and greens were enameled on the cobalt background, their outlines etched in fine gold. Kinu wondered if her grandmother had worn her necklace tucked in the neckline of her favorite blue silk kimono. Gracie would love this gift.

❧ *Chapter Fifteen* ❧

My Mother and Big Daddy
Gracie

Dear Kinu,

I envy you writing about your mother with such intimacy. She sounds like such a beautiful, strong woman. You must treasure your close relationship.

To find out about my mother I went to Jessie, a close relative who would give me an intimate glimpse of the woman I never really knew.

I said to Jessie, "My mother is stuck in my mind as always being forty-two. I see her standing on the top of the ridge at our farm. Her waist-length auburn hair, freshly washed, is swept up by the wind…her day style is the fashionable French twist. She's wearing a belted, bright-blue, plaid housedress, showing a shapely figure after so many children. She appears taller than her five-feet-four against the soft blue sky. The sun reflects on her olive-colored face and her hand shields her green eyes from the sunlight. She's beautiful. I feel like that's almost all I know about my mother…her outside appearance."

Jessie told me she understood what I meant when I said I never really knew my mother. She explained my mother was a private woman, introverted even with her own children. Her shyness bordered on discomfort.

"Your mother was not equipped, mentally or physically, to properly nurture her too-many children. That's why so much of the care fell on your oldest sister. It wasn't because she didn't care about her children; she did the best she could. She loved you.

"Your mother was burdened with trying to figure out a way to scrape by with little money for groceries. Your dad was the chief, and your mother walked the straight and narrow for him. She would do without necessities for fear he would become upset if she asked for a new dress or decent furniture for the house. Her emotions were kept under lock and key when he was around. No one crossed your dad, not even your mother.

"There are secrets about your mother not many people know, especially your dad. It was rumored among some of the women relatives that she was a secret smoker. They said that she would hide in a closet and smoke. There were always whispers about your mother and a redheaded traveling salesman."

Jessie's insight on my mother brought up a memory I thought I had put away for good. Memory of the story had me wondering if there was a non-religious connection between my mother and Preacher Paul.

I remember my mother, our neighbor Gladdy, short for Gladys, and two other women talking about Preacher Paul. They were having a get-together to make paper flowers for Decoration Day to take to the graves. My mother referred to Preacher Paul as "Big Daddy." When she said Big Daddy she took a deep breath and she fluttered her eyelashes. Big Daddy was the pet name used only by closest family members. The women broke out in giggles, covering their mouths with their hands and looking at my mother. One of the women remarked there were other women in the church also secretly in love with Preacher Paul.

This was at a time when everyone in Stretchneck Holler was talking about Preacher Paul. I was not old enough to understand what all went on in the adult world around me, but old enough to sense danger and fear. When I heard the whispers about our preacher, hairs bristled on my arms—Preacher Paul was a holy man. Rumors were he was leaving Stretchneck Holler. What would happen to all the Christians without his leadership—what would happen to Jesus in Stretchneck Holler?

I got a better understanding of what was going on the day I passed by the church on the way to my grandmother's house. My mother needed butter.

I heard Preacher Paul pleading, "Please don't punish me like this. There must be another way I can serve. I know I'm a sinner but do I deserve this?"

I edged silently toward the open church window so I could see who Preacher Paul was pleading with. I was careful to stay out of sight when I stepped up on the log, giving me a slight view into the small sanctuary. The room appeared dusty and ugly without the congregation.

I soon realized Preacher Paul was talking to Jesus.

The Preacher's rumpled, yellowed, white Sunday preaching shirt was dripping wet with sweat and foaming moisture was at both sides of his mouth. He knelt in front of the wobbly altar. The railing swayed back and forth from the weight of his heavy, muscular arms. He wore miners' knee pads to muffle the familiar clicking sound coming from both knees. Coal dusted the floor around him. He wore the same knee pads on his hoot-owl shift each night, mining out the rich coal for Big Conover.

The boards in front of the altar were worn and stained where Preacher Paul knelt slightly to the right of the pulpit, his customary starting point. On this day instead of the loud, demanding voice he used to both bully and praise the Lord, he whined, childlike, sobbing intermittently. As he began to pray, he began to move, eyes still closed and rough hands with deep creases of coal dust pressed together like a child during their bedtime prayer. Effortlessly he traveled on his knees the distance from one end of the altar to the other, as if he were chasing the Lord during this heated one-sided debate. He learned to walk on his knees in the coal mines long before he was called to preach.

"Jesus, I can't talk the African talk. How will I save them after I get there? How will I tell them about you? What will I eat? And the women, Lord they don't cover their breasts, do they? They're unschooled. Why, Jesus? Why, Jesus, are you sending me? Because I've sinned? But in Romans 3:23, you say, 'For all have sinned, and come short of the glory of God.' Jesus, since you have so many to pick from, can you not send someone who is a sinner and wants to be a missionary too? I've never been out of this state."

Preacher Paul wiped the water from his eyes with his shirtsleeve, struggled to his feet and stumbled to the old school piano in the corner. He eased himself down onto the bench. Without hesitation his crusty, dirty fingers floated above the keys. The gift of music transformed Preacher Paul from a backwoods coalminer to a gifted musical instrument. The preacher stopped whining and began singing in a deep-throated baritone voice as smooth as silk. The hymn he chose for this troubled time I had heard him sing many times:

119

Sweet Beulah Land

O Beulah land, sweet Beulah land!
As on thy highest mount I stand,
I look away across the sea
Where mansions are prepared for me
And view the shining glory shore
My heaven, my home forever more.

I eased myself down from my perch, shaken from the voyeurism. I didn't really know the meaning of the song, but it was the singer I was so taken with. At my young age, I understood somewhat why women of the church, single or married, young and old, even my own mother, were strangely attracted to this big, burly, country preacher. It was his velvet voice.

My grandmother noticed I was not myself when I got to her house. She carefully looked me over before asking if someone tried to bother me on the back path. I said, "No." I couldn't say the only thing bothering me was thoughts of the holler without Preacher Paul.

I, like all the others in the community, was afraid without Preacher Paul and afraid of Preacher Paul. He'd been around as the preacher since I was born. The strong focus on religion was nothing new; every living, breathing, plant, animal, and person in the community was there because of Jesus, everyone knew that. They had been told that since birth; the church was the center of power and Preacher Paul was the center of the church.

Life was on a strange hold as everyone waited for a sign from somewhere beyond their coal-filled mountains giving them permission to go on as before, with or without their preacher. I remember my grandmother telling me, "This unrest, this trouble brewing, reminds me of the time when miners tried to unionize Conover and a strike broke out. Two scab miners got shot. Folks get scared and do crazy things when they don't know what's about to happen. We just have to do a lot of praying."

In the heat of the turmoil, without warning, Preacher Paul announced his church was going into revival. This added fuel to the fire by giving people in the community cause to get together and talk up what could happen with the preacher's departure. A prominent political leader said it was not a good time for a revival. Preacher Paul on a local radio interview told his audience and the politician: "Revivals were not scheduled by the preacher or politicians, but by Jesus."

A tent was borrowed from a big church in the western part of the state. The warm summer nights were perfect for the outside revival. Twenty men assembled and erected the canvas structure on Poorman Creek. There was a circus-like atmosphere on the banks of the baptismal stream. Women carried sweet tea and fried chicken to the workers in one arm and crying babies in the other arm. Barefoot kids ran in and out of the tent flaps. Church members laughed and prayed out loud for guidance and deliverance. I saw my mother crying. I never knew why.

During the revival, for the first and only time, I witnessed my mother getting emotional during a religious service. She could have been overwrought with thoughts of losing Preacher Paul to the natives of Africa, or perhaps her blood pressure was acting up over something the boys had done. That evening my mother sat with several of the other regular church women, her eyes downcast as usual. I thought I saw Preacher Paul cast a glance her way when he began updating the church on his call to Africa and what he expected to endure in this third world country. Then, without pause, Preacher Paul broke out in song. My mother lifted her eyes toward the highest part of the tent held up by a big metal pole as if she could see Jesus through the heavy canvas. Then to everyone's surprise my shy, modest mother jumped from her metal folding chair, knocking it over, and twirled around with both arms in the air, either praising or rebuking the Lord in strange sounds. Some said she spoke in tongues. After the third or fourth twirl she fell down into her chair, which had been picked up from the floor and put back in place by the women surrounding her. In a matter of a couple of minutes her face had become flushed, pink lips turned to a bright red, and strands of her long auburn hair fell from the pins holding it in place. She cried softly for a few minutes in the arms of her church friends. She was embarrassed. My dad was summoned to the tent. When he walked down the narrow aisle to where my mother was being cared for by her church friends, the strong smell of moonshine filled the air. He led my mother out. I followed behind.

Word spread like wildfire up and down the holler about the revival. The tent filled beyond capacity after the first night. Many sinners were drawn to the special music provided by a local family playing guitars and mandolins and Preacher Paul's singing.

Each evening when the sun started down over the steep hillside, crowds gathered and preaching and singing filled the muggy night air of Stretchneck Holler. An electric cord was strung from the church to the tent to provide lighting. Services had to finish in time for Preacher Paul to board the mantrip for the hoot-owl shift in the mine.

Sinners were saved during the revival and perpetual backsliders repented again, but on the final night of the revival Preacher Paul understood why he was called to preach. The Blackburn twins, Bobby Joe and Buddy Rae, the most established and respected sinners in the county, came to the altar seeking salvation and forgiveness. The twenty-four-year-old identical twins towered over the preacher's six-foot stout frame. They were the color of autumn, with tan freckles sprinkled up and down their strong arms onto their faces. Their thick, wavy hair was the same color as their freckles. They each had one green eye and one blue eye. Their strength came not from mining coal; their business was lumbering and making moonshine.

Preacher Paul gently coaxed them to their knees, asking them to remove their pistols during the altar call. Later it was reported from Christians on the front row that their breath reeked of moonshine. They wanted to be saved before the preacher went away. They didn't trust their sinful souls to just anyone.

My dad moved my family across the mountain from Stretchneck Holler long before Preacher Paul actually went to Africa. Some said the Lord was waiting for Preacher Paul, Jr., his son with his first wife, to come of age so he could take over his father's church. My mother always attended church on Sunday after we moved, and she went to church socials, but she never joined another church or transferred her membership. She remained faithful to Preacher Paul.

Kinu, looking back at these stories I can see how much I'm influenced by our culture. Please don't judge my mother. She was a woman in desperate times in a desperate place. I can now see she developed coping skills to get by. I believe I've done the same.

Take care,

Gracie

⊱ *Chapter Sixteen* ⊰

Moonlight and Fireflies
Kinu

Gracie,

I've noted the women in both our lives—mothers, daughters, sisters, grandmothers. Backbones of their families, these women dealt with the challenges in their lives, each in their own way. Don't think I would ever judge your mother or mine either; we are all women and our shared experiences give us strength.

Your New York medium told you basically the same thing Delores Lee told me. Look at our histories, our ancestries. Listen to our stories.

I wanted to tell you more about my parents—how they met and why my father ended up back in the Appalachian Mountains—the same place he started from.

My parents met in Hawaii. My mother is Japanese; my father is from Appalachia. World War II was happening.

Dad had been severely wounded while fighting the Japanese in the Philippines; he was sent to Hawaii for rest and recuperation. He met my mother at an officer's dance. Actually, he saw her walking down the road and followed her into the officer's club dance hall, intrigued by her graceful walk and lilting laugh.

When he first asked her to dance, she turned him down. Later, when I was in my twenties and we were talking about how she and Dad met, she said, "He asked me to dance, but he wasn't my type—red hair and too tall for me." But after she watched him move effortlessly across the floor in a slow waltz with another partner, she changed her mind.

I am the oldest of their five children, four girls and a boy.

We were Army brats; we moved frequently to wherever Dad was stationed stateside, but while he was overseas, we lived in Hawaii. There I was what was called a "hoppa haole," half-white. My hair was fine and silky, a reddish brown, not the thick, glossy, black hair of my cousins and my siblings, but my eyes were slanted and heavy lidded. Later, when I was in elementary school in North Carolina, I got into many a fight over the shape of my eyes. One too many boys would pull the outer corners of his eyes tight and chant, "Ching, ching, Chinaman." The first time it happened, I didn't know what they were talking about, but when I realized they were taunting me, I responded. I responded by fighting, which usually ended with me giving the bully a good head-pounding. I was merciless and I got a reputation as someone not to be messed with.

The pattern was the same at every school I attended, but once I established my identity I was left alone and made friends. I was athletic, a good runner and tetherball player, and a good student. I got picked in sports teams first, and they wanted me to be on their side whenever there was a spelling bee. So I made my space. I adjusted more easily to each new school as my elementary years passed. By junior high I felt like I fit in, although I knew then that I looked different from my classmates.

It wasn't until we moved back to my dad's home in the heart of the Appalachians that I really acknowledged my mixed heritage.

That first summer, the summer of '59, we stayed with my grandmother, Rebecca. She and Grandpa Harris had raised their five children on the small mountain farm; it was Dad's home place. Grandpa had worked in the mines. He died in his fifties, taken over by black lung, so it was just Grandma who welcomed us that summer.

She took us in, closing her ears to the church congregation's whispers. She treated my beautiful mother as a daughter and claimed us as her angels. I overheard her telling my Dad, "Always a few will find something to talk about; don't pay them no mind."

We worked hard in the garden that summer, putting up vegetables and canning in the heat of the day. Evenings, we swam in the creek across the road and sat down to huge suppers at the old oak table. I thought Grandma's dining room was the prettiest in the house, with lace curtains fluttering at open windows and the big cabinet at the end of the room holding prized bits of crockery and china. Grandma Rebecca's most treasured possession was an old pipe organ, given to her by her father as a wedding gift; it stood in the corner of the dining room, flanking the china cabinet. The sturdy, tapestry-covered bench seat was

125

needleworked in an intricate climbing rose pattern, somewhat worn over the years from Grandma's considerable weight. She spent time each day polishing the fine wood. On many summer evenings, after the table had been cleared and the dishes washed, we children, replete with good food, would gather around Grandma as she sat at her organ singing church hymns. The magnificent sound would fill the seven-room farmhouse, and even the outside farm animals fell silent in appreciation.

I noticed my dad was quiet at times. He was an authoritative man, having spent nearly twenty years as an officer in the military. He was looking for a place for us to rent or buy, plus he was looking for a job. Jobs were scarce. He'd worked briefly as a young man in the mines and did not want to go back in there. But unless he found another job, he knew that was what he would have to do. Mining was the main industry in the area; there were always jobs to be had if you were willing to go in the deep mines.

When my Dad worked in the mines earlier, before he went off to college and then to the Army, he'd been in a mining accident. He was trapped in a collapsed tunnel for nearly ten hours, his arm mangled and pinned down by a colossal rock in a rock fall. Helpless, he could hear the men outside trying to get to him. He was finally freed by one of the miners, a huge Negro who had worked side-by-side with Dad, and who came in alone to the area where Dad lay trapped. Everyone else was too afraid to chance another cave-in, but this one man was somehow able to throw off his fear; he moved the rock just enough to get Dad's arm loose, and together they made it out. Dad told us this story that summer, and showed us his scar. There was no fine levied against the company, and no newspaper coverage, either. Dad never went back, but the man who rescued him continued to work for his dole.

So now, faced with the prospect of once again working underground, Dad grew silent. Mom tried to stay encouraging and cheerful, but as the summer days passed and in spite of the abundance of food at the table, Mom grew slimmer and seemed to pick at her food. I could hear them talking late into the night after the rest of us had gone to bed.

Then, at the beginning of August, Dad got the good news that he'd been hired as a teacher and principal of a one-room elementary school. Although he had a bachelor's degree, he hadn't majored in

126

education and therefore would have to get some classes in and eventually go on for his master's, but he had a foot in the door. Shortly after that, we found a house to rent and I started in my new school.

By this time, I decided I loved living in the country. Surrounded by my father's family and heritage, I once again adjusted. The community that perhaps once had reservations about the Japanese in their midst had come to know us and closed around us welcomingly with surprisingly little racial prejudice. Fellow classmates at my new school did not taunt me or my sisters and brother, and even the church whisperers claimed other topics. We were comfortable in town, home, and school. The mountains and my father's family had embraced us. I liked where I found myself.

One other thing—it wasn't all moonlight and fireflies. Dad's silences that summer were later explained; he'd rediscovered rot-gut moonshine, a mountain favorite, and had been drinking secretly. Over the following years, his drinking increased, and with it, a change in his personality became evident. If he was once authoritative, now he was dictatorial; once jovial and articulate, now remote and taciturn.

He drank only on weekends, however, and stayed at home. Nobody but his family and his moonshiner knew his secret.

I was the lookout. On Friday evenings I'd watch for his car to pull up the long, steep driveway. I would strain to get a glimpse of his face. All I needed was one clear look and I could tell if he'd been drinking or not. Usually, he had.

I would tell Mom and warn the kids. We would be on edge, but prepared, for when he walked in. We kids would rush to do what he told us to do, mostly housecleaning chores, and then we'd stay out of his way. Mom would give him the silent treatment. Sometimes an argument would break the silence. They'd become angry, the arguments would get louder, and on those occasions I was especially alert.

I only remember three incidents of domestic violence.

The first time I was fourteen. I'd just come in from outside and I heard Mom and Dad's loud voices on the upstairs landing outside the kids' room. The kids were crying. Without thinking, I ran up the stairs just in time to witness Dad push Mom into their bedroom. He slammed the door shut and then he turned towards the kids' room with his belt in his hand. He was drunk.

I moved to block the doorway and he kept coming, so I pushed him back as hard as I could. He staggered a little and looked at me with a curious light in his eye. Then he punched me in the stomach. I doubled over and fell to my knees, gasping for breath.

When I looked up, he was gone. He'd gone down the stairs and out to the car. I heard the car start up through the door he'd left open, and he drove off. Mom helped me up and we quieted the kids. We didn't talk about what had happened, but Mom rubbed my tummy and asked me if I was hurt. She and I were both shaking.

When Dad came home later that night, he was sober. It was like nothing had happened. No apologies from him and none from me either. Something had changed between us.

The second incident was the only time I actually saw my father hit my mother. We were driving somewhere. Dad had been drinking. Mom and Dad were in the front seat, Dad driving, and I was sitting between them. The kids were in the back seat. I don't remember what precipitated it, but suddenly Dad reached around me and struck Mom in the chest. The car was swerving. She cried out in pain and the kids started whimpering, their eyes huge with fright. Dad looked at me threateningly and I was afraid to move or to open my mouth. I thought he was going to try and wreck us. I did nothing. We somehow made it home, and I swore to myself that never would I allow him to hit her again, no matter what.

The third and last time my dad and I had a violent confrontation was because I came to my mother's defense when she called me. Dad had been drinking heavily that evening, even more than usual. He and Mom were in the kitchen, my sister and I were in the front bedroom, and the little kids were in the back bedroom. I heard the sound of glass breaking and Mom's voice rising. I went rushing through the hall and stepped into the kitchen. Mom was cowering against the kitchen table. Dad was weaving on his feet, standing over her in a threatening manner. His face was swollen and red with temper, fists clenched. The rigid muscles in his jaw were twitching. He took a short step toward her, raising his fisted hand. When I yelled at him, he turned to me. At that moment, Mom slipped by him. There was a knife in the sink; I grabbed it and held it in front of me. Dad took another step forward, but stopped cold when his bloodshot eyes focused on the knife in my hand.

I yelled at him to get out of the house, to go outside or I would kill him. His eyes cleared for an instant and, to my amazement, he turned and stumbled out the door. I shut and locked it behind him.

All night I stayed awake, watching him from the kitchen window. He was sitting at the picnic table in the yard, holding his head in his hands. After that, weekends came and went without him drinking. He told my mother I was a strong one, but that was all that was said.

Believe it or not, my dad and I were civil and non-combative the rest of the time I was home. I think this happened during my junior year in high school. I went off to college, and shortly after I left for school Dad began complaining about not feeling well. He quit drinking totally and was once again the father we loved. My sister thinks he may have had a heart attack; he later died of a massive heart attack at age fifty-seven. I think he saw something in me that night that made him stop and think about what he was doing to his family.

I also remember, in that summer of '59 at Grandma's house, him telling me the story of the time he had come home for a visit from college. He heard his father's voice raised in anger. Dad stepped through the kitchen door from the porch. He'd just gotten home. He looked at his father, who had a pint jar of moonshine in one hand with his other hand clenched in anger. Grandma said, "No!" but Grandpa moved quickly to where Dad stood watching him and struck him in the face. He snarled drunkenly, "What are you gawking at?" The force of the blow knocked Dad backward, out the door, and off the porch stoop. Dad got up and left.

I can still visualize the look in his eyes as he told me this story. Was it a look of recognition?

So, now, I watch myself. I stay on guard. Not against others, but against myself. Always watching for signs of violence in me. It was in my father's father and my father. I'm afraid it's my legacy.

Thank you for listening,

Kinu

❧ *Chapter Seventeen* ❧

Gracie

Dear Kinu,

I'm so happy to have a friend like you to share my life's stories without apologies. I've held back simply because I fantasized a different life—a normal life; a home with nice furniture, and company on Sunday who was not always the preacher. I wished for a warm, friendly home to come to after school each day, absent of alcohol and without the silent treatment. At times I even told people I had a family who praised and encouraged my efforts to achieve beyond what I'd done. But that was another one of my fantasies. I've come to realize that if worthwhile benefits come my way, it is from telling the truth to others and admitting it to myself.

My early childhood years have lots of blank pages. I have trouble narrowing down specific events or episodes about growing up. My siblings and I were the children, not the key players in our household. Where I grew up our parents and grandparents lived a life outside our lives. I do have one tender Christmas memory I will never forget. This is one of my earliest memories.

A Christmas Story

"Get up! Get up! I'm leaving, and you have to fix the boys' breakfast." My mother nudged my oldest sister. "I'll be back tonight. I hung the Christmas wreaths. Don't let the boys tear them up while I'm gone," she said as she helped my sister get her feet on the cold floor.

It was the day before Christmas, and at the crack of dawn my mother boarded the long bus that ran up and down the holler hauling passengers to town, mostly women. She was going to do Christmas shopping, as always, the day before Christmas. I ran to the window to catch a glimpse of my mother, but all I saw was the bus with dim lights pulling away. A light blanket of snow covered the dirty coal dust on the road. I imagined the wide tire tracks winding around the narrow road and out of the holler, taking my mother to see Santa Claus. I waved goodbye.

I couldn't go back to sleep with life-sized dolls dressed in green velvet capes and red-and-white striped candy canes dancing through my head. I'm sure we had a Christmas tree with homemade ornaments, but I can't picture it.

The day wore on endlessly. My sister cooked, cleaned, ironed, and took care of us. Those were her normal duties whether my mother was home or absent. Daylight faded in the early afternoon because of the closeness of the mountains. I don't know where my dad was, because he came and went without our knowledge. When darkness finally settled on our little house, I started missing my mother and visualizing the bus going past our house taking my mother and Santa Claus to a place far away, or the bus turning over in the creek, landing in the cold, dirty water. I whimpered as I walked to one of the front windows where a red tinseled wreath hung. Pushing my face through the wreath onto the wet windowpane, I strained my eyes to look around the curves for the long gray-and-white bus that had taken my mother away. No bus was in sight. The outside looked scary in the starless night. My tears soon turned to sobs. Then my sister, who was doing dishes in the kitchen after putting my brothers to bed, heard me crying. She came to me and led me to a rocking chair in front of the fireplace and gently lifted me up on her lap. She took off her shirt, which covered her short-sleeved dress, and wrapped me in it for warmth. Holding me in her arms, she hummed a Christmas tune, telling me, "Gracie, don't worry, your big sister will always take care of you." I stopped crying and fell asleep.

I will always remember that Christmas story.

The Rooster Fight

Another vivid childhood memory is about a rooster fight I watched without my parents' knowledge or permission. It was violent and gruesome. I was too young to realize the violence and harshness we were exposed to growing up in our mountain culture.

When we were about nine, ten, and eleven, my mother and Dad took me and two of the boys on a trip to visit our aunt and uncle on Dad's side. We visited his side of the family often. We rode on the back of the truck. Dad drove slowly over the narrow, winding road. I sat in the middle with my knees pulled up under my chin. A board ran across the bed of the flatbed truck, so I wrapped my long, thin fingers around the board to hold on. The boys were on either side of me. Gnats and June bugs hit us on the side of our faces. Dad drove several miles up Knox Creek on the narrow paved road before making a left turn up a dirt road to our destination. The road was bumpy. My brothers and I jolted up and down when Dad hit the sharp rocks sticking up out of the ground. When he came to a big mud hole, he slowly veered to the side so we didn't slide off, or he went straight into the muddy water with the big tires on the truck. We knew we were almost there when we passed one landmark everybody talked about—the Draper Bottom Cemetery with the graves on the little piece of flat land. That's how you knew you were almost to my aunt and uncle's house. Old-fashioned roses twirled around the uneven, rusty wire fence holding the people in and the larger wild animals out. Faded plastic violets and carnations were blown midway between Mary Doss and her husband Flannel. Dad slowed as we passed the place of human ritual. I could make out names and dates on the larger headstones. This cemetery had a history. People killed during the Civil War were buried in the Draper Bottom Cemetery.

Dad drove on up the rocky creek road until he crossed the one-lane wooden bridge over Knox Creek leading to Russell and Darnell's house. The house was small, covered on one side with some kind of rough green-and-brown siding. Glass-looking drops sparkled in the sun on the rough siding. The front and sides of the house wore the siding. The back was bare wood. Windows in the front room were pulled halfway up. The hot, sticky outside air blew in. My mother braided my hair into pigtails after I jumped off the back of the truck. She turned me around and retied the belts on my pink dress. Turning to Dad she said, "Ah, I see that Harold May is here. Should have left those kids at home."

Dad told us to play outside and not bother anything. Haskell and June, our cousins, came out of the back door when they saw Dad's flatbed truck pull up the hill. The roof, which covered their back porch, touched the back of the hill. The front yard was level and then dropped down an embankment to the creek. We didn't hug like some relatives do; instead my two brothers started rolling down the steep hill in front of the house. They rolled almost to the creek, laughing and yelling for June and me to watch them. Haskell rolled with them the second time they went down. The three boys waded in the creek and started picking up rocks looking for crawdads. A tire swing hung down from the limb of a big beech tree. I wanted to try their swing. In a shed at the side of the house, I spotted a new red Radio Flyer wagon.

June was shorter and rounder than me, but we were close to the same age. Her hair was orange and her face, arms, and legs were sprinkled with freckles. Aunt Darnell was a teacher at the mouth of the holler.

More family members arrived. Uncle Rowan and his wife, Aunt Nora, came. Nora was a teacher, too. She was frail and beautiful. Her skin was white—no brown spots. She wore a long dark coat with a scarf that looked like white silk. She wore high heels and dangling star earrings. You could see her eyelashes, dark and thick, and her lips were pale pink. They couldn't have children. Uncle Rowan carried an open can of Budweiser. He set the beer down on the seat of his truck long enough to help Nora out of the truck and hand her a large dish covered with wax paper. Rowan yelled for us to come over and see what Nora had brought for the dinner. She carefully lifted the wax paper up and bent over to show us a long dish filled with chocolate fudge. The candy was cut into squares with a black walnut half on each piece. The flat side of the nut was carefully placed in the center of each square. Rowan decided to give us our piece of fudge before dinner. Nora, smiling sweetly and obeying her husband's wishes, took a butter knife she carried in a separate container and gouged out five pieces of chocolate fudge. We each got the coveted walnut half. Rowan picked up his beer can and escorted Nora and the remainder of the fudge to the back door. His whiskey flask was visible in his back pants pocket and like the other men, he carried a pistol. Everyone brought a covered dish for the dinner. My mother brought a big pan of cornbread and a dish of fried deer steak.

Uncle Ralph brought his fiddle. Daniel brought his banjo and Greene brought his new Gibson Guitar. We always had music when any of the family got together.

In the yard underneath a grove of Poplar trees, the women put the potluck meal out on a long table made of wide boards placed on sawhorses and covered with clean sheets. The sweet smell of corn-on-the-cob, fried chicken, chicken and dumplings, and freshly-picked half-runner green beans seasoned with bacon drippings filled the air. The men ate first, as was customary. As soon as they finished they gravitated toward a neighbor's house, leaving the women, small children, and the babies at Darnell's to eat, visit, and clean up.

The menfolk were going over to Monk's place. Everyone called him Monk. He was not a relative but a close friend of the family. He lived in a small trailer with a front porch and back porch. A wooden building as big or bigger than his house trailer was behind the dwelling. Monk limped. Dad said he was born with one leg shorter than the other. A hump rose up on his right shoulder. Dad said he had polio. He was bent over. Monk was always clean and neatly dressed in a white shirt and dress pants. He wore red suspenders, western boots and a cowboy hat. Today he wore his cowboy tie, a single braid of thin black strands with a silver medallion pulled up tight on his neck inside his shirt collar instead of the customary trend of wearing the tie outside the shirt collar. His wallet was chained to his belt. Monk was a local businessman. He went in and out of the fork frequently, and people came and went from his place more than other places on the fork.

Women in the family were nice to Pearl because she was Monk's wife, but Pearl was nervous around people. She was withdrawn and didn't talk unless asked a question. When a car or truck pulled up the hill, her big dark-skinned face was the first thing seen from the driveway. She cautiously pulled a curtain back, making enough room to put her face up close to the window to observe the visitor. Then the curtain closed tightly again. Pearl did not speak of her family ties. One of our cousins heard his mom say that someone had sent Pearl to Monk on a Greyhound Bus. She had numbers tattooed on her right arm. Her shoulders were as big and muscular as a man's. She tried to cover the numbers with her left hand when she was with the family. Pearl spent most of her time in the trailer.

My brothers came up the bank running when they heard Harold May's loud voice. Our mother warned us to stay away from Harold May. She said he cussed and we were Christians. Dad told us not to go to the building behind Monk and Pearl's trailer. That was off limits to kids. He told our mother to tell us. Dad did not speak directly to us.

The three boys ran over to Harold May's red pickup to watch him bring out Hercules, his champion fighting rooster. Hercules' cage was covered with a piece of black velvet. Harold said, "Hell, boys, you want to watch a cock fight? Damn, got mud on these new boots."

Dad couldn't see my brothers' close proximity to Harold May. He was inside playing The Wildwood Flower on Ralph's fiddle.

Harold May was an attraction in the community—my mother said that. He was a veteran. While serving in the Navy he had traveled to foreign countries. Harold had gained weight since his discharge. He was over six feet with wavy brown hair and a big face. His brown eyes were round and twinkled. He winked a lot. He wore nice shirts with a crease ironed up the sleeves. Two or three buttons unbuttoned in the front revealed a big chest covered with brown, prickly-looking hair. He had a tattoo of a half-naked woman on his forearm. Rolled up shirtsleeves gave Lu Anne, the tattooed, curvy, woman figure, lots of fresh air and sunshine.

Haskell, June, me, and my two brothers followed in line behind Harold May and Hercules as they marched to Monk's building. We could hear men talking and laughing inside but when we reached the door, Harold turned around and said, "Hell, boys and girls, I'm sorry, but no kids allowed inside. There's a big gap in the boards around back—go try that. You'll be a witness to history. Hercules is going to slice up little Napoleon and I've got my money on it."

We ran to the back and jockeyed for a good place to watch. My place was between June and Haskell. My brothers bent down on their knees in front.

Powder Dalton, who lived about two miles further up the fork and was rumored to be the father of the baby in the Draper Bottom Cemetery, carried his prizewinning rooster, Napoleon, to the pit in a cage embellished with rhinestones. The pit was in the middle of the room, built on a platform to showcase the cockfights.

Hercules was late making his appearance to the pit. Harold May was haggling over a bet with Daniel, who was in charge of handling the money and making the payoffs.

The men surrounding the pit were tanked up on booze and the excitement of winning or losing ten or twenty hard-earned coal miners' dollars.

Harold opened the cage door for Hercules, who strutted about the wire cage. His strong legs and taut body held his large neck in military fashion. Feathers on both birds were as shiny as silk. Cocks trained to fight were given a special diet of protein to increase their strength and stamina. Hercules and Napoleon were trained like professional fighters. One would die.

A razor-sharp spur was attached to the left leg in preparation for this death ritual. Harold May held Hercules close to his chest. He whispered words of love and encouragement and kissed Hercules on the head as gently as he would a newborn baby. He lowered his champion into the pit. Powder Dalton lowered Napoleon into the pit with less fanfare. The slow dance began. Each rooster lowered a wing and circled, edging closer each round. The excitement built as the roosters pecked at each other's neck feathers. In an instant, one attacked. The other met the challenge, attacking in return. A loud round of applause and sounds of yeahs and boos filled Monk's building. Hercules and Napoleon exchanged kicks in midair. They slashed each other with four-inch razor-sharp steel spurs. In a flash it was over. Napoleon lay lifeless while blood gushed out of his neck. He ruffled his feathers feebly. His wattle and comb withered. Hercules limped around the pit. Harold May examined Hercules' injuries, placed him back in his cage and covered his champion with the black velvet cloth. Monk handed Harold the dead Napoleon, as well as a wad of dollar bills—set by tradition. Another round of applause rang out as the gamblers made their way to Daniel's table and settled their bets.

We raced back to the front of the house to watch Harold May carry out Hercules, the champion, and place him in the back of his new pickup truck. In an act of kindness and generosity, Harold said to Powder Dalton, "Well, hell, Powder, you are one of my best friends. Now, take Napoleon and cook him up for Sunday dinner."

Dad came out of Monk's building with the other men. He told my mother to round up the kids, it was time to go home. Hope to hear from you soon. Take care of yourself.

Gracie

☞ *Chapter Eighteen* ☜

The Importance of a Good Hound
Gracie

Kinu,

My dad's work history was sketchy. He scheduled his work around matters of importance: hunting seasons—deer, turkey, etc. That is to say that he did not work during those times, at least not steady. He had a deep, abiding love and relationship with the great outdoors, dogs, guns, ammunition, and hunting. He would not tie himself down to a job that did not allow him the flexibility to enjoy his passions.

He worked in the coal mines, but that was not his regular job. He worked timber. He had a sawmill and hauled lumber. The best pine boards, sawed to perfection, were hauled to a company in Tennessee and made into pine coffins.

After Dad moved us to a small farm across the mountain, he continued to work in timber, cutting and hauling mining timbers, and he continued to spend his Saturday nights at local taverns. On other nights when he was away, he coon hunted with his hunting buddies and his hound dogs.

My mother walked on eggs around Dad as a normal habit, but on those nights when she intuitively knew Dad was out drinking, she was scared to death. She nervously paced from window to window, straining and peering into the blackness. She'd send me and my brothers to bed, but we knew there was a possibility something bad could happen during the night. Our feelings were transferred from our mother. Late in the night when the headlights on Dad's flatbed truck turned into the long driveway, moving as slowly as an old black snake, my mother rushed to our bedrooms, waking us and warning us. She urged and scolded us, "Get out of the house before your dad gets home." She whispered, even though he was still in his truck weaving from side to side in the driveway. "Run to the barn and hide. I'll signal when it's safe to come back in the house." Safe meant when our dad had gone to bed and was sound asleep.

I remember running through the snow barefoot. I can still see the moon shining down on the crusted snow. I can still feel the cold, cutting edge of the ice, which felt like cold steel blades hitting the middle of my bare foot as it broke through the snowy ice. The hard ice crystals cut my bare legs as I pulled them out. We hunkered down as we ran across the snowy field, in case he saw us running and came after us. We hid in the hay in the big, open barn until our mother came out of the back door and gave us a silent signal to come back in the house. Sometimes it was almost daylight. We were just little kids.

I'm not sure what went on in the house during the time we were hiding in the barn. I do know my mother was scared. It crossed my mind after I grew up that if Dad hurt or killed someone during those drinking episodes, she wanted it to be her. She did not want to lose another child. Dad had a large gun collection. Buying and trading guns was part of mountain culture. When drinking, he pulled his guns off the racks on the walls and brought out the ones stashed underneath his bed. He always carried a pistol. He would begin loading the guns and aiming in all directions. I would see his bloodshot eyes flashing around the walls of the room as he dug into drawers where shells were hidden. He'd check the pistol in his shoulder holster and load a shotgun and rifle. He'd quiz Mom on where she'd hidden his shells. He often said he was going to shoot someone. One or two of his brothers were usually traveling with him during these times. They all were on the same wavelength—same actions, thoughts, and feelings.

My mother moved about as a silent robot when my dad was drinking, anticipating his every move and want. She rushed into the kitchen and warmed beans, cornbread, and usually a wild meat dish she'd cooked at supper time. She asked no questions, made no demands. She obeyed.

We never spoke to anyone or each other about what went on at our house when Dad was drinking, or any other time.

Take care,

Gracie

❧ Chapter Nineteen ❧

Gracie

Dear Kinu,

When I was growing up, I would hear kids my age talk about discussing a topic from school with their Dad or about disagreeing with what he said. That was foreign to my ears. I wondered what it would be like. I can best describe my dad, who he was and my relationship with him, through these stories, which come to mind when I think back to my childhood.

My Dad Whistled

My dad never talked to his children directly. We gauged our lives around Dad's moods based on my mother's interpretation of his body language and by the tunes he whistled. It's hard to remember names of many of the tunes—and I'm not sure if all the whistling had names—but the rise and fall of the notes are locked in my head. He whistled on all occasions. During low times when someone in the community died or when one of his hunting dogs got lost or hurt, he whistled a sad, religious verse of the Old Rugged Cross or A Picture From Life's Other Side. The long, low notes were filled with sadness and longing, telling everyone in hearing distance of his pain and suffering.

Dad smoked from the time he was a young boy and he never let other activities get in the way of his smoking. It was perfectly normal for Dad to start whistling a verse of a song and halfway through stop to inhale a long drag on his Camel cigarette. The last part of the verse would hit the air enveloped in gray-blue smoke. He whistled when he was drinking. These tunes were of trouble and sorrow. In The Pines was a favorite. The sound would come out of his rounded lips evenly on verses:

In The Pines
Author: unknown

Little girl, little girl, what have I done,
That makes you treat me so.
You have caused me to weep, you have caused me to mourn,
You have caused me to leave my home.
(Chorus)
In the pines, in the pines, where the sun never shines,
And you shiver when the cold wind blows.
In the pines, in the pines, where the sun never shines,
I'll shiver when the cold winds blow.

Chills raced up and down my spine when I heard this tune. I worried, since we knew nothing about Dad's past life. My mother would cut us off short if we ventured there. She'd say, "You kids don't need to be asking questions. Now go outside. Don't bother your dad."

Whistling was one of Dad's primary methods of communicating. He often combined whistling with patting his right foot. Sometimes it was separate and sometimes simultaneous. If it were a slow deliberate pat—one-two, one-two—with his long, thin foot caressing the bare floor, he could not be bothered, even by my mother. She watched and waited for some sign of invitation to tell him the cow was down or one of his boys was hitchhiking cross-country.

We were warned of his different moods by whispers from our mother, who would grab our dress tail or one of the boys' arms and pull us behind a door facing to whisper, "Don't make any noise, your dad's tired or upset or he's got something on his mind. Don't go in there."

Dad walked for miles up and down the steep hill beside our house and back and forth down the cow pasture whistling, working out a problem, or as my mother would say, "Studying on something." His long, lean, six-four body moved slowly along the barbed wire fence line

140

night or day. This was as much a part of our landscape as the trees outlining the wooded area of our forty-acre farm.

Dad believed that nature provided, and honey from the honeybee was one proof of his theory. My dad was a beekeeper.

My Dad, the Beekeeper

I have an aversion to honeybees. Yes, I know they are a keystone species and our ecosystem depends on their work for balance. My parents may be responsible for these negative feelings toward the hard-working, well-organized honeybee. You see, Dad practically lived outdoors and even the bees were his friends. Electric company right-of-way workers, hunters, and timber men came to our home to tell Dad they had spotted a wild bee tree, or they noticed a bee swarm. When that happened his eyes lit up and the preparation began to bring in the swarm or move the colony from the bee tree to a hive at our home. He always worked with minimum equipment. In the case of capturing wild bees from a bee tree or a swarm, he wore a bee veil (wide brim hat with a veil to cover his face), and used a bee smoker (a contraption that worked somewhat like an accordion). The bee smoker was a box with leather bellows and a metal spout. He gathered up old rags and stuffed them in the smoker for a slow burn and thick smoke. He would squeeze the bellows and the smoke rolled out. He once said the smoke settled the bees. He carried a pair of old work gloves to handle the bees, and a burlap sack for transporting the bees to their new home on the farm.

The beehives were located in a row near the front of the house in the midst of our play area—the field, meadow, and creek; an inconvenience to us, but to him and the neighbors, who were farmers and coal miners, beehives were a status symbol.

Now back to my parents being responsible for my shameful negative feelings towards the honeybee. Bee stings were common occurrences. After she, a female bee, hit me with her ovipositor full of venom (her stinger) for no known reason, I immediately began to swell around the area of the sting. Bee stings were painful and itched for days. I would run into the house with an arm, hand, or the side of my face swollen twice its normal size, announcing I was hurt. My mother or dad would ask, "What's wrong?" Seeing no blood, they assumed it was

141

minor. I would show them my swollen limb or eye, expecting a great deal of sympathy. One look and they would remark, "Oh, it's just a bee sting." My mother would mix up a little baking soda and water into a paste, smear it over the swollen area, and send me back out the door to play as if the sting were no more than a figment of my imagination.

And when there was a bee swarm, when the old queen bee had been pushed out of the hive by a younger queen bee, she took thousands of her workers. They hovered, after attaching themselves to a tree limb, jagged rock, or corner of the house, in an oblong solid-looking mass, humming and doing the waggle dance. The waggle dancers turned and swirled, making a figure eight pointed in the direction of the prospective new home. Each dancer tried to convince the group their choice was best. There is a great deal of discussion among the swarm, explaining all the noise.

When a swarm occurred in the woods or from one of our bee hives, Dad was summoned immediately. Time is of the essence. If he were not around, then a neighbor would step in. In other words, the bees are not hanging around long, this departure from the original home has been planned and they have at least four or five prospective new homes nearby. The swarm is a congregation so a decision can be made which home to choose. Dad always responded to the call with as much enthusiasm as is possible from a six-foot-four, rail-thin, laid-back outdoorsman who got warning tickets for driving too slow. He gathered his hat with the veil, bee smoker, gloves, burlap sack, and a handsaw in case the bees were attached to a tree limb and needed sawed down. After the bees were captured, making sure the queen bee was included, he gingerly and tenderly, as if they were a newborn baby, carried and placed the bees in their new home—a white square box, a beehive. Honey or sugar water was placed inside the hive for food and as enticement to make their home at our home.

Dad enjoyed the quarts of honey harvested from the hives as a natural sweetener. He left some of the comb in the jars. He would hold a quart of honey up to the light and smile at what nature had provided for him. When someone in the community died, a miner got injured on the job, or someone was baptized, Dad often gave them a jar of honey as a token of friendship. Dad was a beekeeper.

Kinu, the act of writing these stories down, describing in words facial expressions, laughter, and fear is an act of cleansing. So beneficial to my soul.

Take care,

Gracie

❧ *Chapter Twenty* ❧

Gracie

Dear Kinu,

As you said in one of your letters, "I'm in a writing mood," and memories are pounding in my head. I've got to get them down for myself and to keep my promise to Andrew. Kinu, I hope you don't mind being the recipient of these secrets hidden deep in my soul. I'm hiding so much. I'm adding my story, "Shattered Lives," at the end of this letter.

I remember writing to you that my marriage failed. I'm sure you wondered why. I'm still uncomfortable talking about such personal issues, but I believe my own mother had something to do with that failure.

If I can lay blame on my mother for my failed relationship, that was only in part. She was never interfering or telling me what to do or talking bad about my husband as you may have suspected, but it was due to the complete failure of her own marriage. It hurt badly to see her literally bow down to my dad, anticipating his every need, spoken or unspoken. She never took anything for herself and he never gave—never a Christmas, birthday, or anniversary gift.

Most of what he earned or was given by his family went for his pleasures, a new hunting dog or new hunting gun, while a worn-out refrigerator sat leaking on the front porch. He drove a newer model truck, even though my mother didn't even drive. She slipped around and tried to somehow come up with enough money for groceries and school clothes. I don't know how she did it.

I never wanted that for myself. I didn't want that for my mother. I wanted her to tell Dad he was selfish, spoiled, and inconsiderate. She defended him and covered for him, out of love or fear, or both.

I wanted someone willing to discuss matters and then make decisions. I wanted someone interested in our home, how it looked on the outside and inside. A showcase for our guests and relatives. I wanted someone who showered me with gifts, remembering birthdays,

144

anniversaries, and Christmas. I wanted someone to share common goals without a need for absolute control of one over the other. I wanted a partner to share my life, and if I could not have that, I would rather be alone. I am alone.

Kinu, I've a confession deeper than my failed marriage, a burden, a family secret I want to share with you. This, what I'm about to tell you, has completely overpowered me since it happened. This, what I'm about to tell you, has worn me to the bone. My emotions are threadbare. This, what I'm about to tell you, is almost too much to bear. This has wrecked my life, controlled my life, and left me a cripple emotionally.

You see, I've never been forthright about why I left college in the middle of the night without even saying goodbye to people who'd become important to me. I couldn't face them. I didn't want to try to explain what was going on and garner their pity, or worse. So there were no proper farewells. I feel as though I'm opening up a forbidden door when I speak of my sister's nervous breakdown.

I hope you'll understand why I kept this to myself as much as possible. You see, I felt not many people went around broadcasting the fact that someone in their family was in a state of mental collapse. When those closest to you are in and out of their right mind, you work hard to build a wall around yourself. You become withdrawn and may appear distant to others. You're only trying to survive. I can't give you medical explanations for what happened, tell you why nothing worked in treatment plans—I don't know. Even putting events in chronological order is difficult at this point because of years of suppression, but when things were normal a year seemed like a minute, when things were chaotic and out of control a minute seemed like a year. So I'm only hitting the high spots, but I think you will get the drift of what it is like for a beautiful, purposeful life to crumble into a million pieces.

I'm writing this story from my perspective. Family members have their own version. I hope you'll try to understand, and please don't judge my sister for failing to withstand all the storms in her life.

Shattered Lives

"Gracie, Gracie, your dad is on the phone," my dorm mother said. "Hurry, hurry now, he's waiting to talk to you."

He didn't waste time with small talk. He said, "Your sister is sick and you need to go there and take care of things. You have a family responsibility."

I didn't question Dad or argue about the importance of an education. He let me know right off this was a serious matter, and it was up to me to get things back in order, post-haste. Besides, I owed everything to my sister. She was my caretaker, mentor, and idol.

"Yes, Dad, I'll do whatever is needed."

My sister had been having problems coping for months. Following an almost full-term miscarriage, she began losing touch with reality. Often she sank into deep depression, unable to focus on household chores, tend to her children's needs, or meet her husband's demands. Doctors said it would pass, that it was stress related. They began with medications to quiet her nerves and relieve the anxiety, but prescription pills, while alleviating mild symptoms, quickly became her crutch for living. In a pace that was sometimes slow and sometimes fast, she began a descent into pure hell. The unanswered question was: how could this be happening to a beautiful, smart, talented, mother and wife? From personal observation, I knew she was falling, but I developed an optimistic attitude, one of denial, that if she got the right medical attention with the latest meds for anxiety and stress-related illnesses, and I was nearby for support, she'd return to her normal self.

That night after I hung up the phone with Dad I went back to my room, pulled out the old army footlocker I'd arrived with, and began packing. I never told anyone all the reasons I left college that night, not even my roommate.

I told her, "I've had enough of this place. The Campus God is demanding more of my time. It's not possible for me to live like a normal college student on this campus any longer. It hurts that I've become the subject of campus gossip and ridicule. I feel like a caged

146

animal with someone watching my every move. Leaving is the only way out."

In my heart, I thought this was God's way of removing me from a situation not right for a young mountain girl. The phone call from my dad was a resolution to a smothering, taboo relationship. That night, the moment when I became a college dropout was bittersweet.

My roommate didn't pry, but tried every way in the world to get me to stay. She argued, "At least wait until the morning and talk with a counselor. Aren't you going to check out properly?"

I don't remember how I got my footlocker to the bus terminal, but I purchased my one-way ticket to a town not far away from my sister, who lived in a small community. I could easily visit weekends, holidays, and many evenings. I needed full-time employment to support myself. I knew I could work out a plan on the bus. There were a many uncertainties, but there was one certainty: if I went to live in that home as a full-time helper with the children, and as her caretaker, my life as I'd dreamed it would be cut short permanently. That may have been selfish on my part.

The bus pulled out of the college bus station that night around midnight. I sat near the front with my face pressed against the damp window, staring at the stately buildings with southern porticos and long windows trimmed in white. Those architectural features impressed me so when I arrived on campus the first time on that Greyhound bus. Through the doors of those buildings was my bountiful, happy future. My eyes swallowed up memories, good and bad, as we quietly zipped into the night and into another world. There was no time for tears; I had a family responsibility.

I arrived at my destination near my sister's home around daylight. After securing a locker in the bus terminal to store my belongings, I opened my army trunk and took out a dress, high heels, and makeup. I went into the bathroom and changed clothes, brushed my teeth, and fixed my hair. I started down the street, stopping at every business left and right to ask for a job.

I didn't know where I'd be sleeping that night, but I hadn't ruled out the bus terminal. Fortunately, I ran into a couple of distant relatives who invited me to their small studio apartment until I found a job and housing.

I accepted the first job offered to me, scheduling photo shoots for a photographer and collecting payments. He failed to tell me during the interview that he expected me to pose for photos. The employment lasted only one day. That evening, the relatives I was staying with suggested I make application with the telephone company. The next morning, I walked to the company's personnel office and submitted my application. I was interviewed and told I could possibly get placement in their engineering department instead of starting out entry level, because of my college credits.

After making several more stops to submit job applications that day, I started walking back to the apartment. My feet hurt in those high heels and I was tired. A car pulled over to the curb beside me, and a nice-looking gentleman dressed in a business suit asked me if I needed a ride. I got in. I had no idea who the man was. I told him where I was going. He drove along slowly and when he arrived at the apartment, he stopped. I thanked him and got out. When I told my relatives about getting in a car with a strange man, they nearly passed out and warned me not to do that again. I thanked God for taking care of me.

The next morning, when the business day began, I got a call from the telephone company. The personnel director told me I had a job. I rushed down to fill out paperwork to start my job the very next day. I was assigned to the engineering department in the drafting division. After getting my first paycheck, I rented a single room close to work. I didn't know, until one of the ladies who lived a couple of doors down the hall told me, that I was in a house where call girls who serviced the Holiday Inn and other hotels lived. The lady asked me where I worked and I told her the telephone company. I asked about her employment and she said, "Honey, I work nights at the Holiday Inn and some of the other hotels. I make good money and you could too."

I know those ladies of the night could sense my lack of experience of living in a large town. They were nice to me. I spent my non-working hours in my room.

After spending a few weekends with my sister, I could see her fragility, both physically and mentally. If I was not in her house, I spoke to her by phone every day. Her baby was only six months old, and the oldest of her four children was eleven. Her husband was busy running a business, so he hired a woman to come in and do the cooking and housework and to help with the children.

My sister was a functioning parent one minute, and the next forgot where she dropped off the kids. She had trouble with the hired help living in her house and caring for the children, especially the baby. The wounds were still open from losing a child through miscarriage, and now it appeared she was losing a child through hired help.

This debilitating illness lasted years, yet now in my flashback I see her only as the tall, slender, beautifully-groomed young woman in her early twenties who divided her time between a good office job working in finance and driving home on weekends to help care for us.

I can't remember the day, minute, or hour when she totally snapped, but it was a few months after I'd left school to help care for her. I'd driven straight to her house after work that day because of unusually bizarre behavior during the day. Three or four of her friends and neighbors were already there when I arrived. They didn't know what to do to calm the situation. They were worried and afraid for their personal safety and the safety of her family, yet they didn't want to desert her in this time of need. And for the first time in her life, she became violent. She slapped one of her closest friends, who was discussing her medical problems and the children's future with others in the room. My sister paced through her house like a wildcat. My extremely modest sister was disrobing as if she were trying to break free of restraints as she dashed from one room to another. The tone of her voice was high pitched and agitated. I can't remember if she cursed, but her words were harsh, and she was almost screaming. I could not make out what she was saying. No one could reason with her or calm her down. An ambulance was summoned and two medical professionals restrained her while she was injected, strapped in a straitjacket, loaded on a stretcher, and unceremoniously transported to a medical center for treatment.

Those of us left behind were in shreds emotionally. My sister snapped. The complete mental collapse was a novelty in the small, rural coal mining community. Word soon got around and my family became celebrities in an odd way.

149

She was medicated and sent home to return to her normal duties. The hired help was kept on and a temporary normalcy returned. But the medication didn't hold. She slipped back and forth from one day of being in reality, to acting out of sync with the normal world the next day. I was called to come to her each time she faltered. The moment she saw me or heard my voice she returned to herself, but half the time it was a put-on and a reaction to someone she wanted to please. Her old self was lost somewhere inside. A totally different personality emerged after the breakdown. She now chain-smoked and talked loudly. She said she didn't like people who'd been her closest friends. Schoolteachers were not safe from her verbal attacks. The people closest to her were uncomfortable in her presence and stayed away. The quiet, respectful, shy person we knew changed. She dressed in costumes. Pocahontas was one of her favorites, with lipstick smeared on her face for war paint and a band around her head with a feather in it. No longer permitted to drive, she walked up and down the highway.

Local doctors exhausted their treatments to make my sister well, but because of her insistence, desperation, and our status as honorable community members, they continued to write prescription after prescription for pain medication, which she continued to abuse. She didn't follow doctors' orders, but instead developed a pattern of overmedicating, then refusing to take the helpful drugs. Her condition worsened.

We searched for help outside our small town, because when the pills stopped working or she stopped taking the drugs or the combination was totally wrong, she sank into deep depression and cried for hours like a baby. Not even I could console her.

My sister and her husband divorced. I never knew the reason, but speculated like everyone else in the community. He didn't know how to handle the situation. He couldn't take the on-and-off weird behavior. He needed someone. She partially blamed him for her breakdown.

The divorce left her without medical insurance for a period of time. I remember one time she had to be admitted to a privately run mental institution for treatment. They would not admit her unless I signed a contract that I was responsible for paying for her treatment in this expensive treatment facility; there was no other way. I was thankful they agreed to allow me to pay on an installment plan. The visits to these facilities were painful. Each time I visited, I was reminded of how frail we all are. I saw teenagers who suffered from drug addiction lying motionless on white cots with blank stares; alcoholics attempting to beat the booze; and my sister, who'd been the most normal person I have ever known until she snapped—all housed together behind lock and key with bars on the windows.

I don't remember hearing one specific diagnosis for my sister's illness after the breakdown, but at first she responded well to antidepressants. Her mood lifted and she laughed and became talkative, but there was a downside: her sleep pattern changed—from sleeping at night to pacing throughout the house all night, often going through medicine cabinets searching for pills and chain-smoking. She slept a little during the day. It became a safety factor because of the cigarettes left unattended.

As a desperate treatment option, I authorized electroconvulsive therapy. The doctor who prescribed this controversial therapy said many patients who didn't respond to drug or psychological treatment for mental disorders responded well to this therapy. I've never been through such torture: seeing her lying on the bed with the gear on, with a frightened, helpless look on her face, like a small child crying for me to help her, to hold her, like she had held me. She wasn't awake during the treatments, but the preliminaries were horrifying to her and me. I can only compare it to seeing someone who had been sentenced to die in the electric chair on television. That series of treatments stabilized her for a time, but the side effects were devastating. She lost part of her short-term memory and her normal personality was gone.

I can't remember when the shock treatment effectiveness wore off and drugs were again prescribed. She needed something to help her deal with hallucinations and demons inside, which she sketched late at night on the walls of her house. Strange combinations of letters, forming what she thought were messages from someone beyond reality, were also written on walls and sheets of paper. She was helpless and sobbed like a little lost child. Proper medical names of drugs are hard for me to remember, but I do remember lithium was prescribed. Doctors had trouble finding the proper dosage for her, so again she suffered terrible side effects, this time from the prescription drugs—her hands shook so badly she could not hold a pencil or pen to write letters to family

151

members. Always slender, she now appeared heavy. She would purposely stop taking the medications in order to drop back down to her normal weight. Her vision was blurred, and she already suffered from a loss of short-term memory and personality change.

Friends and neighbors checked on her regularly, because she wanted to stay in her house. She was on churches' prayer chain lists throughout the community. Our church helped out with food baskets a couple of times and a little cash for the electric bill, but when word got back that she bought Christmas gifts for her children and me instead of paying the utility bill, there was no more help from the good Christians for the incurable mental case. Financially, I gave her everything I could possibly spare.

Everyone in the community cared for the children. They scattered at an early age, getting jobs and growing up fast. They were the most important thing in the world to their mother.

With time, it became increasingly difficult to find a doctor who'd take her case. Her medical records revealed that she wasn't a good patient—didn't follow doctor's orders and experienced harsh side effects from drugs doctors prescribed for her condition. I never gave up on her recovery, but I didn't discuss her condition publicly. When asked about my sister, I usually responded by saying, "She's fine." She spent most of her time inside the house when she wasn't in an institution. I was torn up over her most of the time, constantly on guard, but learned to function in spite of constant churning in my stomach.

The most heartbreaking experience for me occurred in the local magistrate court clerk's office. The medical team said she was suicidal and attempted to take her life. I never believed those actions were intentional—she had too much to live for—but she overdosed by accident. There was nothing left to do but commit her for a stay at the state mental institution. The well-known name of the mental institution itself was like a cross on my family's back, but all efforts were exhausted. She had been a patient at several other medical facilities that offered psychiatric treatment, but none of the treatments were lasting.

This episode was frightening enough, but the doctors recommended confinement to save her from herself. That was what they told me. The day of the mental hearing was the hardest and worst day of my life. The deputies escorted her into the courtroom. She was a patient at the local hospital when this happened. The only thing that separated her from me was a long table. I could not bear to look her in the eye. I knew she thought I'd betrayed her. My knees were shaking so badly I thought my legs would fall off. I thought, as I had many times over the course of those years, I'm not strong enough to handle this. I don't feel smart enough or confident enough to make another decision affecting someone's life in this way. I wondered where God was on that day at that hour. But after the magistrate read the medical order, I said, "Yes, she needs to go for her own protection." The deputies escorted her out of the courtroom and placed her in the back of their cruiser. I watched them drive her away.

My visits to the state mental institution were like what I imagine it would be like visiting someone in Hell. The first time I went, what I saw—the setting—was exactly what I've seen in movies. Big, austere, gray buildings with bars over the windows. Huge latches and locks on the doors. The staff was somber, stiff-looking, dressed in white. The hallways were long and dark. I went there to visit my sister after my regular workday, so it was late in the evening or almost dark before I arrived.

One time, I looked through a round hole in a door so I'd have an idea of what to expect on the other side. Someone looked back at me. You could hear screams on the other side of the doors. After gaining entrance, I'd sit with my sister and hold her hand. Sometimes other patients sat beside me or tried to hug me, get right up in my face, or tried to sit on my lap. They stared at me with their eyes riveted. Many of them thought I'd come as their visitor. Yes, I was nervous and uncomfortable.

I'd go home, go in my back bathroom away from everyone, and drop down on my knees to plead my case with the Man Upstairs. I asked why it had to be her. She was filled with goodness and kindness. She was an artist, businesswoman, and a wonderful mother. I asked if she were ever going to get well—back to normal. I asked if it could be me instead of her.

It didn't take many visits to realize my sister was responding to their care. She was gaining ground, and after a few months she moved to a halfway house. She wanted to come home, but when denied by the medical team, she requested a move to another halfway house. She began struggling again, slipping back into prescription drug dependency and deep depression. She had lost all ground. I wasn't sure why she was taken to a hospital but she had minor surgery and she died there alone.

Three days after her death, a funeral was held in a small Baptist church. My mind is blank on the details. I remember being in the church, but I don't remember driving there or riding with anyone. I remember sitting on the second row. It was crowded and hot. I was sweating profusely and I could barely get my breath. The faces of those who lined the walls and filled the pews are just dim figures in my mind, but I know they were family and friends. What did the preacher say about this angel? I have no idea. I believe God shields those of us who are weak even from sorrow we cannot bear. My sister was buried in a small, well-groomed cemetery.

Kinu, I've been writing for hours. It is past midnight. I wish I knew what I felt but I don't—shattered, battered, torn, free. I never realized how bad things really were until now. I'm exhausted. Will write more in a few days.

Thank you,

Gracie

❧ *Chapter Twenty-One* ❧

Dad's Stories
Kinu

Dear Gracie,

Yesterday I received a small package from Mom. She now lives with my youngest sister, Jenny Ann. She's finally sorting out and getting rid of the rest of Dad's things. Jenny Ann's place is small and there's no room for what we kept of Dad's clothing items. My sister wrote me this note:

Kinu, Mom found this envelope addressed to you in the front inside pocket of Dad's favorite jacket. I thought you would be interested in reading what he wrote.

Coal Miner's Son

"J. C., here's your Mason jar of milk and bread for your dinner," my mother said. She wiped her forehead wearily. She'd been up since before daybreak building a fire in the wooden cookstove and fixing breakfast for her four boys. I was the oldest, seventeen years old, and today was my first day to work in the mines.

I noticed Dad's hard hat and work boots by the door; he was still in the back bedroom. Mom touched my shoulder briefly as I got my stuff and stepped out on the porch to wait for him.

"Take care, son," she said softly. She turned away quickly, but not before I caught the tear in her eye. Mom hated the mines; she'd lost her father and two brothers during a cave-in ten years ago. She'd wanted Dad to quit then. She didn't want me to start now.

This was a temporary job for me. I wanted to go to college (the first of our family to do so), but even with the bank loan I managed to get, I needed more money for books and clothes. Dad got me hired at his job site—a deep mine five miles away. We'd walk there and back and eat our milk and bread so as not to have to spend our fifty cents' pay on food or gas.

I heard Dad's voice and he came out the door; his eyes were ringed with the black soot residue that scrubbing couldn't get off, and he was rolling his Prince Albert. "Ready, boy?" Before I could answer, he inhaled deeply and immediately his thin body was wracked with harsh coughing. He continued to smoke as we started to walk rapidly. "You're almost a man now son...by the end of this summer, you will be a man."

God help me, I worked hard that summer. A pick and a shovel, crawling on my hands and knees, too tired at the end of my shift to barely talk; but if hard, dangerous work was the measure of a man, I became one.

By the end of that first week, my knees were bloody and raw from scrabbling on them for hours on end when the roof wall was too low for a man to stand. I coughed short, hard coughs and spit up gobs of phlegm streaked black; even the snot from my nose and the tears from my eyes ran black.

The men had taken to calling me Junior, and after seeing that I aimed to stick it out, they treated me good. Dad worked deeper than I did, with the experienced old-timers, but he heard tell of how I wasn't no quitter. He was happy with me then.

When I'd first told him how I wanted more schooling, he'd snorted and said, "Are you afraid to work for your living?" I needed to prove I could work at what he thought was a "real" job, but I also aimed to show him I had further ambitions than to work in the mines all my life. On our walks home, I told him of my plans to travel and see the world. He said, "Yep, I had them plans too. Best you settle down and marry some little girl from these hills than take off to God knows where, son."

I kept talking every day, and I wore him down. He began listening, even asked questions about college. That summer, my dad and I actually talked at length for the first time I could remember. I found out that he'd dreamed of going to Texas when he was young. "Out there is wide-open spaces so a man can breathe," was what he said. My dad had emphysema and black lung, also a touch of TB, but couldn't afford medicines or doctors; he just wouldn't talk about his health, although his harsh coughing and shallow breathing were sure indicators that he was not well. Dad had his dreams too, but spent his life working in the minefields of Mercy Mountain just as his father did before him.

I grew big and strong that summer. My six-foot frame filled out with muscle; my hands and knees were callused, my fingernails rimmed with black. My eyes, too, were circled with soot, making them a startling blue against my freckled face.

We'd come home at night to eat the huge country meals my dear mother cooked—fried chicken, buttered corn, buttermilk biscuits, beans, and pickled beets would be ready and waiting for us. Mom made sure there was always a little sweet'ning too, a berry cobbler or apple pie.

Before we ate, we'd bathe out in the wash house next to the river that ran in front of our house. Mom wouldn't allow anyone to come to the supper table dirty. Dressed in fresh-washed clothes and our faces scrubbed pink, we'd come in, set our hard hats, boots, and lunch pails down by the doorway, and go straight in to eat with the family. My brothers were there waiting patiently, having completed their chores for the night, and after Mom said grace we'd begin some hard eating. There wasn't much conversation usually, but a whole lot of eating got done.

By September, I had enough money to buy my bus ticket to school and get some store-bought pants and shirts with enough left over for books. I'd worked hard and long enough to know the coal fields were not for me. Much as I hated to leave my family and the mountains I loved, I was ready to get started on the path I had chosen.

The day I left Mercy Mountain, Mom laughed a little and cried a little. She laughed from relief that I'd escaped the dreaded cave-ins she feared daily; she cried, of course, because she knew in her mother's heart that I wasn't coming home, not for a long time.

Six years after I left Mercy Mountain, I enlisted as an officer in the U.S. Marine Corps. World War II had started and I would do my duty.

Dogs Are Coming

I was wounded at Eniwetok, shot in the stomach by a Japanese soldier. My men killed him as I fell on the open field, clutching my gut in agony. I'll never forget the look of savagery on the soldier's sweating face as he jumped out from his camouflaged "spiderweb" foxhole, shooting me point-blank while screaming something in Japanese. Private Burkhart cradled my head in his arms as he yelled at me, "Captain!" I fought to stay conscious. "We got him, Captain. You're gonna be all right. Medic's coming. Hold on, Captain!"

I must have passed out, but not before I heard the sudden burst of machine gun fire and the screams and tortured cries of wounded men. Not before I saw more Japanese swarming out of their subsurface defense network like fierce yellow spider-soldiers. The private's cradling arms dropped. When I came to in extreme pain, my stomach a mass of fire, no one was left alive around me. I was lying in a field of dead soldiers, American and Japanese. Sounds of gunfire in the distance, somewhere beyond the mangroves and thick clusters of coconut trees; the war on this atoll was still going on, then. Only I was left behind.

The late afternoon sun beat down on me, the stench of death rising in the steamy heat filled my nostrils; as time and reality shifted once again, I faded out of consciousness. I was transported back to the Cumberlands, back to my childhood home on Mercy Mountain.

"J. C., fetch another pail of hot water from the stove for your Pa's bath." I was nine, but big for my age; I confidently swung the heavy bucket of steaming water off Ma's wood cookstove and poured it into the galvanized tub we used for our weekly bath. Pa was stripped down to his drawers, sitting silently in the cane-back chair near the kitchen door, smoking his Prince Albert. His neck and face were black with coal dust, as were his gnarled hands and fingernails. He ignored me, as he usually did, except for when he wanted me to do something. As Ma was drawing shut the curtain that isolated the tub area from the rest of the roomy farmhouse kitchen, she shooed me out the door. "Run to the company store and git your Pa another can of baccer; be back before dark," she said.

It was a good thirty-minute walk if I went down by the river where the path was worn and smooth, but if I crossed through the woods behind our house and went over the hill, I could make it there in twenty. I started through the woods. The rhododendron was thick and the hardwood trees were old in this part of the woods. Pa had never cleared it and he wouldn't allow anyone to cut the timber. Chestnut, oak, maple, and hickory interspersed with pines. I loved these woods; I played Indian fighter with my brothers here and we had hunted this rolling, wooded mountain terrain many times for squirrel. Usually, I'd take my time, enjoying the pure majesty of the century old forest, but that late afternoon, I was in a hurry and, as it was, got to the company store just barely before it closed.

I asked for the can of Prince Albert and a pack of papers; Mr. Fuller, the old clerk, peering suspiciously at me over his wire-rimmed spectacles, wrote it down against Dad in the store book, then rubbed his toothless mouth with his yellowed handkerchief before handing me the items I requested. "Be careful, boy, heading back home. It's near dark and somebody said there's a pack of wild dogs out bawling. I heard tell they've done got after Bobby Dean Jackson's boy the other night. They'll run you if you ain't careful. Run you and kill you if they catch you."

I said, "I ain't afraid of no dogs."

I took my time going home. I wanted to try me some of Dad's Prince Albert. Recently, I'd taken to slipping and smoking whenever I could filch some tobacco from the can. Dad knew it, I think. He'd shake the tin and say, "Prince is getting stingy in the can." Going back the way I came, I rolled a thin cigarette and lit it up.

About the time I took my first drag, I heard some rustling noises behind me. I was standing in a clump of slippery elm; it was getting near dark but I thought I could make out canine shapes among the trees. Minding what old man Fuller told me, I dropped my cigarette and ran. Sure enough, I heard sounds of animals running behind me.

I was fast and strong, but I knew I couldn't outrun the pack coming after me. Looking over my shoulder, I thought I could make out a good-sized pack of dogs, their yellow eyes gleaming in the dusk. They were closing in on me, yipping and barking excitedly. At the last minute,

I shinnied up a big chestnut tree and crouched in the crotch of a stout limb. The pack circled the base of my tree, looking up and barking in discordant unison. Five minutes passed and they showed no sign of leaving; I resigned myself to a long wait.

Full darkness had nearly fallen when I looked from my perch and saw my Pa's mining light coming through the woods and up the hill. I knew it was Pa; I could see the red glow of his Prince Albert cigarette shining below the carbide light mounted on his mining helmet, and I could hear his harsh coughing. I knew he'd be carrying his shotgun, loaded with buckshot; the wild dogs seemed to know he was coming, too. They gave out a few more barks, and then slipped away into the darkness of the night.

"Come on down, boy," Dad wheezed. "You lose my can of baccer?"

I replied quickly as I clambered down the tree, "No sir, Pa...well, maybe a little. I dropped the one I rolled."

He coughed, and then gave a dry chuckle, dropping his arm around my shoulder as we walked back down the hill to where Ma was waiting. I remember the heavy warmth of that arm; it was the first time I felt close to my Pa.

When I again regained consciousness, I clung to the memory of my father, wishing he was here to snatch me, once again, out of the jaws of death. For it was Death that was circling me now; Death yipping at my heels and ready to gnaw at my bursting entrails. The pain in my gut was too terrible to withstand; I realized I was dying and would be dead in a matter of hours. With this thought came an equally strong desire to live. Fighting not to pass out again, I managed to open my canteen and gulp some water. A sudden rain squall came up and drenched me briefly, giving some respite from the stifling heat. A momentary breeze moved over the flat terrain. I tried to yell, but the only words that came out of my mouth were a whispered, "God! Father, help me!" I heard the dogs coming.

When the Red Cross picked me up the next morning, I was delirious with pain and dehydration, barely alive. They had been radioed that an Army tank had passed over the prone body of a Marine officer and the gunner thought he detected some movement. Their doctors operated on me immediately, removing part of my perforated intestines; I was sent to Hawaii for rest and recuperation. Ironically, there I met and married a young Japanese woman. When I came home, my mother and father welcomed my Yoshi to Mercy Mountain.

Stranger in the House

I first saw my daughter, Kinu, when she was fourteen months old. I'd been stationed in north China after the war; I was what was commonly called a China Marine, sent to occupy northern China after the surrender of Japan. I was finally back in Hawaii on leave. I'd left my pregnant wife with her mother eighteen months before, but I was home.

Kinu stood silently in her crib. She looked at me with no evidence of fear or shyness in her dark, almond eyes. Her hair was haloed around her face; I noticed it was a reddish-brown color, like mine. In all other aspects, she looked like her mother.

As I reached to pick her up, she backed away from me and, never breaking our eye contact, cried out for her grandmother. I did not try to pick her up again that first day back.

It took weeks for Kinu to warm up to me, and even then, at best, she was lukewarm. Truthfully, I felt like a stranger to my first-born child. I guess I was literally just that. She'd have nothing to do with me, but followed my comings and goings with alert, dark eyes. Finally, after a week of suffering my presence, she was induced to let me hold her, but she was always quick to want to be put down.

Although I understood that my being absent during the first year of her life kept her from regarding me as anything more than a persistent presence, I was a little hurt and put off by her reaction. I couldn't seem to connect with my own child.

Yoshi said to give it time. "Kinu is like her grandfather, reserved." Taking heart from her observation, I noted to myself that it had taken months for Yoshi's father to warm up to me, yet now we were friendly. He spoke little English, but I interpreted his demeanor as friendly, at least.

While in China, I'd dreamed about the birth of this child and had been positive we would instantly bond upon my homecoming. I told everyone who'd listen, even my Chinese houseboy, all the little details gleaned from my wife's letters. In reality, Kinu was a little stranger to me, a stranger embellished by my imagination and my homesickness.

Yoshi and I had four other children after Kinu—three more girls, and finally a son. By the time our second daughter was born, Kinu was four years old. She continued to be somewhat of a puzzle to me.

I watched her grow with a certain detached curiosity. I noted she was very quiet around her grandfather, who was quietly stern with all children. She was warm and chattering with her grandmother, loving toward her mother, playful with her siblings, and guarded with me. I think Kinu was attuned to those around her, sensitive to the actions and reactions of others. Did she sense my detachment and modify her behavior accordingly?

After we left Hawaii, we moved around a lot. There were new schools to adjust to, new neighborhoods, new friends, and new prejudices. My daughter, with her distinctly Asian features, was the target of children's slurs. This was, after all, the period following the war against Japan and we were on the mainland now.

Kinu asked her mother what a "Jap" was one day, and the next day was sent home from school for fighting. Curiously, once she established that she would fight bullies, she was left alone by them. A precedent was set in that each new school brought another fight and then things progressed smoothly; a peculiar initiation process which continued throughout her elementary school years. Kinu accepted it as a rite of passage. I accepted that she never once came to me and asked for my help.

I picked up a bad habit during my seventeen years in the service. Growing up in Appalachia, I was accustomed to hard-drinking men. My father was one of them. My early initiation to the local mountain corn liquor, moonshine, had been casually accepted as part of growing up male in the hills. I slipped many a swallow from my dad's jug; when my mother complained, he said, "Leave him be. It'll harden up his stomach. It ain't hurt me none yet."

My youthful teenage and college drinking had graduated to steady, albeit slightly more "sophisticated," drinking while in the Corps, where drinking was standard procedure. My indulgence in beer, wine, and whiskey took a nasty turn when we moved back to my hometown in the foothills of Appalachia. I reintroduced myself to rotgut and it said "hello" right back.

Kinu was a teenager now. I was drinking myself into a red haze nearly every weekend. There were barely remembered times when my temper would flare against those I loved the best; I was sometimes violent. My personality changed for the worse when I drank. I noted a change in my children's attitude toward me, especially Kinu. The younger ones were fearful and anxious. Kinu and her sister Sharon were watchful.

During this black period of my drunken weekend binges my wife changed also, becoming uncharacteristically cold and distant. Yoshi, always so brave and beautiful, was intimidated by my Mr. Hyde behavior, and rightfully so. Our arguments were shadowed by the threat of violence. She began threats of her own, saying she would go back home to Hawaii, alternately giving me the silent treatment for the days following my binges and then withdrawing to the little kids' bedroom when I was drunk.

Kinu was protective of her sisters and brother, and especially so of her mother. She watched me warily, studying my face and gestures for hints of my moods and temperament. She was never disrespectful verbally, yet her vigilant presence was a challenge and a warning to me. I remember striking her when she stepped between me and the children once. She went down on her knees, but was still determined to take up her position of defense against me. I could see it in her eyes.

I saw a similarity between Kinu and me then. I remembered watching my own father when he would come in drunk. I too stood between him and those I loved. He struck me for the last time when I was an adult man home from college. I had tried to intercede between him and my mother. He died before I came back from the war, but not before

I realized that alcohol had not only hardened his stomach, but also his heart.

My turning point was when Kinu threatened to kill me one night. I recognized the dangerous light in her dark eyes and I felt the desolation of knowing I had lost my daughter. This girl of mine, who I had never understood, now confronted me with an action that mirrored the violence she'd witnessed. I understood what was important to me now and what was of value in my life.

I quit drinking. I tried hard to regain the confidence and love of my wife and children. It was slow, but I think I succeeded. As for Kinu, we eventually came to an understanding. Kinu was greatly impacted by the events of that night. I saw regret in her eyes, and although we didn't directly address the incident, I knew she hadn't put it out of her mind. It became a deep, dark, family secret. I once told her that I understood. I then tried to show her in the following months and years that I was a changed man—no more drinking, no more violence, no hardened heart toward a mother's child who'd fought the stranger in her house.

164

⇾ *Chapter Twenty-Two* ⇽

Homecoming
Kinu

Dear Gracie,

When my parents brought us to Mercy Mountain to live, we moved in with Grandma Rebecca. The big white house, the home place, stood in a curve of the road. It was set well back with a large, grassy yard flanked on one side by the garden and weathered barn. There was a huge evergreen shade tree in the front, and a grape arbor separated the garden from the house. On the summer day when I first saw Grandma's house, it looked to me like a perfect picture from a book about the country—peaceful, quiet, and comforting.

Actually, I'd been to Grandma Rebecca's once before, once that I could remember anyway: I was about seven years old. We'd driven cross-country from Berkeley, California, where Dad was stationed. Grandpa didn't seem too happy to see us. I could never quite visualize what he looked like later; he hadn't talked or even smiled, and so he left little impression on me. I found out later he was in the last stages of black lung disease.

On the other hand, Grandma Rebecca left a lasting impression. I remember she took me aside when we were getting ready to go back home, and opening a drawer of her vanity table in her bedroom, she gave me a special present. It was the most beautiful thing my young eyes had ever seen—a brilliantly-sequined rooster pincushion. She said, "Think of Granny and her little chickens when you look at this, honey, and keep it in a safe place." As I looked into Grandma's warm hazel-brown eyes, I knew she loved me. I kept that cherished gift tucked away with the memory of her sweet smile and the warm hug she gave me to go with it.

Upon our arrival at Grandma's that summer, I was happy to see she still had her chickens. She had a cow, too, and cats in the barn. Squirrels lived and played in the big tree in the front. Most exciting, and a little terrifying, Grandma had an outhouse. We kids loved the animals, although the outhouse took a little getting used to. It was full of spiders,

165

odors, and splinters. We were expected to use Sears & Roebuck catalog pages for toilet paper. Also, the creek across the road was where we played every day, catching crawdads and looking for elusive salamanders. It was a whole different and exciting world for us city kids to explore.

Grandma cooked that summer like she was feeding the starving. Her long, rectangular table, which Grandpa made for her when they were first married, would be loaded down with our favorite chicken and dumplings, fried potatoes, cat-head biscuits, corn on the cob, fried apples, and fresh green beans with a piece of pork belly cooked in them. Dad always claimed the pork belly. There was also honey, molasses, and sweet churned butter on Grandma's table. Before any eating began, Grandma said a long grace, thanking God for many blessings, including the fact that we were there with her.

Your friend,

Kinu

Porkpie Hat Boy

Dear Gracie,

As you know from my letters, my father and I had a strained relationship during my teenage years, but there were times I was glad I had my father to turn to. I had put this memory out of my mind, but today I saw a man wearing a straw Porkpie hat and it all came back to me.

We were staying with Grandma Rebecca that summer; it was a Sunday afternoon in late August in 1960. I was in the old Buick with Dad; he had picked me up from church. I knew Dad was drinking from the quart of moonshine he'd bought early that morning from his favorite moonshiner, old Alec Sims. Alec and Dad had grown up together. He'd left me in the car while he and the moonshiner walked up the holler to the hidden still. Twenty minutes later he came back down carrying a three-quarters-full Mason jar under his arm. His face was red and he was wiping his mouth. I was familiar with this scene. It had happened many times over the summer.

We didn't talk on the short drive home. I didn't want to make him mad; he'd said earlier in the week that if I got my work done in the garden and everyone's clothes ironed for the school week, he'd let me visit my friend that afternoon. But I knew not to remind him of his promise now that he was drinking. I'd learned that the least little thing would set him off.

Late in the afternoon, after the Mason jar was empty and Dad had fallen asleep on the couch, I slipped off. I told my sister Sharon where I was going. Mom and Grandma were taking naps in their bedrooms and I was careful not to wake them up either.

Elaine was my best friend at school. We shared the usual teenage girl secrets, but Dad's drinking was something I never talked to her about; I didn't tell anyone. Elaine wanted to be a beautician someday. Her bedroom was cluttered with glossy magazines titled Silver Screen and True Confessions. On the few times I'd been allowed to visit her, we sat in her room on the bed checking out the hairstyles and makeup worn by movie stars like Sandra Dee and my favorite, Annette Funicello. We then read and discussed the stories, which had horrifyingly intriguing titles such as I Was Raped by My Mother's Boyfriend. I knew Dad would never approve of me reading anything in True Confessions.

Elaine didn't have a controlling father. Her dad had been killed; he was a scab. A union miner shot him dead one early morning when he was on his way to break the lines. She didn't have any brothers or sisters either, but her mother had started taking in foster children. The monthly check the state paid her helped them make ends meet after her father was murdered. An eighteen-year old foster boy lived with them.

I didn't see the new foster boy much. Elaine explained to me that he was shy and often hid from people who came to the house. "Shy" was her substitute word for mentally handicapped. The only glimpse I got of him was on the last time I'd come for a visit. He was standing in the back bedroom, behind the curtain that drew over the doorway entrance. He didn't speak, just watched from behind the curtain. I was uncomfortable, feeling his eyes on me through the filter of the semi-transparent door cover. I thought I could hear him breathing. My impression from that fleeting glimpse was that he was tall and thin. His name was Zandell.

Elaine lived in the next holler over from us. Dad said that when he was young, there used to be a coal camp and a company store there. The store was no longer, but there was still a small community of identically tarpapered coal camp houses. Elaine, her mother, and Zandell lived in the last house on the row. I took the shortcut through the woods.

About halfway between my holler and hers, I felt like I was not alone. Thinking that Sharon had followed me, I yelled, "Go home." I heard loud rustlings in the dry leaves and heavy footsteps running away, but not in the direction of my house. It wasn't Sharon, then. I started walking faster.

By the time I got to the old coal camp and ran up to the house where Elaine lived, I was breathing hard, wet with sweat. Elaine was standing on the small front porch.

She asked, "Why were you running?"

I didn't answer at first. As I glanced back over my shoulder at the woods, I finally said, "Somebody followed me."

"Probably Zandell," she said. "He's been following me everywhere too. Was he wearing his hat?"

"I don't know. I didn't really see anyone. I thought it was my sister. What hat?"

Elaine laughed nervously. "He's got this crazy straw Porkpie hat. He puts a turkey feather in the band and thinks he's invisible when he wears it. It's kind of spooky, but that's what he thinks. He's crazy." She shivered, paused, and said, "Don't worry about him. Come on, I got a new magazine."

We went into her tiny bedroom, plopped down on the bed, and started looking through the magazine. Her room smelled like cheap Evening in Paris cologne and was cluttered with dirty clothes and candy wrappers. There was a picture of Ricky Nelson, another of my favorite stars, on the cover of her new Silver Screen, but even gorgeous Ricky with his sultry eyes wasn't able to hold my attention long. I looked out the window and thought I detected movement in the bushes by the outhouse. I sat back down next to Elaine and tried to concentrate on her chatter. Then the thought came to me that it may have been my dad who was following me, and I didn't want that scene. With that thought, I jumped up to my feet again and started pacing the room.

"What's wrong with you, Kinu?"

"It's later than I thought. I've got to get back home."

Elaine commented as I rushed past her, "You shouldn't have come just to leave right away." But even her hurt tone couldn't keep me there. I had to get home.

The afternoon sun was bright and comforting, yet my sense of unease prevailed. I began to walk home, looking over my shoulder often. A quarter of a mile from Elaine's, I heard the telltale rustlings once again. Turning quickly, I caught sight of a tall figure all hunkered down in the dense ironweed growing alongside the path. I could see the tip of a turkey feather quivering above the tall grass. He was only fifteen feet behind me. Invisible.

I said nothing, but started walking faster, turning around frequently, watching for what he'd do. When I was thirty feet ahead of him, he came out of the weeds, standing up to his full six-foot height, and I got my first good look at Zandell.

His face was expressionless; his hair buzz-cut so short as to look almost bald. His dead-white skin was oily and covered with acne. The hat was pulled down low on his forehead, making it hard to see his eyes. My own eyes widened as I watched him move closer to me. Was I imagining it, or were his eyes fastened on my breasts? Maybe I had read one too many stories from Elaine's True Confessions, but I didn't think so. The turkey feather stood stiff and straight in the flat-topped Porkpie; it was both ridiculous-looking and somehow threatening.

Paralyzed by sudden fear and nearly deafened by the galloping thuds of my heart, I was like a cornered rabbit; I froze, allowing him to come too close. I could smell the rancid sweat that stained his shirt, could smell his panting breath. At the last possible minute, a surge of adrenaline galvanized me. As I spun away from his hands, knowing I must run for my life, I regained some momentary presence of mind and screamed out, "Your feather is missing, Zandell!"

His expressionless face changed instantly into a frightened grimace as he threw his hand up to his hat. By God's grace, that same hand knocked loose the feather and it fluttered to the ground. He bolted, running away from me fast as I ran, equally fast, home to the haven of family, home to my mother and father.

The next day at school, I got Elaine off to herself and told her what happened. She had a frightened look when I finished. When she went home she told her mother, who laughed it off and said, "Make sure he don't get hold of no more turkey feathers and you'll be all right."

I didn't see Elaine at school for the next three days. On Friday, she returned to school bruised around her face and body; she was not herself. Although she never confessed nor told anyone about her secret, I knew Zandell had succeeded in one of his quests. After that Elaine and I no longer shared secrets. Because Elaine did not speak out or get help, Zandell remained at that house for several months until he finally frightened Elaine's mother with his deadly invisible routine.

Dad never wondered why I didn't ask to visit Elaine anymore. I was afraid to tell him about that August afternoon. Even today, I get a shiver of fear whenever I see a man in a feathered Porkpie hat.

Your friend,

Kinu

⇜ Chapter Twenty-Three ⇝

Kinu

Dear Gracie,

I feel as if I must get it all out—everything I can think of about my family. You are hearing my confessions, my blessings and my curses. I want to tell you more of what I remember about my Japanese family in Hawaii.

I called my grandfather Ojii-san, which means grandfather, and I actually have few memories of him. He was silent and somewhat brusque. Maybe this was because he spoke no English and I spoke only a few words of Japanese. I do remember he'd walk me through his yard, past the koi pond, and we'd stop and feed the giant golden fish. They'd rise slowly to the top with gaping mouths and bulging eyes waiting for their bread scraps. I was four or five and they looked huge and somehow menacing to me. Ojii-san must have realized my fear and would caution me through exaggerated pantomime not to fall in or I would get eaten just like the pieces of bread. He would hold my hand tightly and mutter reassuringly in Japanese, or so I surmised.

My dear grandmother, whom I remember much more clearly, I called Obaba, short for Obaa-san. Obaba was my refuge, my safe haven; she also could speak no English but I understood her implicitly through her body language and her loving face and smile. To Obaba I was special; a special granddaughter born to her daughter, Yoshiko and an American soldier, Captain John Clancey Raines. I was special in that I had the fair complexion of my father, only slightly tinged with my mother's golden tones. My hair was not thick, black and shiny, but rather thin, wispy and brown. My Japanese grandmother marveled at my light skin, as this was admired among Japanese women who thought pale skin was better than being dark-skinned, as so many were. But more than this, Obaba loved the fact that I adored her. I did not want to let her out of my sight, according to my mom, even following her to the bathroom. Poor Obaba, she had no privacy around me.

Obaba had long, shining black hair that I loved to brush. My name, Kinu, means silk, and that's what her shining sheet of hair reminded me of. Every day she'd let me brush her hair, and while I was brushing it she'd sing in Japanese. I always thought the songs sounded lonely, as if she were remembering the family left in Hiroshima when she and Ojiisan came to the island of Maui. She was the daughter of a Shinto priest, and while her family was not rich, she was educated. She'd been taught the women's traditional skills of dance, playing the shamisen, tea-making, and dress-making.

Theirs was an arranged marriage; his family worked in the timber business and was relatively affluent. Her family was educated and respected. Both sides felt they had made a good arrangement. They married at age nineteen and left for Hawaii shortly afterward. They settled on Maui and raised seven children together.

My grandfather loved the sea. He was a boat-builder, the best one on the island, and became known as the "president" because he and his craft were so important to the community of Lahaina. The best catches of the day were proffered to Ojiisan; all the fishermen wanted to stay on his good side, as he not only built but also repaired their boats.

Mom said she remembered that her father would dive for abalone and was a strong swimmer. He was short and had muscular, bowed legs, a thick torso, and a large, well-shaped head. It was said, though, that when Obaba first saw him, she thought he was not handsome, as he also had dark skin, bristly hair and small piercing eyes. His saving facial attribute was a strong chin and a confident smile.

Obaba, on the other hand, was very petite in figure and stature, standing well below five feet. Her hair was her crowning glory, and yet in her pictures it was her eyes you noticed. They were very large and beautifully almond-shaped. Her mouth was unusual too, wide with a strongly defined upper lip and a widely spaced cupid's bow. She was acknowledged by all who saw her as a most striking and beautiful woman. I remember most that she always smelled like the little violet-flavored candies she would keep in the sleeves of her kimono for me to eat. I was heartbroken when we left Hawaii and my Obaba behind.

Your friend,

Kinu

My Obaba

Your hair a silken glory
Your love a glorious story
Your smile of sweet compassion
Old memories I often fashion
I was your darling hoppa haole
Growing up in sunny Maui
Following you for special care
Obaba's love always there
Grandmother with her almond eyes
Tender, happy, free from lies
Always watching, always near
My Obaba, oh so dear
When we left, you cried and cried
It was like someone had died
I too cried and missed you so
Wondering where did Obaba go
Faded memories linger on
Violet smells not quite gone
Still I know you've watched me grow
And you hear me and you know

173

The Foot Washing

Dear Gracie,

After the funeral for Mrs. Ransome, several of the women invited me to come to a foot washing service. I declined, but told them we'd try to come to the next one. They told me they have them once every two months. I had never been to a Holiness church foot washing, but I found myself in need of the solace of prayer, communal spirit, and fellowship in worship. Two months after Mrs. Ransome's death, I accepted their invitation. Maggie and I went to the service together.

The church was small and bare. There were rows of plain wooden pews and an altar up front. On the wall behind the altar area and podium was a picture of Jesus, and to the right of that was another picture of The Last Supper. To the left of Jesus' picture was a smaller, discreet portrait of the pastor and his family. A dark curtain used to separate the men from the women during the foot washing had been drawn and bisected the altar and half of the worship hall; this was for privacy purposes, I supposed, yet was typical of the segregation of men and women in the Holiness churches I'd been to. Generally, though there were exceptions, men sat together on one side and women on the other.

As the women came into the room, they were quiet and dressed somberly in long skirts and modest dresses. Many of them knelt immediately to pray at their pews; there was none of the usual quiet socializing, but many reassuring hugs and condolences were offered to me and to Maggie. I could hear the men coming in on the other side of the curtain. One of the women, an older woman I recognized as a friend of my mother-in-law's, began a soft keening, which led into a beautiful old song sung from the heart by the gathering women, In the Arms of Jesus Are Ten Thousand Charms.

Although I am usually a stoic in church, I was immediately moved to tears and I fell to my knees and prayed. And again surprising myself, I found myself praying out loud, following the lead of the women around me, also praying out loud. I felt gentle touches on my back and hands and allowed myself to be led to the front of the church to one of the wooden chairs that had been placed there. As I sat quietly, still praying and crying, someone carefully removed my shoes and placed my feet in a bowl of warm water.

Mrs. Ransome's old friend, moving slowly and stiffly from arthritis, got to her knees in front of me and tenderly bathed my feet. She prayed loudly, keening when she saw and felt the deformity my joint disease had inflicted on my ankles and arches; I felt the warmth of her tears mixing with the water she laved first over my right foot, and then my left. Other women knelt around me and prayed for God to heal my feet. A soft white towel was used to pat them dry, but one young girl used her long blond hair to blot water from my heel. I had never before felt such love, nor had I ever felt so humble. It was almost as powerful a feeling as when I was first saved, along with my mother, long ago.

I looked around at these women who, in their worship, were praying for forgiveness of their sins and asking for God's help with their problems; I noted that many were praying for their husbands and children and also for themselves. They were asking for help—twenty-five women of varying ages, all asking for help. It dawned on me that we all have a common need. We're taught to be strong, maybe because bad behavior from our men is expected and has come to be somewhat accepted, so we're born and bred to be fighters and to be strong and hold our families together. Our mountain culture expects that too, but we do all need someone to be there to give us reassurance that our lives will be better. My grandmother, my mother, my mother-in-law—strong women who turned to God; these same women were the strength and backbone of their families, and yet they were frail in their need. Even my Japanese grandmother was tested in the new land of Hawaii, far from her home and family, not by domestic troubles or abusive behavior as my mother was, but by separation from those she loved. Yes, we're tested, women more than men because more is demanded of us, and I think it's especially true here in our hills.

I looked at Maggie that night and I wondered at her heartbroken weeping. Later, on the way home from church, she told me of her own ordeal with her first husband. I had only known that she was not happy with her marriage, but she told me about episodes of alcohol and drug-fueled rages, and how the children had been intimidated and terrified by the late-night fights. She, my little Maggie, had been beaten and verbally taunted to the point that she nearly resorted to violence herself, she revealed. So familiar from my own past, I could only say, "I understand."

My test may be in my future. Even at this age, there's a new day dawning. I don't need to look back anymore. Delores was right; it was necessary for me to look back in order to get to this point of understanding, but the time to look back is over for me.

I came away from the foot washing with an idea, Gracie. I want to meet you so we can talk freely. It's been a meeting long in coming, hasn't it?

Kinu

Maggie's Story
Little Maggie
Lyrics by: The Stanley Brothers

Oh yonder stands little Maggie

With a dram glass in her hand

She's drinking away her troubles

She's a'courting some other man.

"Mom, I'm finally going to tell you something I've been hiding. You called me Little Maggie after your favorite song...well, I was the *Little Maggie* Ralph Stanley sang about, for real.

"You knew I was unhappy in my first marriage. You always thought we got married too young and you blamed it on me wanting to get away from Daddy. You were right on both counts.

"Josh started drinking and running around after he got out of the Army and we moved back here to Mercy Mountain. I was pregnant with Jon, remember Mom? I didn't talk much to you or Dad about the arguments; I couldn't stand to worry you and couldn't stand to hear Dad's mouth. So I kept silent, but I counted the nights my husband stayed out; I counted the days when nothing would satisfy him...not his children, not my cooking, not even the money I brought in from my nursing job in Lexington.

It got so that we would take our fights to the bedroom. There was no escape. Oh, I tried. Like the *Little Maggie* in the song, I started drinking. Finally one night, after he'd thrown the food off the table and scared the kids into tears, I came to a decision.

I went to town the next morning—to the gun shop where Daddy traded. I told the man I wanted a gun for protection. It cost me four hundred and fifty dollars; money well spent.

Daddy told me later that the gun shop man called him that same day and said, "Do you have a little red-haired daughter about thirty-five years old? Well, she's been in here this morning and she bought a big forty-caliber Smith & Wesson. I asked her what such a little girl wanted with such a big gun. She gave me a straight look and said, 'When I shoot something, I want to shoot it once and it stay down.' You better watch your girl, John Henry; she's got something on her mind and she means to take care of business."

I went home that afternoon with a bottle and the gun. I cooked supper for when the kids came in from school and straightened the house. Around the time Josh usually came home from the mines, I went to the barn and waited. I took my gun and my bottle.

Josh always came first to the barn after work. I was waiting.

The school bus dropped Jon and Sis off; I hollered out to them that there was food on the table and I'd be there in a minute when I finished in the barn, and for them to stay in the house.

When I heard his old pickup truck coming up our approach, I put the bottle down and stood up. My heart wasn't pounding; my hands were steady. I was dead convinced of what I had to do. Then I heard my son's voice, calling my name. He was standing on the back porch, calling "Mommy."

Josh got out of the truck and slammed the door. He saw me standing just inside the barn door and gave me an ill look. He snarled, "Get inside and fix me something to eat." I started to walk backwards further into the barn; he set his lunch box down hard and came my way.

The sudden heat in my head almost drowned out the sound of my boy's voice. He was hollering, "Mommy, I need you!"

He needed me. Oh my Lord! The murder in my heart retreated and I laid the gun down behind a bale of hay. When Josh came through the doorway, blinking in the dark, I told him I'd fixed a big dinner and I'd heat it up for him. He gave me a little push as he walked by me and muttered, "What's the matter with you?"

I left that night. I waited until he was asleep, woke the kids, and left everything behind…no clothes, nothing. I stopped only to get the gun from the barn. You took me in with tears in your eyes, Mom. Dad was standing on the porch, waiting and watching to see if Josh had followed. He had a gun stuck under his belt. I remember that all Dad said was, "Did you shoot him, Maggie?"

❧ *Chapter Twenty-Four* ❧

Legacy of Violence
Kinu

Dear Gracie,

My grandson Jon is home from college. You would like Jon; everybody does.

This morning, Jon let me read a story he wrote for class. It's about an incident he witnessed between his parents when he was a young boy. I think he was about ten or eleven. His story reminded me of my own childhood experience with domestic abuse.

Stepping Up

I grew up with the sounds of late-night arguing, grew accustomed to the sudden bursts of anger and harsh words exchanged between my parents; it's been going on as long as I could remember. My sister and I learned to stay in our rooms until the storm blew over. But one hot summer afternoon, I didn't go to my room.

Mom and Dad were in the yard, near the horse barn. Dad was filling the water trough with the water hose and Mom had just gotten home from work. She was working as a nurse, driving back and forth from Lexington every day. Dad said something to her as she got out of her truck and walked by him. She answered sharply.

I couldn't hear everything that was said between them, but suddenly, their voices were raised. I stepped off the porch and walked toward them. Dad was spraying Mom with the water hose and she was angry; she told him to quit, but he didn't. Instead, he stepped in closer and grabbed her uniform top tight around her neck, holding her while he sprayed water directly in her face. It was going up her nose and down her throat. She couldn't turn away to get a breath of air. I heard her gasping and saw her struggling, flailing her fist to get loose, but she couldn't. She was drowning, I thought.

"Dad," I hollered as I ran up behind him. "Dad, quit!" When he didn't, I picked up a hoe handle and hit him as hard as I could across the back of his legs. As he turned and grabbed for me, his face a mask of anger and outrage, Mom was able to twist free of his grip. I dropped the hoe handle and ran to the barn. I stood there, waiting for my whipping.

For some reason, he didn't come after me. Later that evening, when I was finally brave enough to come in the house, he was waiting for me. He said, "I'm going to punish you, Son, for striking me. But I know why you did it and I want to explain something to you first." He motioned for me to sit down, but I stood rigidly with my hands clenched at my sides.

"Your Mom and I are having troubles. I lost my temper, but I shouldn't have done what I did. Now, you're not a man yet, but you did what a man would do and I don't hardly blame you. But I can't have my boy striking me, you understand? Now, eat your supper and feed the dogs. I'll meet you at the barn after you're done," he said.

My food tasted like sawdust and I could barely get it down my throat; I could see Mom lying on the bed with my sister snuggled up next to her. She gave me a grim smile and the thumbs up sign. I knew then I could take my little whipping.

I finished eating and was standing by the kitchen door, scraping out the iron skillet into the scrap bucket. Dad came over and bent his head down to put pork chop bones in the scraps.

Something moved inside of me. I looked at his bared neck and I had this thought—I could bring this skillet down on his head, could make him pay for what he did to Mom.

I didn't do it. I wanted to. God, I wanted to. For an awful minute, I felt a terrible anger. Then something told me not to be like him. I put the skillet down and walked out to the barn.

Gracie, I hugged my grandson, knowing in my grateful heart that he had escaped the legacy of violence.

Kinu

After finishing her letter to Gracie, Kinu sat at her kitchen table thinking about her son. Luke's call earlier that morning brought exciting news—he was coming home for a two-week visit at the end of the month. She hadn't seen him in nearly a year; his job as an ocean surveyor for a company based in Connecticut kept him busy, but he was doing what he loved. She understood. He'd been home three times since John Henry's death.

She was excited. She wanted to show Luke that she was doing well and he didn't need to worry about her. The days of wheelchair dependence were over; and in fact the wheelchair no longer sat in the corner of her bedroom. It was banished to a corner of the utility shed. She still used her scooter for shopping purposes, but soon she would be able to step away from it too. Even the dragonfly cane was now only a reminder of what she was once limited in doing. Diet and strengthening exercises had proven successful in her rehabilitation. She was on a journey and the end was in sight.

On impulse, she picked up the phone and dialed his number; she wanted to hear his voice, which sounded so much like his father's. The answering machine on the end of the line beeped, so she left a message, saying, "I love you Matt-mo." She was surprised to hear herself using the childhood nickname, a derivative of his middle name, Matthew. Kinu remembered the day she asked, "Why do you want me to call you Matt-mo and not Luke"? His dark eyes had regarded her intently before he answered, "Because I want it to be Mommy, Maggie and Matt-mo". He enunciated each "m" carefully as if reciting phonics. His answer was matter-of-fact, determined. "What about Daddy?" I asked. John Henry hadn't been spending much time at home. Luke ignored the question.

That night, Kinu found the poems she'd written about Maggie and Matt-mo, the two gifts of her marriage. When Luke got home and she, he, and Maggie (Michele) were sitting around the table, she would give them these poems—a thank you from her heart.

My Michele

First child, you were born early
I remember all so clearly
You were like a tiny baby doll
Fair and beautiful, oh so small
Mommy's girl and Daddy's pride
Everything else was put aside
That first year went by so fast
Despite my wishes to make it last
Hair like red-gold orangutan
Holding on but wanting to stand
Making first sounds, not quite a coo
More like a monkey's "woo, woo, woo"
Eyes of turquoise waters blue
Like your fathers, this is true
Loved your grandma, easy to see
I loved mine too, you took after me
Full of laughter, a joy to see
Talking early, "a, b, c's"
Lots of questions, sharp as a whip
Bedtime stories were always a hit
As you grew older, friendly and smart
I knew you would always try from your heart
Whatever job you chose to do
Whatever life offered you

Determination was your middle name
Nothing ventured, nothing gained
I love your strength of will and fire
Red-gold child of my heart's desire
I'm proud of the woman that you've become
You said you could, look at all you've done
My mother's heart is overflowing
The perfect daughter, my girl, a darling

Matt-mo

Surprise second chance at a son
God's little gift, another one
Your father and I so excited
The entire family all delighted
Large and strong, your nickname Samson
Doctors and nurses proclaimed you handsome
Head of black hair, not like your sister
Dark-eyed and tempered, call me Mister
Fingers nimble and full of skill
Twisting transformers at your will
Puzzles of hundreds of pieces and more
You loved to work them, spread out on the floor
Building tiles would become huge castles
And GI Joes were collected by passels
Fishing and hunting and going to camp
You played video games till you became champ
As you grew older, we sometimes would say
Our son will work hard and hard he will play
Strong-willed and following his path always
Making his choices with no delays
Forever determined to find your own way
Yet close to your loved ones, even today
You were your dad's final pride and joy
He was dependent on his boy

Once you said, in your Matt-mo way
"I plan to travel the world someday"
I never doubted it, this was true
Matt-mo would do what he meant to do
"Also Mom, I want to live by the sea
It's a place I'll feel fully free"
My grandfather also felt the same call
So I understood what binds us all
Know I love the daring spirit of you
And how you do what you set out to do
I am proud of you, my son
All that you are and what you've become
You too are my heart's delight
A child of ours, full of fight
My boy, Matt-mo, young and strong
You are the son we counted on

∼ Chapter Twenty-Five ∼

A Safe House
Kinu

Kinu pulled up to Ratliff's Jewelry and got out of her car. Gilles was waiting for her in the doorway. She smiled at his greeting and noticed once again that he was looking good, fit and trim. He was also looking at her curiously.

"What is it Kinu? You said you had something to discuss with me. Weren't you happy with your ring?"

"No Gilles, it isn't that. You did a beautiful job repairing my ring. I have a favor to ask."

They sat down and she started talking. She told him about her stories and the letters to Gracie. She told him how, in trying to figure out her past history and reconcile her life's choices, she'd realized that she could begin again and move forward. She wanted to help women like herself, women who kept secrets in their lives and relationships. She explained her idea to set up a house for women trapped within these mountains, women who confessed their trials only to God because secrecy and tenaciousness were inherent to their mountain culture, a part of their heritage. She would use the profits from the jewelry.

After listening intently, Gilles said, "Let me help you in any way."

Smiling through the tears in her eyes, she said, "I will, Gilles."

Degrees of Love

Kinu looked at the slip of paper in her hand. She dialed the number slowly. Just as she was about to hang up, a woman's breathless voice said, "Hello?"

"Gracie? This is Kinu." She heard a squeal of delight.

186

They talked for thirty minutes; Kinu suggested they meet this coming weekend, but Gracie had committed to doing volunteer work at the black lung clinic for the next two weekends. Luke would be in for his visit following that, so they set a date in four weeks.

Before hanging up, Kinu told Gracie that she would send one last bunch of letters and stories, all in a single shipment—a purging, a final chapter unbound by secrets and golden with a new light. They had walked a dark path of fears, regrets and revelations; she sensed they were near their destination of understanding and peace of mind. Gracie agreed.

Boundaries

Dear Gracie,

I didn't want to leave you with the impression that I never loved John Henry. I did love my husband, but there are different degrees of love, aren't there?

In our early years together, I set certain boundaries in our relationship. Some people might say that boundaries are a bad thing, but they helped me live within the walls of my marriage. You see, it was like a map; I knew what my boundaries were, so even if I ever stumbled across them, I could stop, find my way back over, and continue to live the life I'd chosen. What would have happened without them?

I would have just stepped out of my marriage. I would have looked for the one I couldn't forget. I would have acknowledged that I'd made the wrong choice. These were the fearful certainties I kept locked in. For my marriage to work, I had to stay within boundaries.

My father labeled me a fighter once. He was right; I fought him hard. But in those first few years of marriage, I fought myself harder than I had ever fought Dad. On the day I took my wedding vows, I swore silently to myself that I wouldn't quit or run away or go looking for another. I swore it because, at the very moment when the preacher said, "Until death do you part," I knew I wanted to run.

The first boundary I decided on was that I wouldn't compare the life I now had to the one I had dreamed of having. "Never mind," was my mantra. So when we started off our married life by moving into a four-room log cabin on the top of a ridge named Backbone, in the heart of southern Appalachia, I didn't allow myself to yearn for city lights or a decent bathroom. When John sometimes adhered to the insistent mountain tradition that allowed men to behave badly, coming home liquored-up from a night out with his coon-hunting buddies, or not coming home at all, I didn't confront. I recognized this behavior as typical to our region and tolerated by women here. Never mind that I'd abhorred my own father's weekend binges, and never mind that I'd vowed I'd never put up with it. And when my dreams were haunted by a certain face, by a voice with an all too familiar timbre, by the racing of my heart—never mind.

Married life was easier for me once Maggie was born. I had only to look at her the first time to realize immediately that she was worth any emotional sacrifice I may have made. With her firmly in my arms, I could face down any subversive discontentment with John Henry and my choices.

Soon after Maggie's birth, I found a job at the high school teaching English; John Henry worked at the tipple for Jewel Smokeless, analyzing and weighing coal samples. Together we were making good money. We moved into a larger house, bought some furniture and a second car, used but reliable. I knew John had his doubts, too. When we talked at the end of the day, our conversations were deliberately and routinely about our jobs and the baby. We paid our bills on the first of every month.

We did our best to be happy. If we weren't happy enough, we didn't talk about it; if we had a restless dream in the night, we didn't acknowledge it. We just tried to make it. This kind of thinking was another boundary, set by both of us and set to keep us both within our carefully- built walls. This is how we got through those first few years.

Then, something happened that changed our life together. John Henry had an affair. This wasn't just a fling that I could ignore; it was an ongoing relationship. I found out about it through the mountain grapevine—at church, via a gossiping church biddy. I was told that John and an old high school girlfriend of his had been seeing each other for six months or longer. My first reaction was to opt for the "never mind" approach, but that didn't work this time. Dampened emotions, so long repressed and tightly controlled, came boiling up from somewhere to lodge in my throat, choking me into two sharp realizations: not only did I love John; I would fight to keep him.

When John came home from work that evening, we went to war. We didn't just argue, we had the mother of all arguments; every doubt, resentment, disillusionment, fear, and secret were thrown into the fire. At the end, he swore he loved me. It all came down to one thing: Did I love him? We were man and wife, yet we had done everything we could to avoid facing that question. It had lurked in the corners of our two years together for too long. Once it was out in the open, I immediately felt a peaceful certainty; I knew my answer. John Henry looked into my eyes and knew it too. We started our lives together all over again and the degrees of love between us began to grow.

Your friend,

Kinu

Groundhog Supper

Dear Gracie,

I am so sorry your marriage didn't work; loneliness is another thing we have in common. As you know, my marriage didn't always work well either, but in thinking back on our time together, although the hard memories seem to come first and foremost to my mind, there were sweet ones too.

The sky was a brilliant, cloudless blue that day, and the crisp mountain breezes ruffled my hair and smelled like the pines lining the road before us. John brought our battered, open-topped Jeep to a dead stop.

"Do you want me to catch it for you?" John asked.

We'd been out for one of our Sunday afternoon drives; it was a pleasant habit we'd fallen into since we'd become empty-nesters. Usually we'd drive for hours, taking scenic routes, sometimes stopping for a picnic or a visit with a friend.

"You can't run down a groundhog!" I laughed.

"Watch me." With that, John stopped the Jeep in the middle of the rutted dirt road leading up to our farm in Salt Lick; he flashed me a dimpled grin and jumped out, hitting the road at a dead run. The groundhog came out of its momentary freeze and scuttled back into the tall underbrush of the culvert with John hot on its trail.

From my seat in the Jeep I had a bird's eye view; I could see John's tall body stooped close to the ground as he chased the deceptively slow-looking groundhog. It was running frantically, looking for shelter, but John's long-legged stride shut it off at every turn. Still, the groundhog gave it a mighty try, twisting and turning, running hard, every quick movement belying its short waddling body.

When John suddenly stood to his full height his triumphant eyes were bluer than ever, and clutched in his right hand by its hind foot was the twisting, growling groundhog. My laughter rang out as he brought me his prize, being careful to keep his arm well extended away from his body, as the struggling groundhog was none too happy about its predicament.

"Do we take it to your mom, or do we let it go?" I asked, knowing what his response would be.

"Many a time, when I was growing up, Mama relied on me to catch us a groundhog for supper. She'd love to have this one for Sunday supper," he said, as he deftly dropped the prospective meal into a thick burlap bag. After securely tying the bag off, he turned the Jeep around and we headed for Mrs. Ransome's.

My merriment over the sight of John running down the groundhog had faded. I could barely stomach the idea of eating squirrel, much less groundhog. I knew from past experience that Mrs. Ransome had a penchant for wild game. Once she fixed squirrel gravy and biscuits for breakfast. The gravy had squirrel heads floating in it. I generously left the heads for her and squirmed as she delicately sucked the brains from them. What would she do with a groundhog?

When John presented the squirming burlap bag to his mom, she threw up her apron in delight. "Take it to the woodshed and kill it. I'll dress it out. We'll have us an old time feast for Sunday supper," she said.

John threw me a glance that said, "I told you so," and obediently stepped out to the woodshed with the doomed groundhog. Mrs. Ransome walked around to the back yard where she had her little herb garden. She broke off several small branches from her spice bush and picked some parsley and thyme. She was singing the opening line of the old mountain ballad, *Matty Groves*, under her breath.

Hi-ho, hi-ho, holiday,
the best day of the year
Little Matty Groves to church did go
some holy words to hear
Some holy words to hear.

"Fill me up a kettle of cold water and drop in a handful of salt," she said as we walked into the kitchen through the back door. While I did that, she sharpened her bone-handled butcher knife. John came up the kitchen porch steps carrying the dead groundhog. Risking a peek, I noticed it was skinned, gutted and missing its head and feet. I averted my eyes, but not before Mrs. Ransome noticed my discomfort.

"Nice and fat. We'll cut 'er up like you cut up a chicken." This comment was directed to me so as to tell me she expected me to watch and learn. The carcass looked like a large, fat rodent. I stood my ground, much to John's secret amusement.

After she painstakingly walked me through all the steps that went into proper groundhog cooking, the simmering, flouring and baking, she shooed us out of her cramped little kitchen with orders to dig some sweet potatoes and bring up three quart jars of her white half-runner beans from the cellar.

John held my hand as we sat on the front porch waiting for supper to be done. "You've been a good sport. Now do you think you can carry it one step further and actually eat with us?"

"After all this...the chasing, the killing, the skinning, the chopping, the cooking...I'll do it or die," I said. The smells coming from the open kitchen screen door weren't actually that discouraging. John suddenly kissed me fiercely and said, "You've always stepped up, never backed down. I know you can do it."

Those few words were sweet to my ear. The honey of John's words still in my ear, I sat down to my first groundhog supper. It was delicious. As Mrs. Ransome said, "Best durn eatin' ever was!"

❧ *Chapter Twenty-Six* ❧

Kinu

Dear Gracie,

Another good memory: In the nineteenth year of our marriage, John Henry told me he wanted to get baptized. I was ecstatic; I recognized his decision to be a milestone, both in his life and in our marriage.

Baptism in the River

There was a crowd gathering on the river banks of the Red Bird River; it was two-thirty on a bright Sunday afternoon in Clay County. The modest white wooden church at the top of the hill was practically emptied now as the church congregation wound their way down the grassy hill to the river. Two of the men were already at the river bank, waiting in their shirtsleeves, their pant legs rolled up. As the people arrived, they segregated into small groups; men stood together, smoking or talking quietly. Women in modest long skirts and unadorned dresses, their hair pinned up in the style accepted by Pentecostal women of the mountain community, wrestled with fussy babies and tried to corral and shush restless young children.

The two who had been waiting for the congregation to settle took off their shoes and waded into the slightly muddy, nearly thigh-deep water. One of the men was an older visiting preacher, bald-headed and slightly built. The other was a deacon of the little church who was a tall, robust man in his early fifties. The preacher raised his hands in opening prayer. After the short prayer, he greeted the crowd briefly and then asked someone to lead them in a hymn while those who wished to be baptized were led into the water.

One of the young preachers started singing the opening line of *Shall We Gather at the River* in a clear, pure tenor, and the women and men joined in. The young preacher's powerful voice filled the mountain valley with the beautiful, haunting notes of the old song. The words were sweet and familiar; a hundred voices joined in on the chorus as three people joined hands and waded into the river.

Years ago, Mrs. Ransome had declared that she'd be re-baptized with her son whenever he made that decision, if she were living. John had asked if I'd join them and get baptized in the river. I explained that I'd been sprinkled when I was thirteen, but he argued that immersion was the true way of baptism and begged that I do this. Because I wanted to stand by John in solidarity, I agreed to do so, although I was convinced that my long-ago "sprinkling" had been a true baptism and was still good.

With Mrs. Ransome on his right and me on his left, John led us through the cool water toward Preacher Napier. The preacher took Mrs. Ransome first.

Checking to make sure her skirts were securely pinned between her legs, so as to prevent any show of immodesty as she was dunked, and clutching a large handkerchief over her mouth and nose, John's mother started praying for the Holy Ghost to fall on her. Brother Troy positioned himself behind her as the preacher turned her to face him so as to receive the words of baptism; supporting her at the waist and across the shoulders, the two men then quickly laid her down on her back in the water until her head went under and her feet came up. She was held under for the space of two or three seconds and when they let her up, water streaming from her face and hair, she lifted her arms up in praise and shouted, "Hallelujah, hallelujah!" Brother Troy supported her as she stumbled back to the riverbank where the women wrapped her in towels and sheltered her with their bodies from the curious eyes of the children.

John Henry was next; he was led out to a slightly deeper part of the river. John was a big man, over six-two and weighing two hundred twenty pounds; the young, singing preacher waded out to assist the other two men.

John's face was calm, but I noted his shoulders were tense and he gripped his hands together tightly in front of his belt. I knew he had a strong fear of water; I'd heard him praying to God to give him the strength to overcome his fear. When it came time for him to be dunked, he fell back willingly into the muddied water, but as he lost his footing and his feet started to rise, John Henry involuntarily started to struggle.

He came out of the water flailing, and although Brother Troy stood solidly, the two preachers, young and old, both got a dunking of their own. There were a few indrawn breaths and a few more nervous guffaws, mostly from the younger crowd, before the men regained their feet. Preacher Napier said a thankful "Amen" and headed John in the right direction, being careful not to get in his way. John's face was again composed and serenely relieved as he carefully walked back toward the bank.

I'd been pinned and handkerchiefed and I was not afraid of the water, but as I walked out on Brother Troy's proffered arm, I felt suddenly cold. I had on a thick shirt, again for modesty purposes, but my body chilled in the warm afternoon sun. I remember thinking, "What if I feel nothing? Am I challenging God to touch me once again with the forgiveness of my sins? Am I doing right? Am I where I should be?" Then, I had time only to think, "Forgive me for my doubts, Lord. Thy will be done," before I too was laid down in the waters of the river.

It seemed like much longer than a mere three seconds before I was allowed up. I found my footing quickly and shook off the supporting hands around my shoulders. Although I didn't lift my hands or say any words of praise or rejoicing, I felt an intense warmth flow through me. My doubts and chills were gone, washed away. Those on the river bank began to sing and the sounds of the old hymn, *Amazing Grace,* guided me back once again to John Henry.

The Obi Jade

Dear Gracie,

I was sorting some clothes I found stored in unlabeled boxes, and I found a kimono that belonged to my Obaba. The intricate embroidery of the cherry blossoms in bloom was still vivid on the pristine watered blue silk. Impulsively, I buried my nose in the fabric; I thought I could still detect the faint smell of her violet candies. Tucked in the kimono sleeve, where a granddaughter used to find candies, was a jade obi pin with my name engraved on the back, and a small journal written in Japanese. There are only three entries in the journal. My sister's daughter, Sara, is studying Japanese at UNC; she translated this for me.

January, 1912

My name is Toshiko Yamamoto but everyone calls me Kinu. I am seventeen and I live here in this city of Hiroshima with my parents and my three sisters. My father is a Shinto priest; I am his oldest daughter.

Today, I saw the one I am going to marry. It has been decided between our families. He is a boy most unattractive, dark-skinned and nearly as short as I with his bowed legs and flat feet. His hair is stiff and stands up like a bristle-brush emphasizing a big head carried on a thick torso. He has a very determined chin, prominently jutted out from under a mouth wide with a smile. I didn't smile. His name is Kasaku Masunaga.

Perhaps he will not want me, either. I am small and thin-boned, my body has not enough curves; still, it was said by the wise woman who can see into the future that I would be a great beauty. My only beauty now is my silken hair, although my mother says my eyes are large and well-shaped and my skin is fair and smooth. My father says nothing of my looks—he notes only that I am obedient and virtuous. He is relieved to have a good marriage arranged for me to the second son of a wealthy family. His family is newly wealthy through success in logging timber. They have built a big house; unfortunately, they are not well-educated.

Although he is not wealthy, my father has seen that I received an education. I am well-trained in the arts and I have even studied alongside my brothers. I will be an accomplished wife; perhaps this is why the Masunagas desire a marriage arrangement. I possess something that they do not; I will bring status to the family.

February, 1914

I have been married four months; tomorrow my husband and I will leave Hiroshima and our families behind to start a new life in Hawaii. I do not want to go. I will never see my mother again; this I know in my heart. Still, I must be obedient to my husband. Kasaku wishes to strike his own fortune; he will leave his inheritance behind and build fishing boats for the fishermen of Hawaii.

I have no doubt that my husband will be successful. Although I did not fall in love with his looks or his family's wealth, I have learned to love Kasaku's strength of mind and heart. He is most confident in his skills as a craftsman of boats; he is further inspired by his adventuresome spirit. He promises me daughters to educate and train. I, in turn, promise him sons to help build his boats.

I do not tell him I am afraid. I will have my firstborn shortly after we land at our new home. My mother has taught me well; I will adjust to a new way and a new home far from loved ones. Tonight, she brought me a treasured gift. "From my mother to me, from your mother to you," she said, "this jade has passed through chosen daughters of our family. Our secret name is inscribed on the back; it is a luck charm. Keep it, my daughter, as a part of me and then later, give it as a part of you."

December, 1946

Kinu, your birth name and your secret name are the same. You were born today, first child of my youngest daughter and her American captain. Many years ago I started this journal, only to leave it untouched until now. I leave it to you along with your jade. I ask you to write your story and to remember your Obaa-san, a Kinu from long ago.

❧ Chapter Twenty-Seven ❧

Final Comfort
Gracie

Dusk was settling over the steep, protective mountains. Night was closing in. Gracie, without thought, strolled out to her Jeep and drove the familiar route to Draper Bottom. Her heart was lighter—almost peaceful for the first time in a long time. Was that Kinu, her kindred spirit's presence with her? Although they still had not met face-to-face since the last time they saw each other in college, they had exchanged countless letters since reconnecting. They were planning to get together soon. When she reached the gate to the cemetery, she pulled over, parked, and got out. First she checked on the little plastic wreath, which was still intact on the unmarked baby's grave. She quickly surveyed graves of the war veterans, coal miners, and their family members who rested in peace, protected and lovingly cared for by people who placed them there. They were all someone's past. Then her thoughts turned to her past and her people who had lived and died in this place, this land of hardship and violence. This place of resilience, independence, and broken hearts. This place of timeless and unexplainable beauty. This place and these people, alive and dead, were a reflection of her, regardless of where she lived or how she had turned out.

As she drove the narrow one-lane road back to her house, retracing her steps, she passed by the four-room (Jenny Lind) houses, built all alike, boxlike with four rooms, and perched on wooden posts on the steep hillside. She passed by children playing in the yards dressed in bib overalls, and little girls with pigtails. She passed by old people sitting on the porch rocking in rocking chairs. And in the distance she saw the coal tipple, built of tons of steel and wide boards from the strongest timbers. The tipple cast a shadow so large the houses and all the people were no bigger than thimbles. That was the history of the coal culture—David and Goliath. She could not change her ancestral roots, but knowledge she gained from understanding where they came from, how they lived and died, defined who she was and gave her power which came from knowing and accepting the truth—"Then you will know the truth and the truth shall set you free." Where had she heard that?

She had so many to thank: Andrew De Soto had become the pillar of strength to her. They were so close now. He turned out to be that person she'd needed for so long. Someone who didn't judge, but looked at what makes a person who they are, such as their cultural roots. Kinu, of course, was her kindred spirit—they felt, thought and reacted to each other's hurts and healings. God had reconnected her with Kinu. Annie Lynn, Little Jimmie, Preacher Paul, Jr. and all the other people in Stretchneck Holler. They loved her, cared for her and allowed her to be less than perfect when she needed it most.

Tired from the day's work, she was ready for bed. Gracie happily fluffed her pillow and beamed at herself in the mirror. She felt almost euphoric—happiness and peace. Not terms she normally used to describe her feelings inside. She fell down on top of her bed and pulled the handmade denim quilt over her. Gracie fell into a deep slumber.

Sometime during the night Gracie drifted from the deep slumber mode to the dream mode in the brain. Once again she was in the blue dream room. Kinu was there also, dressed in her pale blue kimono, not caring for an ailing person on a bed, but serving as goodwill ambassador, handing out pleasantries and positive thoughts, and as appointed intercessor between Gracie and her deceased sister.

Kinu smiled widely at Gracie, sitting in the straight-back chair in the dream room. She held an envelope in her hand addressed to Gracie Justice in handwriting Gracie grew up with. It was her sister's writing. The alphabetic letters were neat and flowing. Gracie's name was underlined. Her sister always did that to make sure Gracie knew she was important.

IN THE DREAM, Kinu carefully opened the envelope and began to read the mysterious letter from Gracie's sister:

To My Gracie,

I know you have so many questions. But those serve no purpose now. Just know I am in the hands of my Maker. Details about my sudden death will only cause more confusion. I was sent to the hospital from the halfway house for minor surgery on my leg from a fall I had taken. I'm not sure what was recorded as my cause of death, but Gracie, it was simply my time to go. I was sinking into a deep hole again. The doctors on earth could not cure that, but the Doctor in Heaven could and He did.

My Gracie, do not grieve. Give all that up. Enjoy your life. Find peace and love. That is my message to you. I'm surrounded by so many people I love.

We had a long road together as sisters and best friends. Our lives intertwined from your birth—me caring for you as long as I could while you were growing up, and you caring for me in my darkest hours.

Gracie, there are so many things humans cannot control. I lost all control along the way. I became a burden on you and my entire family, and when that happened I stopped wanting to live the life I had been given. I never stopped loving you and the rest of my family. My family was my world. I knew you were always there.

Gracie, don't think of this as an ending for either of us but a new beginning. I know you worried I died alone. I didn't. When I was nearing the end of this labor of life on earth, a friend was at my bedside. I'd never seen him before. He was tall and wore a beard. He was kind and caring and a light from somewhere illuminated around his head. He told me I was in God's hands and that I was on my ultimate journey. He took my hand in his.

Life on earth is a pilgrimage, and on our journey each stage of events prepares us for greater things. You are now ready for a greater purpose. You have the strength and ability to teach others. Help our people who are struggling with abuse and neglect. Looking back at our roots as you did reminds us of where we came from, who we are, our strengths and weaknesses, and above all that life has purpose.

I love you.

Your sister

Kinu folded the letter and placed it back in the envelope. She walked to Gracie with outstretched arms.

Gracie woke from her dream smiling.

❧ *Chapter Twenty-Eight* ❧

The Meeting
Kinu and Gracie

In another small Appalachian mining town not far from Gracie, Kinu dreamed. The dream was vivid, in Technicolor. She was walking in a pasture alongside a shallow stream. It was a bright, sunshine-filled afternoon and she could hear crickets chirping and the soft sounds of the stream's slow waters. Gradually, she noted that the path she'd been following was going downhill; there were rocks and even boulders that she had to climb over or around. The stream ended inexplicably at an old mine entrance in the mountain; staying true to the absurdity of dreams, she stepped without hesitation through the entrance and into a dark train tunnel. She followed the tracks, noting she was in a narrow mine shaft, which she realized was closing in around her. Her breath came short; she could feel the pounding of her heart in her ribcage.

It was now nearly totally dark in the tunnel, yet she could see brilliant splashes of reds and blues glowing around her as she moved forward. At that moment, she realized she was not alone.

Other people were moving down the path with her. She saw a man resting on a bench and when she turned to speak to him, he smiled and closed his eyes. She left him sleeping.

A sense of urgency possessed her. Resisting the temptation to look back the way she'd come, she looked ahead and saw a soft yellow light. There were people gathered there—was it an exit to this tunnel? As she moved quickly toward the light, she recognized the dark red jacket that a tall, blond man was wearing; he was leaning against the exit wall. She studied his profile and came to the realization that this was John Henry—he turned slowly with his blue-eyed smile and stretched out his hand in greeting. He'd been waiting for her.

Kinu woke from her dream with the sure knowledge that she'd touched John once more; her country boy had told her through that touch that everything was all right. He was there, in the light, and they'd see each other again. She got out of bed happily and began to prepare for her day.

The green hills, edged here and there with early autumn gold, were tipped in mid-morning sunlight. A light breeze carried a hint of the coming cooler weather and was fragrant with the smell of the wildflowers growing profusely in the patchy grass bordering the secondary road. A clearing hosted a small recreational area with several picnic tables and sheds placed beneath a sheltering grove of majestic pines.

The solitude was broken by a white Jeep, which pulled into the narrow, graveled parking lot in front of the shelters. Sounds of Bluegrass music came from the rolled-down car windows. The driver cut the engine off and sat waiting, her blond hair ruffling slightly in the breeze.

In a few minutes another vehicle, a small Toyota sedan, pulled into the lot and parked. Its occupant was wearing a pale blue kimono. The car doors opened simultaneously.

On a country road near Stretchneck Holler, two women run toward each other with tears of recognition, joy, and a newfound purpose in life.

The End

❧ *About the Authors* ❧

Betty Dotson-Lewis

Betty Dotson-Lewis was born in the coalfields of southwest Virginia in Buchanan County where her family had deep roots in the coal and timber industries. Her dad moved his big family to a forty-two-acre farm high in the remote hills of Nicholas County, West Virginia when she was still a young girl. He was in pursuit of bigger game to hunt and bigger timber to cut. There in the mountains, Betty was raised surrounded by coal miners, coon hunters, and storytellers.

She hadn't considered writing and publishing as part of her immediate plans since she was already employed in a time-consuming job for the Nicholas County Public School system. However, if you believe there is a Master Plan for each of us, then, you will understand how it came upon her to write. The Girl from Stretchneck Holler became her passion and purpose. Through a series of unusual visionary dreams and a continuous stream of support from those whose stories she documented, she realized this was, indeed, part of her Master Plan.

Dotson-Lewis has a son and daughter. Her hometown is Summersville, West Virginia although she currently resides in North Carolina. She graduated from Nicholas County High School and studied at Berea College in Berea, Kentucky.

Kathleen Colley Slusher

Kathleen Colley Slusher is the eldest daughter of a World War II veteran and his Hawaiian-born Japanese bride. Upon her father's retirement from a career in the Marine Corps, the family of seven resettled in his hometown of Haysi, located in the Appalachian foothills of southwest Virginia.

Blending her mother's cherished stories of growing up in Hawaii with her stories of the mountain culture that her father so loved, Kathleen began writing about her rich and diverse heritage when attending Berea College.

Kathy lives with her daughter in Crab Orchard, Kentucky.

CPSIA information can be obtained at www.ICGtesting.com
Printed in the USA
LVOW01s1548170813

348385LV00003B/314/P